Mark of Drelves

(Elves, Drelves & Dragons: Book One)

C. Star

Join my mailing list to receive the latest news about my books (and extra goodies!)

Community:

Mail: Cynastar019@gmail.com

My Website: Cstarbooks.com

Signup for Newsletter:
https://cstarbooks.com/#newsletter

Thank you for reading my books!

www.Cstarbooks.com

Dedication

Dedicated to Rowena Xena.

A true princess, fierce warrior, and a loyal friend.

Table of Contents

The three Realms
Dreif Kingdom
Dragon Graveyard
Larimar Falls
Shrouded Vale
The Arden
Elf Kingdom
Rivenmoor
Fae Bridge
Dragon Kingdom

Prologue

Long before memory, the realms stood united beneath a fragile covenant—forged between elves and dragons. But time breeds pride, and pride breeds betrayal.

The Covenant shattered.

Now, silence gathers in the corners of forgotten places. Old magic, once sealed by sacrifice, begins to stir. In the heart of the Dragon Realm, something ancient twists awake, coiling through the dark like smoke. Vartharax, ruler of the dragons, feels it—the hum of power long thought lost.

A mark has appeared.

Faint at first, like a flicker on the edge of a storm. But it is enough.

Enough to rouse fear in those who remember the prophecy. Enough to summon death to chase the one who bears it.

Far from thrones and banners, a being flees through forest and shadow, wings hidden beneath cloak and ash. She does not yet know what lives inside her blood—or what hunts her through the trees.

But the world is watching.
And the first thread has been pulled.

Chapter 1

Vartharax, dragon ruler of the Abyss, loomed at the center of the darkened chamber, his massive wings furled against his obsidian-scaled back. Shadows shuddered along the jagged walls, cowed by their master's presence. His smoldering eyes locked onto the dragon kneeling before him—smaller, weaker, but dangerous in his own way.

The oppressive weight of Vartharax's power filled the chamber, making the air heavy with malevolence. His tail, lined with jagged spikes, curled behind him, twitching with impatience as he awaited the news.

"Did you find her?" Vartharax's voice was like the grinding of stones, low and dangerous, filling the space with dark, resonant energy.

Drakor, known as the hand of Vartharax, stood with his head bowed, his slender, crooked form a sharp contrast to the overwhelming physical presence of the dark ruler. His scales, a mottled mix of ashen gray and sickly green, were dull and patchy in places, bearing none of the majesty that Vartharax's gleaming black hide possessed. The discolored patches seemed to writhe like shadows under the dim light, adding to his unsettling appearance. Smaller and weaker—a runt by dragon standards—his narrow frame twisted with age and malice. His eyes, a sickly shade of yellow, glinted with both fear and satisfaction as he answered.

"We have found her, master." Drakor's voice was rasping, but there was a sharpness in it, a hunger.

Unwavering in his confidence, Drakor stood before his master and met his gaze. Ancient artifacts and symbols of power adorned the room, serving as a testament to the black lord's dark reign.

"Are you sure this time?" Vartharax's voice coiled through the chamber, low and venomous. He stepped forward, molten eyes narrowing, reading Drakor like a blade poised above his throat.

Drakor's heart hammered, but he held his ground. He had learned long ago—Vartharax had no patience for failure. And no mercy for the weak.

"I am certain, my lord." He swallowed back the fear that always threatened to crawl up his throat in Vartharax's presence. He knew how little the black dragon thought of him—a runt in the shadows, tolerated only because of his cunning.

Vartharax's eyes blazed with fire, his towering form shifting as he loomed closer, the air thickening with his dark presence. He began circling Drakor; his steps were heavy and deliberate, each one making the stone chamber tremble beneath them. "The prophecy..." Vartharax murmured, his voice filled with both fascination and loathing. "And the covenant that once bound us... will shatter through her."

A thrill of satisfaction at Vartharax's words coursed through Drakor. He knew the prophecy had long haunted the dark lord, a potential threat to his rise. But now—this one with the mark—it could be the answer to breaking the balance once and for all.

"She is the one," Drakor insisted, his voice rising with false confidence. "She bears the mark, master. The one we have sought for so long."

Vartharax paused, his enormous head tilting as his eyes bored into Drakor's very soul. The silence between them was heavy and suffocating. Then, at last, the dragon lord growled, "If you are wrong, Drakor, there will be no mercy." His breath rippled with heat and in his gaze burned a promise not of death, but something far worse.

Drakor's muscles coiled with tension, but his mind raced. He had to be right this time—Vartharax did not tolerate failure. His last mistake—chasing a false mark—had almost cost him everything. Another misstep and Vartharax would cast him aside like carrion.

What Drakor lacked in brute strength, he made up for in cunning—the sole reason he stood at Vartharax's side. But he wanted more. More power. More Respect. More fear from the other dragons.

And this—this was his chance.

Vartharax paused as he peered down at the smaller dragon. A heavy, oppressive silence enveloped them as if the darkness were expecting the black dragon's next words.

"Good." Vartharax's mouth twisted into a dark smile. "Then bring her to me."

Drakor bowed low, heart racing. He turned, already thinking of the next steps. The plan was in motion, and soon, Vartharax's vision for total dominance would come to pass—and Drakor, loyal and ever-watchful, would secure the power and respect he had yearned for.

"As you wish, my lord."

Drakor turned, striding from the chamber with measured steps, though Vartharax's gaze burned into his back like a brand. His master's power-loomed behind him, a reminder that he couldn't afford to fail.

Not this time.

For centuries, Drakor had scoured the ancient prophecies, dissecting every cryptic verse in search of the truth that could shift the balance of power. While others dismissed myths, he traced their threads, watching the celestial alignments, sensing the magic shifts, and listening to whispers of unease. It all led to this moment—a convergence of forces, a storm he could either break or bend to his will.

While larger, stronger dragons craved brute dominance, Drakor had taken another path. Mocked for his size, underestimated by his lack of sheer might, he sharpened his mind instead, hoarding secrets like others hoarded gold. He had witnessed empires rise and fall, kings grasping for power only to watch it slip through their fingers. Strength was not in force alone—it was in knowing the currents that shaped the world… and how to turn them in his favor.

Now, with the mark emerging, the pieces were falling into place. It was his moment to prove that cunning could surpass strength, that the shadows held power greater than any fire or fang. And if he could bring this being—this key to the prophecy—to Vartharax, then the jeers and whispers of the other dragons would mean nothing.

Drakor slunk through the stony corridors, the heavy door to Vartharax's chamber groaning shut behind him. His thoughts raced as he considered the steps he needed to take, the pieces of his plan falling into place.

A burst of fiery light flared ahead, stopping him in his tracks.

"Well, if it isn't the runt himself," came a deep, mocking voice.

Drakor's gaze snapped up, locking onto Korrath—a towering beast of molten crimson, his ember-like eyes burning with amusement. The glow from his scales cast shadowy figures along the passage, the very air heavy with the heat rolling off him.

Korrath stood unmoving, wings half-spread, blocking the corridor like a living wall. He surveyed Drakor with the lazy satisfaction of a predator toying with prey.

"I suppose our glorious master didn't eat you this time," he mused, baring a row of sharp teeth with a wicked grin. "Pity. I could've used the entertainment."

Drakor's yellow eyes narrowed, but he masked his irritation with a cool, measured smirk. "Shouldn't you be off torching something? Or has your intellect finally caught up with your appetite?"

Korrath let out a deep, rumbling laugh, the sound vibrating through the stone. "And you're still trying to talk your way to the top. Exhausting, isn't it? All that scheming." He took a deliberate step forward, his massive frame dwarfing Drakor. "So, tell me, what's the runt's trick this time? More prophecy nonsense? Or are you just spinning another lie to keep yourself useful?"

Drakor's claws flexed, but his smirk remained. "You'll find out soon enough. Some of us use strategy, Korrath—you'd have to think beyond your next meal to understand."

Korrath's grin faded, his ember eyes narrowing with quiet menace. "Careful, Drakor. Even the smallest creatures get crushed if they bite too hard."

Drakor stepped closer, his voice falling to a venomous whisper. "Try it. I'd enjoy watching Vartharax flay the scales from your hide."

The corridor crackled with tension—Korrath's searing heat against the cold venom in Drakor's stare. Then the red dragon snorted, stepping aside with a derisive flick of his tail. "Run along, runt. Your master's leash is waiting."

Drakor didn't spare him a glance as he passed. But as Korrath's hulking form disappeared behind him, a dark smile curled Drakor's lips.

"Leashes are for the predictable," he muttered under his breath. "Before this is over, I'll be the one holding the chains." His eyes gleamed with dark satisfaction as he vanished into the shadows.

The passageways twisted upward, leading him toward the surface. The moment he breached the cavern's mouth, a gust of chilly night air rushed over his scales, sharp and invigorating after the oppressive heat of Vartharax's domain. He inhaled, sensing the power of the world above—a realm on the brink of change, a future he would mold with his own claws.

Spreading his wings, Drakor launched himself into the sky. The thin, membranous stretch of them caught the wind, lifting him into the storm-laden air. The night whispered with unseen forces, the wind humming with ancient secrets, carrying the distant echoes of dragons long forgotten.

His sharp gaze cut through the darkness, locked onto the distant horizon. Somewhere beyond those storm-clouded peaks, power and destiny awaited—his for the taking.

Let Vartharax believe he held all the strings. Let Korrath revel in his brute strength.

In the end, Drakor would dictate how this game was played.

The realms teetered on a knife's edge.

And Drakor intended to be the one who tipped the power in his favor.

Chapter 2

Morning light filtered through the towering trees of the Elven kingdom, casting golden rays that danced across the forest floor. Branches intertwined high above like the vaulted ceilings of a grand cathedral, creating a canopy that whispered of timelessness. Streams of crystalline water meandered through the city, their gentle murmur mingling with the rustling leaves and distant birdsong to weave a melody as eternal as the land itself.

The Elven kingdom was alive with magic, tangible energy that shimmered throughout and lingered in every stone pathway. Spires of silver and emerald rose with graceful precision, catching the light as though kissed by the dawn. Homes nestled among the trees seemed to grow as part of the forest, their curved designs attuned to the natural world around them. Here, nature and artistry were not separate but fused, each enhancing the beauty of the other.

Strength in this realm was more than physical—the elves wove it into their traditions, discipline, and delicate balance, which they held sacred. Though the kingdom thrived in peace, beneath its serene exterior lay a readiness born of centuries of resilience, an unyielding spirit etched into its core.

Eldrin strode down a cobblestone path lined with trees whose golden leaves glowed in the morning light. His long, dark hair flowed down his back, with a portion tied to keep it from falling into his face. Across his forehead, an intricate braid adorned with a silver clasp bearing the royal sigil of his house gleamed in the sunlight. The braid, both practical and symbolic, marked him as a son of the Elven King. Loose strands framed his face, softening the sharp angles of his jaw as his vivid green eyes scanned the path ahead, their intensity betraying a mind already focused on the training to come.

"Don't tell me you're planning to show up at training with that scowl," said a familiar voice.

Glancing over his shoulder, Eldrin spotted Finnian catching up to him, his twin swords strapped across his back as always. His friend's perpetual grin was as disarming as his quick wit. Finnian's dark green tunic, slightly rumpled, gave him the look of someone who hadn't quite finished getting ready but somehow looked roguishly confident, anyway.

"You're late," Eldrin said, though a smile tugged at his lips.

"I'm exactly on time," Finnian replied, falling into step beside him. "You, however, are absurdly early. Again."

Eldrin glanced at his friend, hiding the smile that threatened to give him away. Finnian's chestnut-brown hair, long with loose braids framing his temples, defied any attempt at neatness, just like Finnian himself. His piercing blue eyes twinkled with mischief, revealing a sharp mind constantly at work behind his carefree demeanor. Though he often masked it with humor, Finnian's prowess as a scout was unmatched. His agility and skill with twin blades had earned him widespread respect, but his tendency to poke fun at authority often landed him in trouble.

"I wanted to get in some extra practice," Eldrin said, a faint edge to his voice. "Before my brother shows up and steals the show. Again."

"Of course you did." Finnian shot him a knowing grin. "Today might be the day you best him—or at least make him break a sweat for once."

Eldrin huffed. "Thalendir doesn't need to work for anything. It all comes naturally to him."

"Which is why it's so satisfying when you make him try." Finnian nudged him. "You will not beat him by sulking about how easy he has it, though."

"I don't sulk."

"Right. You brood. Like an artist who just painted the wrong flower."

"I'm not brooding. I'm focused," Eldrin said, rolling his eyes.

"Focused on taking down Caelith, I hope, because he's your first match today." Finnian's tone was light, but his grin sharpened. "He's fast, but you've got the advantage. Your form is better, and if all else fails, you've got me on the sidelines shouting invaluable words of wisdom."

Eldrin raised a brow. "Wisdom?"

"Well, technically, just words. Occasionally, clever ones."

The two emerged onto the quiet training grounds, the dew-dappled grass shimmering in the soft morning light. The air was still, save for the faint rustle of leaves in the breeze. A few elves were setting up for the day's drills, their movements deliberate but unhurried. The sharp clink of a practice sword being tested against a post echoed faintly in the distance.

"Another day, another chance to show them all what we're made of," Finnian said, clapping Eldrin on the back. "And by 'we,' I mean you. I'm just here to make everyone laugh and look good doing it."

"Modest as always."

"Someone has to balance out all your brooding." Finnian grinned. "Of course, if your brother is late, maybe his effortless charm won't work this time."

Eldrin snorted. "Charm? Is that what we're calling it now? If he even bothers to show up at all."

"True," Finnian replied with mock seriousness. "Punctuality might interrupt his beauty sleep. Can't have that, can we?"

Eldrin couldn't help but chuckle. "Not unless I want him to spend the rest of the day telling me how lucky I am to train with him."

Finnian tapped his chin, a mischievous glint in his eye. "Well, if he shows, maybe today's the day you'll knock him off his pedestal."

Eldrin's smile turned sharper, almost wistful, as he imagined the moment. A hint of satisfaction crossed his face as he pictured his brother's golden hair falling in disarray, his smirk wiped clean, and his sword clattering to the ground. The vision was fleeting but sweet. He glanced toward the training area, his green eyes thoughtful.

"Yes..." he murmured, his ambition betraying the wistfulness in his tone. "Wouldn't that be fun?"

Familiar sounds pulled Eldrin's attention forward. The clang of steel on steel rang out, sharp and rhythmic, intermingling with the occasional bark of a trainer issuing corrections. Low murmurs spread among the gathering elves as warriors lined up, some tightening the straps on their armor, others testing the heft of their swords. The cool morning air carried the scent of dew-soaked grass and a subtle tang of polished steel, a grounding reminder of the discipline and tradition that defined their world.

A young elf passed by, her bow slung over her shoulder. She offered Eldrin a polite nod, her gaze lingering longer than necessary. "Good luck today, my lord."

He nodded back, his voice catching. "Thank you."

As she walked away, Eldrin glanced back, catching the faint sway of her golden braid disappearing into the crowd.

"Careful," Finnian teased, leaning in with a grin. "You're supposed to be thinking about winning, not daydreaming."

A faint flush crept to his cheeks. "I'm focused."

"Sure you are," Finnian drawled. "Just make sure you don't get distracted by, well... other interests."

The crowd near the sparring ring parted as Eldrin approached, eyes following him with both expectation and curiosity. Eldrin caught snippets of conversation—whispers about his matches, murmurs of bets being placed.

Eldrin ignored the remarks, though they stoked the quiet fire in his chest. His fingers flexed around his sword upon entering the ring, his dark locks falling forward until he brushed them back. The familiar weight of his blade was steady in his hand, grounding him against the rising tension.

Across the ring, Caelith waited, his stance poised for the match. Eldrin's eyes met his opponent's, and the crowd's clamor faded into the background. The match was all that mattered now.

Eldrin adjusted his grip on his sword. Dark strands clung to his damp forehead, and his gaze darted to the opponent before him—a skilled warrior named Caelith. They were in the sparring ring, a worn circle in the grass where countless matches had incised faint grooves into the soil. Spectators, eager to see which of the kingdom's warriors would shine today, surrounded a ring of trampled greenery that marked the edges.

"Don't let him trip you up, Eldrin!" called Finnian from the sidelines. He leaned against a wooden post, one boot propped up behind him, arms draped loosely over his chest. A lopsided grin played across his lips. "He's all footwork and flair. Not a lot of substance."

Eldrin smirked but didn't look away from Caelith, whose stance shifted, ready to strike. Caelith lunged first, his blade cutting through the air with speed and precision. Eldrin parried with ease, his movements fluid and deliberate.

Finnian added, "Don't let him rattle you, Eldrin. Just picture Thalendir's smug face, and you'll cut him down in no time."

Eldrin ignored him, his focus narrowing to the match at hand. His opponent was fast, but Eldrin had dedicated years honing his reflexes, often in the shadow of his elder brother, Thalendir—the golden heir to the Elven throne. Thalendir's effortless mastery of the blade had been both a source of inspiration and frustration for Eldrin. While Thalendir excelled, Eldrin had clawed his way to mastery through sheer determination, long hours of practice, and the unshakable belief that one day, he could surpass his brother.

Caelith thrust forward, aiming for Eldrin's midsection. Eldrin sidestepped, spun, and, with a deft flick of his wrist, sent Caelith's blade flying. With a single fluid movement, Eldrin's sword stopped at Caelith's throat.

"Yield," Eldrin said.

Caelith froze, then lifted his hands in surrender. The watching elves murmured their approval, a few applauding. Finnian gave a loud whistle, grinning broadly. "Now, that is how you do it!"

Eldrin sheathed his sword, stepping back. But the minor victory was short-lived.

"Well done," rang a familiar voice. Thalendir advanced, his hair gleaming in the sunlight, his signature smirk firmly in place. The eldest prince exuded confidence; his tunic was pristine despite earlier matches. "But let's see how you fare against someone who's not so easily disarmed."

The murmurs started before Thalendir even entered the ring, a ripple of excitement sweeping through the crowd. Eldrin wiped beads of sweat from his brow after his victory against Caelith, but the growing buzz around him brought new tension to the air.

"Thalendir's here."

"Think Eldrin's got a chance?"

"No way. Thalendir's untouchable."

Eldrin heard the whispers but kept his expression neutral. Thalendir's golden hair caught the sunlight as he entered the sparring circle; like he owned it. In some ways, he did. The crowd parted for him, and even the trainers paused their instruction to watch.

Thalendir smirked, his keen eyes finding Eldrin through the crowd. With a careless turn of his wrist, he spun his sword, the blade gleaming as if it belonged to him as equally as his breath—a natural extension of his skill and arrogance.

The air shifted. The gathered elves fell silent, their anticipation palpable. Sparring with Thalendir was not just a match—it was an event.

Eldrin squared his shoulders. "I'm ready."

Thalendir chuckled, a low, condescending sound. "We'll see."

A flurry of motion started the match. Thalendir's strikes were swift and relentless, his blade a streak of silver. Eldrin countered each blow, his muscles straining as he pushed himself to keep up. He held his own until Thalendir's sword twisted around his, disarming him in one smooth movement.

A clang from Eldrin's blade striking the ground echoed throughout the training grounds. Thalendir's sword hovered just inches from Eldrin's chest.

"Not bad," Thalendir said, stepping back with a satisfied smile. He sheathed his sword, his tone dripping with mock encouragement. "You're improving, little brother. Almost made me try this time."

Eldrin bent to retrieve his sword, his jaw tight. "One day, I'll beat you."

Thalendir's laugh rang out as he walked away. "When you do, maybe I'll start taking you seriously."

Finnian patted Eldrin's shoulder. "Hey, you had him for a second there. I think you even made him sweat. That's a win in my book."

Eldrin managed a small smile, though his frustration simmered just below the surface. "Not good enough."

"Well," Finnian said, stretching, "I guess I'll just have to stick around to watch when you finally wipe that smug grin off his face."

Eldrin chuckled, but the sound lacked warmth. Finnian's words echoed in his mind, stirring a familiar ache. He had always been in Thalendir's shadow. Even their father, King Eldermyst, seemed to favor his eldest son. His tone carried an edge of pride reserved only for him. It wasn't outright favoritism—at least not in a way anyone else would notice—but to Eldrin, it was like a shadow he could never quite step out from.

The thought stung, but it only fueled his resolve. Eldrin glanced at the worn sparring ring before him. One day, he vowed silently he would prove himself, not just to Thalendir or their father, but to the entire kingdom.

As the sparring matches concluded, the focus shifted to other drills. Groups of elves moved seamlessly between stations, practicing their forms, testing their balance, or refining their aim under the watchful eyes of their trainers.

The clamor of clashing steel and murmured instructions underscored the discipline of Elven life.

Eldrin lingered by the perimeter of the grounds, watching the others as he set aside his sword. The tension from his match with Thalendir still thrummed in his muscles, but he welcomed the weight of his bow as he retrieved it from where it rested against a nearby post. The smooth curve of the weapon sat naturally in his hands, its presence grounding him like nothing else could.

He loosed an arrow, watching it soar before striking just shy of the target's center. Eldrin frowned, adjusting his stance, and drew another arrow. This one flew closer to its mark but was still not as precise as he'd hoped. The cadence of drawing and releasing the bowstring was meditative, the repetitions sharpening his focus as he worked to improve each shot. Comfort with the bow was one thing; mastery was another.

He faced the target once more, drawing another arrow. This time, the shot grazed the bullseye, closer to perfection. He exhaled a quiet breath, a trace of determination sparking to life within him.

Eldrin lowered his bow, the ache in his muscles a satisfying reminder of his efforts. Nearby, Finnian leaned against a wooden post, his twin blades still strapped to his back, watching the activity with a relaxed grin.

"Good work out there," Finnian said, his grin as easy as ever. "Though if you want pointers on disarming a smirk, I'm always available."

Eldrin huffed a laugh. "I'll keep that in mind."

The sharp whistle of Master Trainer Aldareth pierced the din, silencing the elves and drawing them to attention. The chatter faded, replaced by a collective focus as Aldareth's piercing eyes looked over them.

"Line up," he barked, his voice carrying the authority of years spent shaping warriors.

As the elves assembled, the trainer's tone grew grave. "The council has received reports of disturbances near the western borders. Signs of dark forces moving closer to our lands."

A murmur spread throughout the group, uneasy but restrained. Eldrin's pulse quickened. Dark forces could mean many things, but few of them were good.

Aldareth let his words linger before continuing. "We will send a group of you to scout our kingdom and protect us, if necessary, based on your skills. This mission is not a choice—it is a duty. Look sharp and report any disturbances to me."

He focused on Thalendir first. "Thalendir," Aldareth said, his tone softening. "Your father has requested your presence. You're excused."

Thalendir nodded with a grin that became wider as he was departing, but not before he glanced at Eldrin, gleaming with subtle amusement. He paused long enough to throw a verbal dagger. "Don't trip over your blade out there, little brother."

Eldrin's jaw clenched, but he met his brother's gaze with steady determination. The words he didn't say burned within him: One day, I'll prove you wrong.

"Finnian," Aldareth continued, his voice regaining its commanding edge, "your skills as a scout will be valuable. You'll take the northern border. Eldrin," he said, turning to him, "you will lead a patrol into the forest, take Caelith and Aelor with you. Dareth, you and Eryndor will cover the outlying roads and villages."

Eldrin straightened, his heart racing. This was his moment—a chance to show what he was made of. Not just to the council but to everyone.

Finnian clapped him between the shoulder blades. "Looks like we're splitting up this time. Try not to get into too much trouble without me."

Eldrin managed a half-smile. "I'll try. But no promises." As the others dispersed to prepare, he turned toward the treeline beyond the training grounds. The wind stirred the leaves like a whisper.

His patrol would begin at dawn. And this time, he wouldn't just be following.

He'd be leading.

Chapter 3

Lyria's fingers brushed the glowing tattoo on her neck, wishing she could erase the mark etched into her skin. Her clawed fingertips, sharp yet delicate, grazed the spiraling symbols just above her collarbone, their faint luminescence casting a soft, silver glow in the dim light. These were not the hands of an elf—slender and graceful—but something entirely other. Talons tipped with a faint emerald gleam reflected the storm-charged sky above, a vivid testament to the Draconic power coursing through her veins. She flexed her hand, feeling the strength behind those claws—a sharp difference to the soft, almost ethereal glow of her Elven features.

Her appearance was a paradox: beauty intertwined with danger, the result of a forbidden union between elf and dragon kind—a living reminder of a covenant broken and a bloodline shrouded in shame. Her very existence was a blend of two worlds that loathed her kind, a fusion of elegance and ferocity. The shimmer of natural scales along her shoulders and sides hinted at Draconic armor, blending with her Elven frame. The green widow's peak of her hair cascaded into blue braids, framing her face and emphasizing her sharp features as well as the haunting beauty that set her apart. Tucked behind her, red wings glimmered, a vivid counterpart to her graceful, pointed ears. Yet it was her amethyst eyes, alive with determination and conflict, that betrayed the tempest within—a battle fought not only with those who scorned her kind but with the legacy written into her very skin.

Drelves thrived in obscurity of the three realms, carving a path of survival in the cracks between power and prejudice. But that survival came at a cost. Lyria endured the plight of her people's exile like a mantle, the burden of a life lived between two worlds that refused to claim her. Now, the mark glowing against her skin threatened their fragile existence, a silent beacon to the darkness hunting her.

They would come for her, the marked one. Darkness hidden for centuries would rise from the abyss, from every corner of the world, to stop the prophecy. She received a warning in a dream the night before when the mark appeared. A white dragon, its luminous scales shimmering with an otherworldly light that seemed to pierce through the veil of her subconscious, spoke to her. Its voice was both commanding and serene, resonating with a power that made the air hum in her dream. "The mark you now bear," it had said, "is the spark that ignites the prophecy—a force that can reshape the realms. But with it comes great peril. Darkness will seek you out, for it knows what you represent."

Lyria had awoken drenched in sweat, the spiraling tattoo glowing upon her skin as if reacting to the dragon's words. The white dragon's voice echoed clearly in her mind, its tone heavy with urgency: "The nemods are coming. You must leave before they find you. Seek the enchanted forest. Trust its magic."

Leaving her people had cut deeper than any blade, but staying would have doomed them. She had fled in haste, knowing each mile put more distance between her and the only home she had ever known—yet every step seemed to sever a piece of herself. Their safety depended on her absence, no matter how much it tore at her.

The nemods, monstrous creatures bound to the Abyss, would stop at nothing to erase her—and the prophecy she carried. If she remained among her kind, she would be their undoing. They would destroy the drelf kingdom to claim her.

That thought chilled her far more than the dragon's warning ever could.

Hours of flight had rendered her wings straining with each beat, cutting through the dense, storm-charged air. Below, the land blurred into a distorted patchwork of darkened forests and jagged ridges, shrouded further by the brewing tempest. Overhead, clouds churned with unspent fury, flashes of lightning casting fleeting silhouettes across the terrain. The air pressed down on her as icy drops of rain mixed with the sweat on her skin, each one a sharp sting as thunder growled in the distance.

Her muscles burned, wings trembling from the relentless effort of staying aloft, but she dared not slow. She wasn't just fleeing the storm—she was escaping the hunters sent to track her. Wyverns, unleashed by the nemods, had been shadowing her for miles, their sleek, sinewy forms tearing through the turbulent skies. Much smaller and more feral than dragons, built for speed and precision, with powerful taloned legs and wide, bat-like wings. Their charcoal-gray scales, streaked with veins of crimson, shimmered against the storm's flickering light, blending them into the chaos above. Long barbed tails whipped in their wake, and their glowing predator's eyes blazed with feral hunger. Each piercing screech they unleashed echoed with primal savagery, a sound that clawed at her nerves.

Below, her sharp eyes caught movement. Nemods—hulking, twisted shadows against the storm.

Wolf-like heads, hunched and predatory, turned upward, their ember-filled voids locking onto her like soulless beacons. Their charred, cracked hides, like burnt stone over molten veins, pulsed with flickers of unnatural light. Jagged obsidian fangs, serrated like shattered glass, gleamed as they snarled. Sparse, wire-stiff hairs jutted from their stone-like flesh, remnants of something that had once been alive—before the Abyss twisted them into something far more dreadful.

Their mounts—just as grotesque—were nightmarish horse-like beasts, their blackened hides stretched taut over unnatural frames, clawed hooves carving deep trenches into the earth. They moved with unnerving, synchronized precision, their glowing eyes penetrating the storm's darkness like twin lanterns of malice.

The nemods did not wander. They hunted.

And with every beat of her wings, their grotesque silhouettes drew closer.

Her pulse quickened as she glanced behind her, scanning the skies. Two wyverns were converging, their leathery wings unfurling with a sickening crack. They ascended, their shrill cries piercing the tempest like a hunter's call.

Lyria gritted her teeth, pushing herself harder, her focus honing in on the distant trees. Its dark canopy shimmered through the storm's haze, a glimmer of hope against the shadows pursuing her. She had to reach it before they caught up to her.

The assassins were relentless, their piercing screeches penetrating through the thunder's roar as they circled closer. One dove at her, talons outstretched, forcing her to roll away. The maneuver strained her already battered wings, but she kept pushing forward. Below her, the wind-battered landscape gave way to the mysterious silhouette of the magic forest, its towering trees a looming promise of refuge—or more danger.

A sudden dive from another wyvern forced her to veer sharply, her wings protesting the strain. Before she could right herself, the winged devil struck from her blind side. Talons raked against the base of her left wing, and a sickening snap reverberated through her body. Pain exploded across her back, and her wing crumpled beneath her weight.

The storm blurred into chaos as she fell. Branches clawed at her as she plummeted from the forest canopy, the ground rushing up to meet her. The wind screamed past her ears as she fell. Branches shattered beneath her — one, then another, then another — snapping like brittle bones as she plunged through the canopy. And then the ground. She hit with bone-jarring force, rolling to a halt amid the underbrush. Every muscle screamed in agony. Her wing hung behind her, blood trickling from shallow cuts, the vivid blue-green hue of her heritage staining the leaves. Her breaths came in ragged gasps.

Above her, the wyverns circled before retreating toward the nemods, their task complete. Their cries faded into the wind, leaving only the pounding of hooves growing louder.

Lyria staggered to her feet as pain seared through her. Blood oozed from her broken wing and grazed flesh, but she pressed on, her steps faltering as the forest loomed ahead, its towering trees dark and foreboding.

Before she could take another step, a sharp whistle pierced the air.

Her instincts screamed—too late.

The nemod's spear struck, its jagged edge tearing through flesh and grazing her ribs. She gasped, her cry obliterated by the storm as agony flared through her body. Blue-green spilled between her talons as she clutched the wound, her vision blurring.

Gritting her teeth, she seized the shaft and wrenched it free. A fresh jolt of pain seared through her, but she couldn't afford hesitation. She tossed the spear aside, stumbling toward the forest, her wings flattened to her back as she forced herself forward. She had to keep moving.

The white dragon's words lingered in her mind. "Trust the forest. There, you will find refuge."

A roar of pounding hooves renewed her determination. Clutching her bleeding side, Lyria staggered into the woods. The air shifted—cooler, heavier as if the forest itself breathed. Shadows deepened, twisting and coiling around her, muffling the storm's fury.

Following close behind, the nemods reached the forest border and slid to a halt, their mounts carving deep gouges in the sodden earth. Rain pounded down around them, steam rising where it struck the beasts' overheated flanks. The creatures snorted and shifted, talons raking at the ground—but none crossed the threshold.

Something in the air pulsed.

A low, thrumming vibration rolled outward from the trees—ancient, watchful. The forest loomed like a living sentinel, its shadowed canopy whispering with old magic. Magic that had not stirred in an age. Magic that warned.

The leader snarled, his yellow eyes narrowing. He felt it in his bones—a boundary not meant to be crossed. A warning etched into the marrow of their kind.

And yet…

Through the haze of mist and storm, a glimmer of light caught sight. Faint and fleeting but unmistakable.

The mark.

Silver light traced the curve of her shoulder as she disappeared into the gloom.

A guttural cry tore from the lead nemod's throat, and the others answered, their rage overwhelming their fear. They would not let her vanish. Not now. Not with the mark alive and burning.

With howls of fury, the nemods drove their mounts into the trees—into the forbidden wood—into the arms of the ancient power that waited there.

Chapter 4

Eldrin glided through the grove, his steps keeping time with the drumming of rainfall on the leaves. Around him, the forest thrummed with life: the hiss of rain cascading through leaves, the rich scent of damp soil rising, and the low groan of branches bending under the weight of water. It was a symphony of nature's raw, untamed power, each element harmonizing with the quiet hum of enchantment in the atmosphere.

This was no ordinary forest. The enchanted forests' magic pulsed with unseen energy, each leaf, stone, and tree tied to an ancient power. Hues of green and gold glowed, their light blending with the elves' ethereal essence. For Eldrin, the forest remained a place of solace and strength. But tonight, it seemed different—watchful, as if it braced against an unseen threat.

The young elf slipped into the hollow of a towering tree, its blackened core a scar from a fire that had long since been extinguished. The dense scent of moss and decaying leaves mingled with the rain-soaked air, grounding him in the present. Around him, ancient giants stretched skyward, their branches intertwining like cathedral arches, each one bearing the marks of centuries of storms, fire, and flood. They were pillars of resilience, yet even they seemed to sway under the storm's fury.

Eldrin crouched low, steadying his breath as he replayed the events of the last hour. The tempest had dispersed his patrol, separating him from the others and forcing him onto a different path. Then, through the persistent beat of rain, came the faint sound of hoofbeats in the distance—unnatural, out of place, and discordant with the forest's melody. His instincts had kicked in, urging him upward. With effortless grace, he climbed into the canopy, his sharp green eyes surveying the area.

That was when he'd seen them: nemods. A small band of shadowy creatures on their monstrous horse-like mounts galloped at a determined pace toward the forest's perimeter. Their beasts, with jagged spines and dark fur that merged with the shadows, ground to a standstill at the tree line, their sharp hooves digging into the wet earth. A faint, smoky mist flowed from their flared nostrils, giving them an eerie, spectral presence. The nemods' glowing eyes gleamed like embers in the rain, their guttural snarls carrying through the downpour. They shouldn't have been here—not in Elven territory, much less about to enter the sacred realm. Yet here they were, a blight moving against the natural order.

Eldrin's chest tightened at the memory. He had never seen a nemod before, only heard the grim tales of their malice and their unyielding loyalty to darkness. From his vantage point, he had counted two dozen, their movements precise as their mounts paced at the wood's border. But there could have been more lurking within the storm's shadows.

As the tempest raged on, he had descended quietly, intending to loop back and warn the others. But the relentless downpour conspired against him, drowning out sound and muddling his way through the trees. Now alone and unsure of his comrades' fate, he sought refuge in the hollowed tree. Its charred, gnarled core offered a fleeting sense of safety, a place to wait out the storm—and to remain hidden should the horrid beasts dare to enter the grove.

Behind the curtain of rain, Eldrin heard hoofbeats. They were unmistakable—clawed hooves slashing through the thicket, moving toward the interior of the forest. They had crossed the unseen border and entered the sacred realm. His grip tightened on his bow as his watchful eyes examined the rain-soaked shadows for movement. The dark riders were coming.

He covered his pointed ears with the hood of his cape while raindrops fell off his back. The wool repelled the rain, but he knew it would become heavy if soaked. His hand felt for the dagger, sheathed in well-worn leather on his belt. It had been a gift from his father, King Eldermyst, decades ago on his coming-of-age birthday. Over the years, the handle had melded to his grip as if it had always been a part of him. The sturdy blade could split a hair and slice through sinew with ease. Adrenaline coursed through his body in anticipation. His heart pounded like a war drum, the rhythm echoing in his ears.

A bead of sweat trickled down his forehead, combining with the rain dripping from his hood. His hand reached for an arrow in his quiver, but his fingers met only the smooth, empty lining of the leather casing. Panic flared as he patted the quiver again, disbelief spreading like wildfire within his chest. The heavy weight on his back now felt mocking—a hollow reminder of what should have been there.

Frustration twisted into desperation. His trembling hands searched once more, numbed by the damp cold, as his breaths quickened, shallow and uneven. He clenched his teeth, trying to steady himself, but the realization settled like a stone in his gut.

How could I forget my arrows? Idiot.

The first rule for a warrior, broken. The remembrance of his brother's voice, sharp with derision, transcended the pounding storm. If Thalendir ever found out, Eldrin knew he'd face endless ridicule.

Moments like this gnawed at him, a cruel testament to how far he still had to go. He wasn't ready—not yet—not to meet the battles he dreamed of or the looming presence of his brother's effortless skill. Rain hammered the forest, matching the beat of his frustration. All he could do was hope Thalendir was still sprawled across his silken bed, unaware of the storm and this humiliating failure.

His fingers abandoned the empty quiver and shifted to his sword, the familiar weight a slight comfort against the growing unease twisting at his core. The blade, secured at his hip, acted as a lifeline, its sturdy presence grounding him amidst the storm of uncertainty. He had trained for years to wield it, mastering every strike and parry with painstaking precision, but this was no sparring match. This enemy was real, and he was alone.

Rain muffled the hoofbeats, but Eldrin could still sense their steady rhythm reverberating through the woodland, faint but relentless. The hair at the nape of his neck prickled, and his stomach churned at the idea of the evil creatures entering the forest. *Why were they here?*

He knew they hadn't detected him, and if he remained still, they would pass him by as his dark cloak against the charred tree rendered him almost invisible. Still, his muscles tensed, ready to spring.

While the storm roared around him, the rain beat against the trees, each drop heavy, as if the heavens themselves were warning of the danger. The howling wind twisted through the branches, shrieking as if the forest were alive.

He might have missed her if a jagged streak of lightning hadn't flashed overhead, illuminating the forest in stark relief. For a heartbeat, the world froze. A lone figure darted among the bushes, her braided locks glimmering in the flash before darkness swallowed her again.

Was that a…?

Eldrin's breath choked, his heart thumping harder than the downpour on the canopy above. He blinked, trying to clear his vision, then strained his eyes to pierce the gloom. There was no mistaking the colored braids—that was definitely a drelf.

What was she doing here?

Drelves didn't belong in these parts—didn't belong anywhere. For centuries, they had been outcasts, banished from both the Elven and dragon realms. To the elves, they were living reminders of broken oaths and forbidden unions, creatures to be feared and despised. And the dragons regarded them as an abomination. Half-breeds. Part dragon, part elf, they survived in obscurity, unwanted by either world.

Yet here she was, in the Elven realm where her kind had not set foot in centuries.

Another flash of lightning split the heavens, lighting up the ground ahead. He caught the glistening trail of blood pooling in her erratic footsteps. A twisted wing hung, dragging with each labored stride, flapping against her ridged, saw-toothed back. Her injuries were severe. Whatever strength she had left was fading fast, her movements unsteady and uneven.

And then the unmistakable shrieks of nemods rising over the tempest, chilling and primal. The guttural cries merged with the relentless beat of hooves, increasing in intensity with each second. The realization struck him with sudden force.

They're hunting her.

His thoughts hurried. She didn't belong here, and neither did they. The drelf was an enemy of his kind, an outcast by nature and blood—but the nemods were a blight, their presence defiling the sacred forest. That fact alone unsettled him, the peace of the grove already straining under their dark intrusion.

If he stayed hidden, the nemods would never know he was there. But they would find her. Wounded and unable to fly, she didn't stand a chance.

Eldrin's stomach twisted with indecision. He had to decide—now.

Helping a drelf would be an act of treason, a betrayal of his kin that could shatter his reputation, his family's honor, and everything he had worked so hard to achieve. The logical choice was simple: stay hidden, let the nemods finish her. She wasn't his concern.

And yet, something in her broken, desperate form reached into his very being, and he couldn't ignore it. The way she stumbled forward, bleeding and struggling, as though sheer will alone kept her on her feet, it ignited a response beyond reason, beyond even fear.

Before he could stop himself, his feet moved.

The driving rain stole his breath, but before doubt could creep in, his legs propelled him forward. A strong wind whipped through the trees, tugging his hood back and stinging his face with icy drops. He didn't slow. Committed now, he surged through the undergrowth, his cape billowing behind him, tracking the trail of shimmering blue-green blood.

Her injury was the only reason he could catch up. Without it, she would have vanished into the darkness, another ghost lost amidst the trees. Each stride sent fire through his muscles, his lungs burning as the damp, frigid air clawed at his throat. The soaked mass of his cape dragged at his shoulders, but he pressed on. His boots skidded over the rain-slick earth, every misstep forcing him to lurch forward to keep his balance.

He saw her just ahead, gasping for air as she rested on a towering redwood. Her face was ashen, contorted with pain, as she pressed trembling hands against a gaping wound on her flank. Each ragged breath seemed a battle in itself. Blood dripped in uneven splatters upon the forest earth. The vibrant blue-green liquid glistened against the rain-slick ground, its stark hue a vivid testament to her injuries. Her armored shell, once shimmering with Draconic elegance, was now smeared with her life's essence, the metallic sheen dulled by streaks of battle and pain.

The redwood she leaned against was no ordinary tree. Towering above the grove, it was ancient and commanding, its bark etched with intricate patterns that seemed to ripple with magic. This was the entrance to the Elven realm—a hidden portal veiled within the tree's colossal form. Its branches stretched toward the heavens, cradling the storm, while its enchanted bark pulsed with a faint light, a barrier visible only to noble elves. The veil shimmered, guarding the secret route that led into their mystical realm—a sanctuary few could find and even fewer could enter.

For outsiders, attempting to pass through without permission could lead to disastrous consequences—becoming trapped between worlds, lost in a void, or worse. Eldrin's pulse raced as he weighed the risk, but with the nemods closing in, the hesitation was no longer an option.

He had to act.

Murmuring the ancient incantation, his voice trembled but refused to falter. The words flowed from his lips, each syllable pulling at the magic woven into the tree as the ground below them rumbled. A shimmering doorway materialized within the bark, light spilling out in ethereal waves as the hidden entrance revealed itself.

The drelf stared at him, her eyes wide with a mix of confusion and defiance. She attempted to move, but Eldrin was already in motion. With one final, determined stride, he surged forward, colliding with her as his shoulder drove into hers. The impact forced her backward, her cry of pain swallowed by the roar of the storm as he propelled them both through the portal.

Behind them, the veil of magic swallowed the guttural snarls of the nemods and the splintering crack of wood. Soft light enveloped them, the forest vanishing in an instant as they tumbled into the safety—and uncertainty—of the elf kingdom. The portal sealed behind them, cutting off the howling storm and the relentless pursuit that had driven them here.

The rain continued, but here, it fell in a steady, rhythmic drizzle.

It wasn't his most graceful entrance—or the softest. The impact left them prostrate on the floor of the Elven passageway, its cool air filled with ancient magic that hummed in the walls. But they'd made it. The storm's roar faded behind them, replaced by an eerie calm. Within the stronghold of his father's realm, they were safe for now.

The fall left them both stunned. Eldrin stirred first, his body pressing against hers. The unexpected warmth of her scales jolted him, but before he could react, her tail snapped with surprising speed. It coiled around his legs before whipping outward, sending him sprawling a short distance away. The force wasn't enough to hurl him far, but it knocked him off balance, leaving him gasping as he landed hard and struggled to catch his breath.

Pain etched every movement she made, but adrenaline pushed her onward. She clawed at the dirt, her tail swaying behind her to keep him at bay. Blood seeped from her side, her breaths uneven and strained. The blade in her hand trembled, catching his eye. Sleek and deadly, it bore the hallmarks of exceptional craftsmanship—strong and elegant, forged with skill. Outcast or not, the drelves hadn't forgotten their Elven roots.

Eldrin scrambled to his feet, his sword ready in his grip, though he hesitated to raise it. His blood surged while observing her struggle, her frame trembling to rise. Smaller than he had imagined a drelf to be, she was still an imposing figure. Her scaled skin was dulled by grime and streaked with blood. The damaged wing hung awkwardly behind her while every ragged breath seemed to drain her remaining strength.

A guttural snarl escaped her as she attempted again to get to her feet, the blade dipping as her arm shook under the effort. Desperation burned in her eyes, but it was dimming fast, the fight in her fading like sparks in a dying flame.

With one last faltering attempt to push herself upright, her knees buckled. She crumpled to the floor, the blade slipping from her grasp as her tail fell motionless.

Eldrin froze, his sword still raised, his breaths coming fast and uneven. She lay broken, her strength spent, her trembling body suspended between life and death. The sight of her vulnerability extinguished his hesitation.

He approached cautiously, each step measured as the rain fell around them.

Kneeling beside her, his eyes caught the shimmer of something on her neck—a pulsing spiral of ethereal light. It seemed to call to him, tugging at something deep within. For several seconds, the light mesmerized him. But there wasn't time to linger on its mystery.

Her wounds were severe. The fractured wing hung limp, and her side gaped open, spilling her lifeblood in sickening rivulets. She needed help—quickly. But why had she risked entering the Elven lands—and what could compel the nemods to chase her into the forbidden territory?

Those answers would have to wait. Eldrin knew only one thing—he had to get her to safety before her presence became a danger to them both.

Chapter 5

Eldrin's breaths came ragged and uneven.

What have I done?

The thought struck him. Sharp and unforgiving. He had acted on instinct, driven by something he couldn't name, and now the significance of that choice felt like a crushing tide. A lifetime of rules, of boundaries ingrained in him from birth, had shattered in a single reckless moment. And he had done the unthinkable.

He brought a drelf into the Elven kingdom.

The portal had closed behind them, and there was no undoing it now. Blood was soaking into the soil like ink seeping into parchment. The metallic tang of it permeated the air, thick and rancid.

His stomach twisted into knots. Rainwater dripped from his hair and cloak, trailing down his skin in icy rivulets, but that paled compared to the chill settling in his bones.

What if the others return and find her?

His thoughts raced to Caelith and Aelar—the elves he had patrolled with. The storm had separated them, but if they had regrouped and come back through the portal, there would be no hiding what he had done.

For a fleeting moment, he almost wished he had abandoned her in the forest. Eldrin pressed his knuckles to his lips, fighting to quiet the storm rising inside him. His gaze dropped to the drelf. She looked fragile. Smaller than she had seemed in the woods. The feral snarl he had witnessed before was gone, replaced by the quiet, desperate struggle of a being clinging to life.

A low groan escaped her lips, weak, twisting his resolve tighter. The sound permeated the night, frail and haunting—a reminder that her life hung by a thread. The weak glimmer of her life force—something unique to beings of magic—flickered against the damp earth like the last gasp of a dying ember.

His hand drifted to the pouch tied at his waist. The small vial of healing potion inside felt cool against his trembling fingers. Gantar had given it to him months ago, insisting it might save a life one day. Eldrin uncorked the vial, a faint herbal scent permeating the damp air, and poured a few precious drops onto her open wound.

At first, nothing happened. Then, a gentle, golden glow spread from the injury, illuminating her pale face. Torn flesh knitted together—imperfect, but enough to slow the worst of the bleeding. Her shallow breaths grew steadier, her ashen complexion gaining a touch of color.

It failed to heal her fully, but it bought him precious time.

Time he couldn't waste.

His eyes scanned her battered form, noting the broken wing sprawled beside her. If he dragged her like this, it would catch on roots and stones, tearing the wound open again. He had to secure it.

Gritting his teeth, he ripped a strip of fabric from his tunic. The noise of the tear seemed to echo in the stillness, louder than it had any right to be. He slipped the makeshift bandage beneath her wing, fingers working to bind it against her side. The knot wasn't perfect, but it would keep the damaged appendage out of harm's way.

"That'll have to do," he muttered, brushing rain off his forehead.

Straightening, he hooked his arms beneath her shoulders and lifted with a grunt. She was heavier than he expected, her scaled armor slick with rain. He shifted his stance, planting his boots into the wet earth, and pulled.

Eldrin made his way along the winding pathways, dragging her limp body, his boots scuffing against the stony walkways slick with rain. Ancient trees loomed overhead, their canopies woven into the structures of Elven homes—seamless blends of nature and civilization. Lanterns flickered from windows, casting a golden glow against the misty night.

He could only hope that the rain would wash away the trail of blue blood and drag marks left behind.

Through the haze, the familiar outline of a cottage emerged, nestled among the towering oaks. Gantar's home. A beacon of quiet wisdom and safety. If anyone could help, it would be the old sage. He was a healer, a seer, and in this moment, Eldrin's only hope.

Eldrin felt his heart race as he staggered to the doorway, his breathing labored. Whatever came next, he would have to face it. He rapped against the wood.

"Gantar," he whispered. "It's Eldrin. Please—I need your help."

For what seemed like an eternity, there was no reply—only the steady drip of rain from the eaves. Eldrin tapped his boot as each second stretched unbearably. He fought the urge to knock again.

A faint shuffling came from within, followed by the groan of the door hinges. A dim glow spilled out, casting silhouettes across the rain-slicked ground. Inside, shelves lined with vials, herbs, and ancient tomes stretched to the ceiling. The warm, earthy scent of dried sage and lavender permeated the night air—a marked divergence from the dampness outside.

Gantar stood in the doorway, his silver hair tousled, his robe loosely fastened. His eyes squinted under the low light, their sharpness cutting through his otherwise disheveled appearance.

"Eldrin? What's the—" His words faltered as his gaze fell on the drelf in Eldrin's arms. His expression shifted from mild curiosity to alarm, his silver brows knitting together as his gaze swept over her battered form.

"Is that a…?"

"Yes," Eldrin interrupted, his voice raw with desperation. "It's a drelf. I didn't know where else to go."

Gantar's eyes darkened when he noticed the bluish-green marks spread across Eldrin's hands. His voice became low and measured. "You realize what you've done? The risk you've taken? This could destroy you—your reputation, your family, everything."

Eldrin locked eyes with him without flinching, his voice calm despite the turmoil clawing inside him. "I know," he said, his jaw tight. "But she'll die if we delay any longer. Are you going to help or not?"

A hush fell between them, broken only by the faint crackle of the hearth inside. Gantar's sharp eyes searched Eldrin's, his stern expression softening just enough to reveal a hint of reluctant respect.

At last, he stepped aside. "Bring her in."

Eldrin crossed the threshold, the gentle warmth of the cottage enveloping him, a welcome reprieve from the storm's relentless bite. The air was saturated with the fragrance of herbs and the sweetness of burning incense, a balm against the weight heavy on his soul. Shelves crammed with cracked leather tomes, vials of glowing liquids in an array of colors, and bundles of dried plants hung from the rafters, creating an aura of quiet mystery. Enchanted lanterns cast a soft light, their flickering shadows playing across like whispered secrets.

Eldrin maneuvered the drelf onto a cot, her weight sagging lifelessly in his arms. "It was nemods, Gantar. They followed her into our forest, crossing the wards. Almost two dozen of them, moving among the trees like they owned our forest. The wards that should have held them off were useless. And the storm… it was unnatural. The roots, the wind—it all felt alive like nature itself was trying to push them back."

Gantar's expression darkened. "Nemods, here? The wards have held for centuries. For them to falter now…" He grimaced, his voice grim. "The nemods don't act alone, Eldrin. An ancient force drives them. More dangerous than any you've encountered."

Eldrin hesitated. "Like what?"

Gantar dropped his voice and looked around before speaking as though someone might hear him. "Vartharax. A being of shadow and greed, whose name time has lost but whose presence lingers in obscurity. He shapes their every move, spreading corruption like rot through the veins of the realms. If the creatures were hunting her, it's because she is more dangerous to their master than we can yet understand."

The idea of such a being—one powerful enough to unravel wards that had stood for centuries—was almost impossible to grasp. Still, the storm, the nemods—it all pointed to a threat far exceeding what he'd imagined.

Gantar remained silent, his focus narrowing as he worked. Eldrin noticed the strain in the sage's hands, the slight pause in his movements as if he, too, sensed something vast and dangerous weighing upon them. His fingers stilled as a silver glow appeared, the faint light chasing the shadows over her body. His sudden gasp shattered the quiet.

"What is it?" Eldrin asked, stepping closer.

There, obscured by blood and grime, was a tattoo—a mesmerizing silver design of spiraling symbols and ancient runes. It pulsed, the ethereal glow casting soft light across her pale features, rendering her both fragile and otherworldly.

Gantar's breath caught. His countenance changed from curiosity to something far deeper—reverence, fear, and disbelief mingled in his piercing eyes. "By the ancients..." he whispered, "The mark."

Eldrin stared at the tattoo. A subtle warmth seemed to radiate from it, brushing against his senses like a suggestion of something ominous. In a brief instant, he felt a connection, an invisible thread linking them, pulsing as if it carried the echoes of ancient knowledge. He dismissed it as exhaustion—or perhaps the strain of carrying her so far. "You know what it is?"

Gantar's hand lingered close to the tattoo as though touching it might invoke some irreversible power. "This … is no ordinary drelf."

Eldrin frowned, his unease growing. "What do you mean?"

The sage hesitated before replying. He straightened, his look a combination of reverence and alarm. "This mark…" Gantar paused, his words heavy. "It matches the descriptions from the oldest texts. They speak of a reckoning, of a time when the kingdoms will either mend or fracture. I never thought I'd see it in my lifetime." His eyes lingered on the mark, and Eldrin saw a suggestion of doubt in the sage's eyes.

"A reckoning? What kind?"

"The prophecy doesn't give simple answers," Gantar admitted. He paused, then recited softly,

"A child of fire and shadow shall bear the mark,
A spark to ignite what was lost in the dark…
When the realms stand at the edge of despair…
A union of foes…"

His words ceased, his voice heavy with meaning. "Riddles shroud the rest. But it's clear—the balance hangs on forces that were never meant to align."

A worried look crossed Eldrin's face. "You're saying she's… what? Part of this prophecy?"

"I'm saying she bears the mark," Gantar replied, his expression darkened as he leaned closer, his gaze tracing the intricate patterns of the tattoo. The delicate lines twisted and spiraled, alive with an inner light that shimmered like moonlit water, casting gentle shadows that danced along her skin. The glow seemed to shift as if responding to unseen forces, carrying a quiet hum like the ring of distant bells. "What that means… we don't yet know, but the prophecy warned it held great power… and great danger."

The drelf stirred, a low groan escaping her lips as Gantar worked with practiced precision, examining the wound with a steady hand. His calming presence and quiet focus eased Eldrin's fears, though tension still simmered beneath his composed exterior. The sage's every movement bore the mark of experience; his touch was careful yet confident, even as his mind raced with unspoken questions. He poured a few drops of a shimmering liquid onto her wounds. The mark glowed brighter as the healing magic took hold, knitting the torn flesh together.

"I used some of the potion you gave me," Eldrin said, breaking through Gantar's thoughts. He patted the leather pouch at his belt, his tone tentative. "I hope that was the right thing to do?"

"It's likely the only reason she's still alive," Gantar replied, his voice gentle but weighted with the seriousness of the situation. His eyes reverted to the mark, the glow reflecting in his eyes. "But if what I suspect is true, keeping her alive might have consequences far beyond what either of us could imagine."

As the sage bent over the drelf, Eldrin's anxiety eased, finding comfort in Gantar's steady presence. With practiced touch and careful movements, the sage instilled Eldrin with a small measure of hope that the drelf might survive the ordeal. But a shadow lingered in the room, the unspoken questions that no one could yet answer.

"She'll live," Gantar said. "But this wing may never be the same. I'm not sure she will fly again."

Eldrin's shoulders sagged — the thought of her being grounded forever was disheartening. But he pushed it aside. Gantar was the best healer they had, and if anyone could mend her wing, it was him.

Better to focus on the questions still gnawing at him.

"Why would she risk entering our forest in the first place?" he asked, his voice tight with confusion. "A drelf crossing into Elven lands? It's reckless. She had to know she wouldn't be welcome here. It makes no sense."

Gantar studied the unconscious drelf, his expression tightening as he traced the faint shimmer pulsing at her throat with his eyes. The silver mark glowed softly, bathing her in light, as if something ancient, long hidden, was trying to surface. He faced Eldrin, his tone quiet but confident. "We may not yet grasp it, but one truth is certain. You and this drelf… are bound to something much more significant than either of you knows."

"You think I'm part of this… prophecy? Eldin asked.

Gantar's expression softened. "Perhaps. But the storm that brought you to her, the nemods breaking through our wards, her mark—these are not mere coincidences."

Eldrin didn't answer, but he recalled the moment he'd caught sight of the drelf's symbol. He had felt something—an inexplicable warmth, a connection that defied reason. It unsettled him. "What do we do now?"

"We protect her," Gantar said. "And we learn. The council must not know of her presence. If they discover she's here…" His voice faded, his expression grave.

"They'll kill her," Eldrin finished. He squeezed his fists, uncertainty curling within him like smoke. "And if the nemods come back?"

"Then we fight," Gantar said. "But make no mistake, Eldrin—this is only the first wave. What lies ahead will test us all."

Eldrin didn't answer. He stared at the drelf, her brand casting a pale shimmer upon the walls like ripples in still water. Whatever this prophecy meant, he could feel its pull — steady, relentless — drawing him toward something unknown. He had prepared to face blades, not omens. But this… this was heavier than steel.

He emitted a gentle sigh, the turmoil inside him shifting—not gone, but quieter, like distant thunder. He was unaware of what path lay ahead, but he knew one thing: Whatever had brought him here, he couldn't walk away.

Chapter 6

Eldrin wove through the quiet streets of the Elven city, avoiding the main roads as the predawn shadows were waking. His footsteps light against the cobblestones, slick with lingering moisture from the night's storm. The grand spires and elegant arches of the city rose around him, bathed in the soft hues of early morning. Ancient trees, their roots intertwined with the stone pathways, rustled softly as if the city itself were stirring from its slumber.

When he got to the palace, he opted for a less conspicuous entrance—a side door used by the servants and guards. Slipping inside, he ascended the stairs toward his chambers, careful to avoid any patrolling sentinels. He paused for one last glance at the city. Somewhere out there, forces were moving—forces that could alter the destiny of all realms. And somehow, he was now entwined in that destiny.

He stepped into his room, closing the door behind him with a weary breath, and stopped cold. Thalendir lounged on his bed, twirling Eldrin's quiver of arrows between his hands.

With a sly grin, his brother said, "Lose something?"

Eldrin forced a casual smile, though the thunder within betrayed him. "Ah, there they are. I've been looking for those."

Thalendir leaned back, his hair shining with the first rays of sunlight, giving him an almost ethereal glow. "Out on patrol without arrows? That's careless even for you, little brother."

"Didn't think I'd need them," Eldrin said, shrugging off the tension as best he could. "Did you sneak into my room just to admire my quiver, or are you angling for my patrol shifts?"

Thalendir's laugh was soft and sharp, like a blade drawn in jest. "Please. You and I both know Father only sends me on the *important* assignments." His grin widened, but something flickered beneath his smile—something weary, though it was gone as quickly as it came. "Judging by your state, though, I'd say you were the one angling for excitement. Wrestling shadow panthers, were you?"

Eldrin chuckled, avoiding his brother's piercing gaze. "Shadow panthers are myths, stories to scare young elves. You know that."

"Are they?" Thalendir's voice dropped, his gaze sliding to Eldrin's hands. "Because it seems you had a run-in with something-or someone—you'd rather not mention."

Eldrin stiffened as Thalendir's gaze flicked down, his gaze locking onto the stains on his hands, bluish-green. His fingers twitched, then balled into fists before he shoved them into his pockets, heat creeping up his neck.

Thalendir's brows knit together, his stare lingering for a beat too long. Then his gaze shifted, taking in the torn fabric of Eldrin's tunic, the frayed edges damp with rain and darkened by something else.

Eldrin ground his teeth, tension ticking in his cheek, willing himself to stay steady under his brother's scrutiny. But the moment stretched, charged with an unspoken question Thalendir didn't need to voice.

"Just stumbled into some thorn bushes. Nothing exciting," Eldrin said as he tugged at his torn sleeve, trying to hide the scratch beneath.

"Thorn bushes that leave a bluish stain on your hands?" Thalendir's eyes fell upon Eldrin's fingers.

Eldrin's stomach lurched, but his demeanor was light. "Just tree sap from blackwoods. Sticky stuff, hard to wash off."

"Hmm." Thalendir didn't look convinced, though he let it slide. "No nemods, then? Father's eager for any news from the borders."

Eldrin paused for the briefest of moments. "Quiet night. The storm made tracking difficult."

Thalendir's gaze lingered, but then he rose from Eldrin's bed and laid a hand on his brother's shoulder. "Well, I hope you're ready for breakfast. Father expects your report. Try not to make it sound *too* dull." He turned to leave but took a parting shot. "And Eldrin, wash up. Father's not the only one who notices when someone's chasing shadows."

The door closed behind him, leaving Eldrin alone in his chambers. He sank onto the bed, his breath unsteady. Thalendir knew more than he let on—he always did. The jests about myths and shadows had a way of cutting too close to the bone. Eldrin stared at his hands, the faint stains still visible under the morning light. Rising, he crossed to the washbasin, scrubbing at his skin until it stung.

He peeled off his tunic, examining the torn sleeve. Mud streaked the fabric, and a dark stain from the drelf's blood marred the weave. He couldn't risk anyone finding it. Tossing the tunic into the fireplace, he watched as the flames consumed it, the cloth curling and blackening until it was nothing but ash.

Changing into fresh clothes, he caught his reflection in the mirror: dark circles beneath his eyes, his hair in disarray. He brushed it with his fingers and straightened his tunic, forcing himself to look more like the son his father expected.

Eldrin entered the dining hall, his boots reverberating against the gleaming stone floor. The tall, arched windows allowed shafts of golden morning light to pour in, illuminating the long table where Thalendir already lounged, sipping from his goblet. Across from him, at the head of the table, sat King Eldermyst.

The Elven King's presence was a force unto itself. Regal yet restrained, he carried himself with a quiet authority, his posture unshaken by the burden of ages. His silver hair, streaked with pale gold, fell in elegant waves past his shoulders, untouched by time's heavy hand. Though the years had passed, his face bore an ageless quality—sharp, refined, and carved by both wisdom and war. His emerald eyes, clear and unyielding like sunlight filtering through ancient leaves, held the onus of countless battles, victories, and the responsibility of the entire kingdom.

A subtle, ever-present magic hummed around him as if the Elven lifeblood pulsed within him. His long emerald robe, embroidered with silver thread, mirrored the twisting branches of the oldest Elven trees—a tribute to their enduring legacy. Upon his brow rested a thin circlet of white gold—unadorned yet unmistakable. More than a symbol of rule, but of duty, sacrifice, and the ever-watchful guardian of their realm.

To Eldrin, his father had always seemed more legend than flesh. He was the keeper of Elven wisdom, the unwavering force that held their kingdom together. Yet, for all his power, there was a distance about him—an untouchable quality that often left Eldrin unsure of where he stood.

"Sit," Eldermyst said, conveying the quiet authority of a ruler who did not need to raise his voice to be heard. The tone was formal but not unkind.

Eldrin took his seat, mindful of his father's gaze, which lasted just long enough to make him feel scrutinized. He slipped into his seat across from Thalendir, doing his best to avoid his father's piercing gaze. The gravity of the night's events settled upon him, but he schooled his face into an impassive mask. He reached for a goblet of water, gripping it as if it might steady the chaos in his soul.

Thalendir, not one to let a moment of discomfort pass unnoticed, leaned back in his chair and turned his head to their father. "It appears to have been an uneventful patrol. Eldrin's here in one piece, after all."

Eldermyst silenced him with a glance before shifting his focus to Eldrin. "Tell me what transpired. Did you see any nemods?"

The directness of the question cut like a razor. Eldrin was aware of his father's unwavering gaze pinning him in place, waiting for an answer. He had rehearsed his story, but now, under his father's scrutiny, every word appeared fragile. "There were signs of movement near the border," He began, his voice controlled, notwithstanding the constriction around his heart. "Tracks that could have been nemods, but nothing conclusive. It felt as if they were testing the boundaries—probing, but not crossing."

Eldermyst's sharp green eyes narrowed, searching for any cracks in his son's words. "No other signs of trouble?"

The image of the drelf flashed in Eldrin's mind: her fragile form, the luminous brand at her nape, the blood that would not wash away. He made himself hold his father's gaze, though his stomach churned. "Nothing else, Father. The storm made it difficult to track anything further."

A long silence followed, during which Eldermyst studied him. His majesty possessed the ability to peel back layers with a single glance, and it seemed to Eldrin that every unsaid truth was etched across his features. At last, Eldermyst gave a curt nod. "Very well. The borders remain a concern. I will discuss further precautions with the captains."

Eldrin nodded, though the anxiety within him only tightened. He was uncertain how long he could keep this charade intact.

Across the table, Thalendir smirked, leaning forward. "No nemods? I'm almost disappointed. I was hoping for an exciting tale over breakfast."

Eldrin glared at him, but Thalendir pressed on, his grin widening. "Although judging by those circles under your eyes, I'd say your patrol wasn't as quiet as you're letting on."

"Enough," Eldermyst said, severing the conversation with sharp precision. "We have no time for games, Thalendir."

Thalendir threw up his hands in mock surrender, though his smirk didn't falter. "Of course, Father. My apologies."

The rest of the meal passed in tense silence. Eldermyst finished quickly, rising from his seat. "I expect you both to resume your studies," he stated, his demeanor leaving no room for debate. His eyes rested on Eldrin briefly, as if searching for something unspoken, before he turned and swept out of the room.

Thalendir lingered, swirling the remains of his drink. "You know, brother," he said, his voice subdued, "you almost look like you've got secrets worth keeping."

Eldrin stiffened but showed no emotion. "I'm just tired, Thalendir. Patrols take their toll."

"Of course," Thalendir said, his grin sharp. He stood, brushing imaginary dust off his garment. "But whatever kept you out there… I hope it was worth it." He paused as though contemplating his next words. "Oh, and Eldrin? Don't let Father catch you slipping. His patience is thin these days."

He left the dining hall with the same effortless ease he carried in everything, leaving Eldrin alone at the table.

Eldrin sat staring at the untouched food on his plate. The sunlight streaming through the arched windows was too warm, too bright for the storm that raged within him. The drelf, her mark, the prophecy—it was all unraveling faster than he could make sense of it. Thalendir's parting words lingered in his thoughts, needling the fringes of his carefully constructed composure. Did his brother suspect something more? Or was Thalendir just being his usual sharp-tongued self?

He scrubbed a hand over his face, exhaustion tugging at him. Somewhere in the city, Gantar was tending to the drelf, and forces vastly more powerful than he could comprehend were in motion. The truth was a burden he couldn't share, but how long could he bear it alone?

Rising, Eldrin straightened his tunic and forced his thoughts into order. The day was just beginning, and the shadows of last night were already clawing at his resolve. But for now, he could only move forward—step by step, lie by lie.

As Eldrin wandered through the dimly lit halls, his steps heavy, the familiar walls of the palace offered little comfort. The ancient tapestries and glowing lanterns, once symbols of peace and home, seemed to loom over him now, their presence suffocating. He knew he should head to the library, as his father had instructed—duty called, and duty was everything—but events of the night before kept replaying in his head, dragging at his every step. Sleep tugged at him like an unseen hand, insistent, yet he doubted that rest would come.

In his chambers, Eldrin pushed open the door and collapsed onto his bed, the cool linen doing little to still the whirlwind of thoughts. He closed his eyes, willing himself to forget—briefly—the prophecy, the drelf, and the nemods. But his mind refused to settle.

Desperation to quiet his thoughts prompted him to hum an ancient Elven song, one his mother, Thariel, had once sung to him. The melody rose unbidden, soft and fragile, a relic of a simpler time when her voice still filled the palace. Thariel had been the heart of their family, her presence a balm to even the sharpest wounds. It was a lullaby—one she used to sing to him and Thalendir when they were young. Its verses spoke of warriors returning to peace, of rebirth from the ashes of war. The tune filled the room, weaving through the quiet like a whisper from the past, carrying the memory of her warmth, her smile, and the way her voice could calm him, even in his darkest moments.

The tightness in his shoulders eased a bit. Thoughts of the prophecy and the drelf's mark still pressed on him, but the song quieted the noise in his head, if only for a few minutes. As the last notes left his lips, his eyelids grew heavier, and finally, sleep claimed him.

His dreams were restless, fragments of shifting images and shadowed terrors. He ran through dense underbrush, the thud of heavy paws behind him. Shadow panthers—those creatures of myth—watched him with glowing eyes, their movements as fluid as the darkness they stalked. The low growl of nemods reverberated among the trees, their shapes flickering in and out of sight like the shadows themselves hunted him.

And then there was the drelf. She stood before him, her silver tattoo glowing like moonlight against the dark. Her eyes pleaded as she reached for him, but regardless of how fast he ran, the forest pulled her further away, swallowed by shadows closing in around her. The growls grew louder, the cold pressing against him like an icy dagger.

A chill swept over him, and Eldrin jolted awake, his heart hammering as he fought to orient himself. Dim morning light seeped through the heavy curtains, casting muted shadows across his chamber. The dream held onto him, its urgency like a haunting refrain he couldn't escape.

Sitting up, he rubbed his face, willing the fragments of the dream to dissolve. But the images stayed with him: the pleading look in the drelf's eyes, the shadows that filtered through the foliage, the ominous sense that the storm wasn't over. It felt less like a dream and more like an omen.

Rising, Eldrin crossed to the window. Sunlight stretched across the horizon, golden light spilling into the fog, but it brought no comfort. The tempest remained in secret places, reaching beyond the borders as forces moved, shadows deepened, and the world crept closer to the verge of something immense and dangerous.

Chapter 7

Drakor's rage had settled into a cold, simmering fury as he neared the enchanted woods. The dark forms of his nemod army shifted, eyes downcast and wary. They sensed the storm within him, the darkness he could unleash at any moment. The air rippled with his presence, tension crackling like lightning before a storm.

Their mounts grew impatient, their hooves scraping at the ground. They were equally menacing beings—massive and muscular, that melded with the shadows. A thin, smoky haze escaped their flared nostrils as though they exhaled the shadows themselves.

A harsh snarl shattered the stillness as Drakor spotted his commanding officer, Skalvorr, leading the group. His broad shoulders squared, even though his eyes remained lowered in deference. The silence stretched on for an unbearably long time as Drakor stopped in front of him. When he spoke, his voice was a low, venomous hiss, every syllable laced with barely contained fury.

"You let her escape."

Skalvorr flinched. "We-we wounded her, my lord. Almost brought her down..." He faltered, his voice cracking like brittle glass. "But she fled… into the forest."

Drakor's eyes darkened. "You followed her into the Enchanted Forest?" His tone was cutting, each word a shard shattering the silence.

Skalvorr gave a stiff, halting nod. "We… had no choice," he rasped. "She crossed the boundary into the trees, and we pursued her."

For a beat, Drakor said nothing. The forest's ancient wards were near impenetrable to creatures of darkness; their mere presence on its sacred ground was an impossibility. A shift, then—a disturbance in the forces at play, tilting toward the darkness.

A slow, twisted smile crept across his maw, his eyes shining with dark pleasure. Yes, this was good. Proof that the shadows were growing stronger.

But the satisfaction was fleeting. His claws flexed, digging into the moist earth. "How did she escape you?" he demanded, voice low and deadly.

Silence hung thick between them, suffocating the air. Skalvorr trembled, his shoulders quaking under his master's gaze. The other nemods stood motionless, silent witnesses to their commander's unraveling.

"I asked," Drakor hissed, "how?"

The nemod's head jerked upward as he choked out the answer, his breath rattling. "An elf, my lord. An elf appeared, snatched her, then vanished into the trees."

Drakor froze the words like ice in his veins. He rose, his claws uncurling. "An elf?" The atmosphere seemed to darken, the cold deepening as Drakor spoke the words.

How could that be?

The broken covenant ensured hatred among the realms—elves, dragons, and drelves alike. There was no alliance left to unite them, and yet — an elf had risked life and honor to rescue a drelf.

Why?

His thoughts spiraled, as the ancient prophecies and fragmented murmurs of the Great Covenant long ago broken, came to the forefront. Could there be something more? A truth hidden even from Vartharax?

Drakor's attention shifted to the shadowed edge of the enchanted woods, his eyes narrowing. Whatever secrets that drelf carried—whatever knowledge she possessed—had just become far more dangerous. "So, the fools meddle," he growled, his voice like crushed gravel. "The realms stir, daring to disrupt the master's design."

The seething anger in his words was undeniable, but beneath it lurked something colder—unease. For all his cunning, Drakor had not foreseen this. The prophecy's threads were pulling taut, twisting in ways he had not expected. And somewhere in their shifting, the drelf had escaped.

Drakor turned, his sickly gaze falling once more on Skalvorr. "Do you know what you've done? That mark she bears—it is power, Skalvorr. The power that we need."

The nemod captain tensed. "She is one drelf, my lord. We will find her—"

"*One drelf?*" Drakor roared, his tail snapping with a sound like thunder. Skalvorr recoiled, baring his teeth in a hiss of instinctive fear. Drakor hung over him, his crooked neck lowering until his eyes blazed inches from Skalvorr's own. "One drelf bears a mark that threatens everything we have built. One drelf has already eluded you. And now, Skalvorr, I will show you the importance of one drelf."

"My lord—" Skalvorr began, but Drakor straightened with a sudden, sinister calm. "Please—" Skalvorr began, but the utterance hadn't left his mouth before Drakor struck.

With a speed that belied his wiry frame, Drakor's tail snapped with the force of a whip, coiling around Skalvorr's throat. He ripped the nemod from his mount, slamming it against the earth as the nemod's eyes bulged and its claws scrabbled against the unyielding hold. Mud splattered across his charred hide as he choked, his breath reduced to strangled gasps.

Drakor towered above him, his eyes blazing. "Failure," he hissed, tightening his hold until Skalvorr's vision swam. "An *elf* aided her, you pathetic wretch. And you let them slip away."

Skalvorr's claws twitched, his chest struggling with futile attempts to draw air. His mount snarled and backed away, knowing better than to interfere.

Drakor's gaze looked toward Varagos, Skalvorr's younger and hungrier second-in-command, who remained at the outskirts of the group. The nemod's eyes shone with anticipation, and his fangs bared in something too eager to be called a smile.

"Varagos," Drakor said, his voice like silk wrapped around a blade. "Take command of the hunt. Skalvorr has proven himself… inadequate."

The ambitious young beast dipped his head, satisfaction gleaming in his ember-lit eyes. "As you command, my lord."

Drakor released his hold on Skalvorr with a violent shove, letting the disgraced nemod collapse into the mud, gasping and wheezing like a dying animal.

"Get out of my sight!" Drakor spat. "And hope I don't find a better use for your bones."

Skalvorr dragged himself away, his shame palpable, his claws digging furrows into the muck in an attempt to crawl away.

Drakor's gaze swept the assembled nemods, his voice a cold, merciless lash. "Station guards at the last place you saw them. The forest cannot shelter her forever. If she reappears, you will deliver her to me—alive. And if you fail…" His eyes glowed brighter, a promise of pain and fury. "You will wish for a death as swift as Skalvorr's should have been."

The ensuing silence was thick and stifling. Skalvorr remained prostrate, gasping for air, his humiliation and rage barely concealed. The other nemods shifted, claws scraping against the ground as if trying to root themselves against the coldness of Drakor's gaze.

But where Skalvorr trembled, Varagos moved with cold efficiency. His predatory gaze swept over the others, eyes simmering with cruel determination.

"Well?" Varagos barked, his voice a whip-crack of authority. "You heard the orders. Move!"

The creatures sprang into action, spurring their mounts with frantic urgency. Their monstrous mounts reared with piercing cries as they reared on hind legs, then thundered forward, their hooves striking the earth like war drums.

Varagos's laughter followed them into the night, a sound filled with twisted delight.

Drakor stood motionless, watching them fade into the night. A blast of icy wind swept across the wasteland, tugging at the ragged edges around his wings as the shadows at his heels writhed like serpents, whispering and curling around him in anticipation.

His gaze moved to the distant treeline, where the mystical woods loomed like a barrier of secrets. Somewhere beyond its impenetrable veil, the drelf and her Elven protector lingered. For the time being, the ancient wards would shield them, but nothing lasted forever. Wards could crack, just as alliances could shatter.

Soon, the balance would shift further. Darkness would bleed across the boundaries that struggled to hold it back.

Drakor unfurled his wings. The gust from their movement sent the shadows writhing at his feet, coiling like hungry spirits. A cruel smile curled his lips. "You can hide mark bearer," he murmured, his voice carrying like frost on the wind. "But the shadows always find their prey."

In one thunderous flap, he ascended into the skies. The power of his ascent cracked the frost-laden earth below, sending fissures spattering outward. The land trembled, and above, the sky darkened as though unwilling to bear his passing.

As Drakor rose higher, the shadows pooled beneath him, stretching like dark fingers across the land—a harbinger of the storm yet to come.

Chapter 8

The claw was the first thing he noticed.

It jutted from the mud at an awkward angle, its jagged edge glinting as the morning sun broke. He crouched beside it, his sharp blue eyes inspecting the ground. The claw was small but unmistakably drelf. He softly whistled.

"What in the name of the stars are you doing here?" he muttered, plucking the claw from the muck. Haste—or desperation—had splintered its edge, breaking it off.

The elf's sharp gaze swept the trees ahead. He wasn't certain of what he expected to find—since it must have been hours since the drelf passed this way-but his senses were on high alert, sharpened by the hours of searching for signs of the other patrol. Master Trainer Aldarath dispatched him to the forest to locate Caelith and Aelar, whose patrol of the deeper woods failed to return. His search had turned up little but unease and unanswered questions—until now.

Around the claw, the ground told its story in faint details. A line of tracks departed from the spot, uneven and erratic. Nearby, bluish-green blood pooled in a footprint, the edges dried and cracked. The scout knelt closer, sniffing as the slight hint of drelf blood mingled with the damp, earthy scent of the soaked forest reached his senses.

However, it wasn't merely the claw or the blood that caused him to shudder.

A short distance past the drelf's footprints, there was something else—far more troubling. Pressed down into the soil were tracks with clawed hooves and an elongated stride, the unmistakable marks of Shadowmanes. And there was only one creature that rode those nightmares...

The elf stilled, his heart thudding against his ribs. A drelf and nemods in the elves' forest? The very idea was unthinkable. The wards that protected this place should have kept such darkness in check. However, here was the proof, plain as the claw he held.

He moved cautiously, his boots silent against the sodden earth. The trail was anything but faint now. Deep gouges, carved into the mire where the Shadowmanes had charged, tore the ground ahead. Their clawed hooves had carved a chaotic path, shredding the underbrush and uprooting smaller plants. The elf's frown deepened, his steps faltering as he examined the destruction. Sacred land, scarred by darkness.

The blood trail grew fainter, lost amidst the upturned soil and broken branches. Then, a second set of tracks caught his eye—lighter, deliberate, and unmistakably Elven. The young scout crouched, tracing a finger over the impression.

Whoever had left these prints was quick, their stride determined, as if they were fleeing—or chasing.

The tracks veered toward the massive redwood at the grove's center, its towering presence impossible to ignore. Like a sentinel, the tree towered, its wood scored with elaborate patterns that pulsed with magic, even under the pale morning sun. The portal. A knot formed in the elf's stomach at every step.

The nemods and their Shadowmanes had diverged, vanishing into the deeper forest. But the Elven tracks—lighter and precise — led straight to the base of the colossal tree. There, just before the bark's shimmering surface, the trail stopped.

The elf crouched, his keen eyes examining the earth for any evidence of a struggle. The faint bluish-green blood smeared across the roots and mingled with the mud told a simple story: the drelf had been here. But she hadn't been alone. The Elven tracks had merged with hers as if whoever had been with her had pulled her through the portal.

His hand brushed against the rough bark of the redwood. The soft drone of its magic vibrated under his fingertips, confirming his suspicions. Someone recently opened the portal; its residual energy still lingered, sharp and raw, as if the woods protested the intrusion.

"Well," the elf breathed, slipping the claw into his pocket. "This just got interesting."

Straightening, he traced the churned path deeper into the woods. The enormity of what he'd uncovered descended upon him. If the drelf was inside the kingdom, there would be consequences. And because the nemods had dared to follow her into sacred ground, the danger wasn't over.

Whoever had traversed the portal—elf or not—was now behind Elven walls. And Finnian intended to find them.

A dim light throbbed within the fog of her mind, flickering like a heartbeat amidst the dark void. Lyria groaned, her body heavy and uncooperative as consciousness dragged her out of the depths. Her head throbbed, each pulse sending tendrils of pain spiraling outward, and her shallow breaths prodded the pain in her ribs, tugging her further from unconsciousness.

Where am I?

The thought crept sluggishly into her mind, tangled with fragments of memory—the tempest, the forest, the relentless pursuit by the nemods. And then... him. The elf.

Her eyes fluttered open, though the world remained blurred, her vision swimming. What she noticed first was the warmth beneath her. Blankets. Not the cold, wet forest floor. Her fingers touched the soft fabric and, beneath it, the smooth surface of carved wood.

The surrounding room was dim, lit by the flickering orange glow of a fire. Shadows danced across stone walls etched with intricate carvings, their twisting lines almost hypnotic. Somewhere nearby, the light fragrance of herbs infused the air, mingling with the sharper tang of salve on her skin. A low, muffled voice reached her ears, barely within earshot.

A jolt of panic shot through her chest, her breaths shallow and uneven as she fought the instinct to flee. She shifted, testing her limits. A dull ache flared at her side—not the searing pain she remembered, but the lingering ache after fresh wounds. Her hand drifted toward her back and froze.

Her wing.

Clawed tips brushed the bandages wrapped around its base, and her stomach sank. A sharp pang of pain shot through the joint as she flexed it—raw and fragile, a bitter reminder of the wyvern's talons and her own weakness. She clenched her fists, frustration boiling inside her. How could she have let herself get captured?

Memories surged back: the nemods, their snarling Shadowmanes, the spear of pain that had racked her body. But more vividly, the elf—the sharp angle of his ears, the piercing green eyes, the cascade of dark hair catching the storm's light. And something else. A glint of silver.

Her heart hammered. This wasn't the forest, nor was it anywhere familiar. The intricate carvings on the walls, the soft thrum of magic around—this was Elven territory. Enemy ground.

Lyria's hand drifted to her throat, where the tattoo burned under her fingertips. Its edges pulsed in synchronously with her heartbeat, dim but unyielding. She squeezed her eyes shut, willing the sensation to fade, but it only stoked the unease coiling in her gut.

The mark was the reason she was here. The mark had ruined everything.

A creak of wood startled her, jerking her attention to the door. She stilled, her breaths shallow as the footsteps approached, slow and measured. Her hand slid toward her side, seeking her dagger that wasn't there.

The door opened, spilling a sliver of golden light inside. Shadows shifted near the threshold, and Lyria froze as she braced for what—or who—would step inside.

The trail was faint but clear enough for Finnian's sharp eyes to follow. The churned mud and shattered branches leading to the portal had given him plenty to work with, but here, inside the elf kingdom, the signs were subtler. A scuff in the ground, a bent blade of grass—minor details only a practiced tracker could piece together.

He crouched near a shallow depression in the dirt, his gloved fingers brushing over a faint line where something—or someone—was drug along. Drops of aquamarine blood dotted the ground, and their hue was muted now as they dried in the morning air. Finnian's gaze narrowed. Whoever had moved the drelf had been careful but not careful enough.

The signs brought him to a small clearing, where a humble stone cottage nestled beneath the boughs of a massive oak. Smoke curled from the chimney, and the subtle herbal aroma drifted nearby. Finnian's mouth tightened into a grim line. Gantar's cottage. The healer. Of course.

He stayed hidden, his instincts guiding him. If Gantar was involved, this was no simple matter. The ancient sage didn't take sides or dabble in mundane affairs. Whatever had driven someone to bring such a creature into the kingdom—and Gantar's care—was something far bigger than a reckless mistake.

Finnian circled the cottage, staying low and silent. The faint drag marks stopped at the door, but a fresh trail caught his attention—lighter, quicker, and unaccompanied. He crouched to study them, tracing the path as it departed from the cottage and back toward the palace.

The trail wound its way into the forest, growing firmer as the ground transitioned from soft forest loam to the kingdom's heart. Finnian's jaw tightened as the tracks became familiar. Whoever had been here was an elf, and they'd left Gantar's cottage in haste.

When the tracks brought him to the palace's outer wall, Finnian scanned the doorway and the surrounding stones. The subtle trace of bluish green near the entrance remained on the grey stone. Someone had left a side door ajar, a faint smudge of dirt marking its edge. His fingers brushed against a shred of fabric clinging to the stone doorway's edge. He pulled it free, holding it up to the light.

A voice, smooth and sharp, interrupted the quiet. "Interesting place to find you snooping around, Finnian."

Finnian's stomach dropped, his fingers encircling the thread he'd just found. He turned, erasing all emotion from his expression. Thalendir stood nearby, his arms crossed, his golden locks cascading over his shoulders. The faintest smirk tugged at the corners of his mouth, yet his eyes glinted with something far colder—curiosity edged with suspicion.

"Thalendir," Finnian said, tucking the fabric into his pocket. "Didn't expect to see you here."

Thalendir raised his brows, his eyes glancing towards the door. "Funny. I could say the same about you. Find anything I should be concerned about?"

"Nothing for certain," Finnian replied. "Something worth checking out further."

"Something?" Thalendir's brows rose, his tone sharpening. "What kind of something?"

Finnian held his jaw rigid; however, his tone remained calm. "Just some strange signs—figured it wouldn't hurt to be thorough."

Thalendir took a step closer, his gaze tightening as he studied Finnian with the precision of a blade. "Thorough is good," he breathed. Thalendir's sharp amber gaze fell to Finnian's hand, curled tight before flicking back to his face. He smiled, but his eyes remained cold. "You aren't chasing shadows along with Eldrin, are you?"

The words hung suspended, a veiled warning that made Finnian's pulse quicken, but he forced a grin. "If I find anything more concrete, you'll be the first to know."

Thalendir's smirk widened. "Good. Because whatever my little brother found out there—if it's not nemods—it's something far worse."

He hesitated, his expression flickering as if suspended between a jest and a genuine thought. "Keep an eye on him, Finnian. Eldrin has a gift for stumbling into trouble, and I'd rather not see him dragged into something he can't handle."

Finnian blinked, surprised, but nodded. "I'll do that."

Thalendir's gaze lingered, the sharpness returning. "And Finnian? Watch your step. The forest has enough shadows without you adding to them." With that, Thalendir turned and disappeared around the corner, leaving Finnian alone in the taut silence of his words.

Slowly, he uncurled his fingers, the thread's familiar weave sending a jolt through him.

His jaw clenched, his thoughts racing.

Eldrin. What have you done?

Chapter 9

The door creaked open, and Lyria's breath hitched, her muscles tensing despite her weakness. She expected to see the elf from her fractured memories, but someone else entered the room. An older elf with weathered features and soft green eyes beneath heavy brows. His movements were deliberate, his presence calming but authoritative.

"You're awake," the sage remarked. He carried a small wooden tray laden with steaming tea and a bowl of something that smelled faintly herbal.

"Who are you?" Lyria asked, her voice hoarse but sharp, her gaze tracking his every move.

He placed the tray on a nearby table, unfazed by her tone. "I'm Gantar," he replied. "Healer, sage, and occasional fool for getting involved in matters far beyond my station." He paused, his expression softening. "You're safe here, for now."

Lyria's gaze hardened. "Safe. That's a bold claim, considering what's hunting me."

Gantar's expression tightened, his tone tranquil but resolute. "Bold, yes. But not baseless. The wards around this place are ancient, and they will hold for now. He stopped, letting the words settle. "But safety, like trust, must be earned — and defended."

Lyria's fingers gripped the blanket's rim as she eyed him warily. "Where am I?"

"In my home," Gantar replied, pulling a chair closer to her bedside. "Someone brought you here after your grave injuries in the woods?"

Her jaw clenched. "Him."

Gantar nodded. "Yes. Eldrin."

The name hit her like a chord she hadn't expected, resonating through the tangled mess of her thoughts. "Why?" she demanded. "Why did he help me?"

"Perhaps you should ask him that yourself," Gantar said. "Though I imagine even he doesn't fully understand his reasons yet."

Lyria scoffed, shaking her head. "Do you have any idea what he's done? We are enemies," she hissed.

"I'm aware of that. And the risks of having you here," Gantar said. "But those risks don't outweigh the consequences of doing nothing."

Her gaze narrowed. "And what consequences are those?"

Gantar leaned back, his gaze unflinching. "You carry a mark of great significance, Lyria."

She stiffened, her breath hitching in her throat. "How do you know my name?" she demanded.

He gestured toward the sign on her neck. "You spoke it in your sleep," he said. "And the mark... it whispered your name," he said, his tone thoughtful. "This is no ordinary magic. It carries something ancient, something alive. It recognized you even before you woke."

Her hand brushed the spirals, her unease deepening. "The mark knows my name?"

Gantar nodded. "Magic works in curious ways. It has a will of its own, and it seems bound to your identity. But I'm more interested in what brought you into our forest. What led you into Elven territory?"

She paused, her eyes darting to the fire as if its glow could shield her thoughts. "I saw... a dragon," she muttered, her voice faltering as the words escaped. She hung onto the blanket as if bracing against a storm. "In my dreams. She warned me the nemods were coming for me."

Gantar stilled as the room held its breath with him. "A dragon?"

"Yes." Her fingers tightened against the blanket. "But not like the ones you've heard of, not like the black beasts in your songs of war. It was white, with scales like starlight, its eyes blazing with something... ancient. She instructed me to 'Seek the enchanted forest. Trust it's magic."

Her words lingered, infused with an unspoken gravity. Gantar's sharp gaze softened, his thoughts racing. "A white dragon," he murmured. "No one has seen such a thing since the Great Covenant fell. They all vanished..."

"Well, there is at least one left," Lyria said.

Gantar studied her, then spoke with quiet conviction. "If a white dragon appeared, then you are here for a good reason. The nemods, the mark, even your entering Elven lands—it's all a piece of a larger thread."

Lyria met his gaze, her defiance faltering under the pressure of his certainty. "You don't understand," she said, her voice softening to a raw edge. "I don't want to be part of anything except my kingdom. And I had to leave that behind. The mark — It's a curse. And curses destroy everything they touch."

"Curses can destroy," Gantar agreed. "But they can also remake. Whether it breaks you or forges you, depends on the strength you bring to bear."

Lyria's hand brushed against her neck, where the mark pulsed beneath her fingers as she searched his eyes. "Do you know what it means?"

"Not yet," Gantar admitted. "I've seen it's like only in the oldest texts—fragments of prophecy most would dismiss as legend. That mark has drawn dark forces to you, and it will continue to do so until its purpose has been fulfilled. But I know this: it's no coincidence you are here. The storm brewing around you isn't one you can face alone."

Lyria's gaze dropped, her fists curling in her lap. "But why me? I didn't ask for this." Her voice cracked, but she bit it back, refusing to show weakness.

"No," Gantar said. "But it's yours. And denying it won't make it go away."

The words hung in the air, heavy with truth. Lyria's breathing slowed, though her expression remained taut, her emotions hidden beneath the surface. She averted her gaze, her eyes glued on the dancing flames.

"Why do you care what happens to me?" she muttered.

Gantar studied her briefly, his expression softening. "Because there's more at stake here than your survival. Or your kingdom. If you fall, the balance of the realms will fall with you."

Lyria flinched, the force of his statement sinking deep into her chest. She didn't want to believe him, but the urgency in his tone was impossible to ignore. Her fingertips grazed against the mark again, seeking answers in its glow.

A faint knock at the door startled them both. Gantar's head spun toward the sound, his calm demeanor hardening.

"Stay here," he said. "And don't move unless I say."

Lyria opened her mouth to argue, but the sharpness in his gaze silenced her. She watched as he crossed the room, his steps measured but purposeful, and disappeared through the doorway, closing it behind him. Left alone, the fire cast restless images on the walls, matching the turmoil within her. Confusion, fear, and a hint of unwelcome hope swirled in her core as she strained to hear what might unfold beyond the door.

The muffled creak of hinges broke the quiet as Gantar opened the front door to a familiar figure. Eldrin stepped inside, his boots making no sound against the worn wooden floor. His eyes darted around the room, tension clear in the way he carried himself.

"She's awake," Gantar said without preamble, closing the door behind him. His attention was fixed on Eldrin, sharp and assessing. "And she's not pleased to be here."

Eldrin released a breath, passing a hand over his hair. "I wouldn't expect her to be. Where is she?"

Gantar nodded toward the rear room. "Resting. She's wary—and rightly so."

Eldrin paused, his hand hovering near the door's handle. "Can I see her?"

Gantar scrutinized him; the old sage's gaze was sharp but not unkind. "If you're prepared for what that means. She's angry."

Eldrin swallowed, the repercussions of his actions settling over him again. But he couldn't ignore the need to understand more. To understand why he had risked everything for a stranger.

He drew a steadying breath, then grasped the handle, his pulse quickening as his fingers encircled the cool metal.

He pushed it open.

Lyria's eyes snapped to his, sharp and defensive. Her posture was stiff; her bandaged wing draped to one side. Though her complexion was pale, her expression was defiant, her hands clenched.

"You're the one," she said, her voice edged with suspicion. "Who brought me here?"

Eldrin nodded, entering the room. "I am."

Her gaze flicked over him again, searching for some trace of mockery or malice. She found none, and that unsettled her more than she cared to admit. "Why? You had no reason to help me."

Eldrin replied. "I couldn't let those creatures kill you. Not on my watch, anyhow."

Her expression hardened, and she looked away, her fingers fidgeting against the blanket's edge. "You have put us all at risk."

The words hung in the silence, thick with meaning. Eldrin inched closer. "You were being hunted like an animal. I couldn't just stand by."

Lyria's eyes darted back to his, searching his expression for some sign of deceit. "And what now? Do you expect me to thank you?"

"No," Eldrin said. "I expect nothing from you."

A faint scoff escaped her lips. "You're a fool, elf. Helping me only puts you in danger—and your kingdom."

Tension tightened in Eldrin's jaw, but before he could respond, Gantar's voice broke through the tension. "Enough," the sage said, approaching with a small tray of herbs and salves. "Neither of you gains anything by snapping at each other."

He set the tray on a small table near the bed, his gaze shifting between the two of them. "We're all in the same storm now. And if you think this is the end of your troubles, you're both sorely mistaken."

Lyria's eyes narrowed. "What do you mean by that?"

Gantar's shoulders sagged. "The mark on your neck draws attention, and not the good kind. They hunted you once already. Do you suppose they'll stop now?" His voice softened, yet his words carried an edge. "This is only the beginning."

A heavy silence settled in the room, the crackling fireplace the only sound between them. Eldrin shifted, his fingers grazing his dagger as though its familiar weight might ground him.

Gantar's gaze settled on Eldrin, laden with the seriousness of what he was about to say. He paused, his countenance hardening. "The beasts are still lurking, and they won't stop until they've accomplished their purpose."

Eldrin's chest tightened. "And their purpose is... her," he said, glancing toward Lyria.

Gantar nodded, his expression grave. "The mark calls to them. As long as she remains, they will keep coming. And it's only a matter of time before the elves discover she is here. Attacks from the darkness will escalate. The kingdom will suffer for it."

Eldrin shifted from one foot to the other, his mind racing. "Then what do we do?"

Gantar moved closer, his voice calm but unyielding. "You've seen what's happening. The nemods aren't gone. They're waiting. For her. She must leave."

Eldrin's face hardened, his gaze flicking to Lyria, who confronted his stare with defiance.

"There must be another way," Eldrin said. "She could hide—"

"Hide?" Gantar's tone mellowed, but his words spoke the truth. "For how long? Days? Weeks? The nemods won't give up, and neither will the palace guards if they find out we're sheltering a drelf."

Lyria stiffened at the word, her eyes narrowing. "And what happens if they find me?" she asked, daring him to answer.

"They'll execute you," Gantar said. "And the mark's loss will leave the realms vulnerable to the darkness that hunts it."

Eldrin flinched, the decision looming over him. His mind whirled with the implications, each more damning than the last.

"She must go," Gantar continued, his voice softening but still firm. "Tonight."

"Leave? And go where?" Eldrin asked, his voice rough with disbelief.

"The Shrouded Vale," Gantar said. "It's dangerous, but it's your only chance."

Eldrin's mouth opened, then closed again. He glanced at Lyria, her face guarded and unyielding.

"But it's—" Eldrin hesitated. "It's dangerous. The creatures there—"

"Are hostile to some," Gantar interrupted, "but not to all. The magic there is ancient, connected with the harmony of the realms. It will recognize the mark she carries. And if it doesn't..." He let the silence hang heavy between them.

Lyria's hand brushed her neck, her expression unreadable. "And if I refuse?" she asked, her voice low and bitter.

"Then you'll die," Gantar said.

Eldrin's protests faltered, his fists tightening. His gaze lingered on Lyria before shifting back to Gantar.

"Silverwind can carry you," Gantar said to Eldrin. "But she'll need her own mount. She certainly can't fly."

Lyria's lips thinned, her gaze turning toward the window. "We?" she asked, but her tone carried a challenge.

Eldrin hesitated, then squared his shoulders. "You can't go into the Shrouded Vale alone," he said, his voice heavy. "Gantar's right. You can't stay here. I will go with you."

Her face hardened, but she didn't argue.

"I'll prepare what you'll need," Gantar said, moving toward the door. "Food, water, and whatever supplies I can spare. But you can't wait. The longer you stay, the greater the risk to all of us."

He paused, his gaze softening as it shifted to Eldrin. "There's one more thing," he said. "Come with me."

Eldrin exchanged a quick glance with Lyria before following Gantar out of the room. As they walked into the main chamber, the healer crossed the room to a small wooden chest tucked into the corner. Gantar knelt and opened the chest with a gentleness that seemed almost reverent.

From within, he retrieved a leather pouch hidden among folded clothes. As he rose, Gantar extended the pouch toward Eldrin, his expression solemn.

Eldrin hesitated, his eyes searching the sage's face for answers he wasn't sure he wanted. But Gantar only nodded, his gaze steady, urging him to accept what was being offered. His fingers trembled as he held out his hand. The weight of the pouch was strange. Heavy, but not heavy.

How was that possible?

Eldrin loosened the drawstring, tilted the pouch, and let the cool, smooth stone slide into his palm. It was pale gray, streaked with faint blue swirls that shimmered even in the low light—like veins of frozen lightning caught within the stone's surface. It felt warm against his skin, a subtle thrum of energy pulsing through his fingertips.

"This is the Aetherstone," Gantar said, his voice hushed as if this moment demanded reverence. "It was your mother's. She left it in my care. To give to you when the time was right. It will guide you when you are lost. If danger is near, it will warn you. And if doubt takes hold, let it remind you—you are not alone. Your mother's faith in you will be with you even when she can't be."

"But…" Eldrin murmured. The stone was grounding in his hand, a tether to something beyond himself. Thoughts of his mother flooded his memory. This stone had once been hers, and now it would be like having a part of her with him. "Thank you," he said, his eyes moist.

Gantar placed a firm, yet gentle, hand on Eldrin's shoulder. "You'll carry much on this journey, Eldrin. Let this remind you that you needn't carry it alone."

Eldrin's shoulders slumped as the weight of the decision settled over him. His fingers closed around the stone, its warmth a fragile comfort against the chill of uncertainty.

From Lyria's room, the faint creak of wood signaled movement. The door was ajar, and through the narrow gap, her gaze met his—steady, unyielding, and filled with something he couldn't decipher.

"We leave at nightfall," he said, the words like stones lodged in his throat, though his eyes remained locked on hers.

Chapter 10

Sheltered by the darkness, Gantar led Eldrin and Lyria through a maze of narrow, winding trails deep within the Elven kingdom. The surrounding forest grew denser, and the air became cooler, as the path sloped downwards.

"This way," Gantar whispered, stopping before a thick wall of ivy cascading down a stone outcropping. He reached forward, his fingers tracing a series of hidden runes carved into the stone. As he murmured some ancient Elven words, the ivy shivered and parted, revealing a narrow tunnel carved from ancient stone.

"What is this?" Lyria asked, scanning the shadowed entrance.

"A hidden path," Gantar replied. "Few know of its existence, and even fewer have used it. Centuries ago, the elves created it as a safeguard, a way to leave the kingdom should the portal ever fall into enemy hands."

Eldrin frowned, holding Silverwind's reins. "Why haven't I heard of this before?"

"Because there was no reason before now," Gantar said. "The passage will take you to the border of the forest. But tread carefully—it has lain unused for many years."

The moon hung low over the forest as Eldrin and Lyria guided their mounts onto the trail that went deeper into the forest. Silverwind moved with practiced ease, her hooves silent on the soft moss beneath her. Beside her, a smaller, dark-coated gelding—Duskrunner, hastily saddled and borrowed from Gantar's meager stables—shifted under Lyria's uncertain grip on the reins.

Lyria winced as the motion jostled her bound wing, but she gritted her teeth and adjusted her grip on the reins. She muttered under her breath, frustration close to the surface.

"This is ridiculous," she snapped. "I'm a drelf—I should be in the air, not... bouncing around on this stubborn beast!" She hated being grounded and relying on this elf, who looked at her with equal measures of concern and mistrust. *I've survived worse,* she told herself, clenching her jaw. *I don't need him. Not really.*

Eldrin turned to her, his expression blank. "It's not the horse's fault you're tense. Relax, and he'll settle."

"Easy for you to say," Lyria shot back. "I've never ridden a horse before, and I'm not exactly in peak condition, in case you hadn't noticed."

Eldrin exhaled, forcing his voice to remain calm. "Just keep him steady and follow close."

As they rode on, Lyria's frustration grew. The makeshift strap Gantar had fashioned for her wing dug into her shoulder with every step, and worse, her tail kept catching on the saddle.

She shifted again, trying to find a more comfortable position, but the motion only unsettled Duskrunner further. "Do your kind ever think about practical design, or do you assume everyone is tailless?" she snapped, her voice filled with irritation.

Eldrin turned to look at her, one brow raised. "You're blaming the saddle now?"

"Yes," Lyria shot back as Duskrunner tossed his head. "This thing is clearly unusable for someone with a tail. It's like I'm sitting on it and trying to ride at the same time."

Eldrin bit back a smirk, though he couldn't resist a slight trace of amusement in his tone. "Tuck it to one side. Or maybe wrap it around yourself."

She glared at him, her eyes flashing. "I don't need your advice, elf."

"Suit yourself," Eldrin said, turning his focus on the trail before them. "Just don't fall off. I'd hate to explain that to Gantar."

Muttering, Lyria shifted her tail again, draping it over one leg. It wasn't comfortable, but it was better than the alternative. Duskrunner seemed to sense her change and settled into a smoother gait, though Lyria's frustration lingered. "At least he doesn't spook at every shadow."

Behind them, the lights of Gantar's cottage had long since disappeared, obscured by the dense trees. The road ahead twisted and narrowed, shrouded in shadow. Gantar's directions had been clear: avoid the main roads, stay hidden, and reach the Shrouded Vale before dawn.

The night air seemed to hum with anticipation, every rustle of leaves or snap of a twig drawing Eldrin's attention. He looked back at Lyria, her face pale but determined.

Hoofbeats. He was certain now. The rhythmic thud echoed among the trees in intervals, faint but steady. Eldrin's hold of the reins tightened, his senses attuned to every flicker of shadow and whisper of movement around them.

"Do you hear that?" he whispered.

"Hear what?" Lyria asked, her voice low, her mount shifting beneath her.

"Hoofbeats," Eldrin said, his tone taut. "Someone is following us."

Lyria glanced toward the path behind them, her unease sharpening. "Do you think it's patrols? Or worse?"

"I don't know," Eldrin admitted. "But we can't stop to find out. Keep moving."

Eldrin's fingers felt for the stone, its faint warmth grounding him. Gantar's words echoed in his mind: "It will guide you when you are lost. If danger is near, it will warn you." The soft pulse of the stone was a constant reminder—something or someone was out there. Lurking. Watching.

As the kingdom's lights disappeared behind the twisting trees, Eldrin cast one last glance over his shoulder. Doubts gnawed at him; every step away from home seemed more difficult. But the road forward allowed no space for hesitation. Too much depended on their survival—and on the faint hope that the Shrouded Vale would provide more than just safety.

A faint shadow flitted through the trees, just beyond the moonlight's reach. The watcher urged their horse forward, maintaining a deliberate distance. Their eyes fixed upon the twisting path ahead, the forest's unnatural stillness pressing in like a warning. Something ancient stirred, and for a fleeting moment, they wondered if they were following shadows—or stepping into a trap of their own.

Nestled within the woods, glowing eyes blinked into existence, then vanished. The air thickened, the ancient trees shifting as if stirred by an unseen breath. Magic coiled within the gloom, unfurling like a breathing presence. The forest appeared to awaken, its unseen power watching and waiting, poised to act.

Chapter 11

Suffocating darkness enveloped the Obsidian Hall, jagged spires of black crystal refracting flickering firelight. Shadows slithered through the vast chamber, their restless movement twisted and sharp, elongating the figures gathered before the throne.

Korrath stood, his scaled head bowed, yet his tone remained steady and deliberate. His fiery tail quivered as he delivered the news to his master. "Drakor has proven unsuccessful," he began, his voice penetrating the heavy silence. "The drelf remains free. Worse yet, an elf protects her within the kingdom's walls. The prophecy stirs."

Vartharax's eyes narrowed, the faint scrape of his claws against the armrest echoing.

Korrath pressed on, his voice gaining weight. "The realms teeter close to collapse, my lord. I propose we unleash the shadows. Let their hunger sweep the forest clean."

Vartharax leaned forward, the flickering light creating ragged shadows across his features. "Hmmm…" he said, his tone thoughtful. Black smoke filled his nostrils and spewed forth, creating dark clouds around his face.

"They will sow fear and devastation. Any unity the realms seek will crumble under their terror," Korrath pushed his idea further.

The black throne groaned under Vartharax's shifting weight. His talons flexed, gouging fresh scars into the obsidian stone as his molten gaze bore into Korrath. "You speak of unleashing chaos," he rumbled in a deep, resonant growl. "Yet you forget, Korrath, that chaos is fickle. It devours without distinction."

Korrath remained steady under the dragon lord's scrutiny, his red scales shimmering in the low light. "My lord, that is why we use them now. Their destruction will know no bounds—all will face their wrath. The realms will fracture, crushed by their own fear."

The corners of Vartharax's mouth formed into a sinister smile. "And what of our forces? Will your ambition see them torn apart as well?"

Korrath hesitated for only a moment. "Sacrifices will be necessary. But the cost of inaction is far greater."

Vartharax reclined on his throne, exhaling another plume of thick, acrid smoke. The tendrils coiled around him, weaving ominous shapes that seemed almost alive. "So… Drakor has failed me," he said at last, his voice hushed and dangerous. "And here you are, eager to offer solutions."

"Yes," Korrath said, his confidence returning. "The shadow panthers will take care of the problem. Lord, let me summon them, and they will tear apart this fragile alliance before it begins."

Vartharax was silent, his contemplation filling the chamber with an oppressive stillness. The flickering firelight seemed to dim, casting deeper shadows that stretched out like reaching claws.

Finally, the dragon king spoke. "Very well, Korrath. You may release them. Chaos it shall be."

Korrath's eyes shone with triumph, but Vartharax's following words froze him in place.

"But know this," the dragon lord continued, his tone razor-sharp. "If your plan fails, you will share in the panthers' appetite. Their hunger will find you next."

A low, guttural growl rumbled from the opposite end of the hall. The heavy doors creaked open, their groan echoing as Drakor entered. His eyes blazed with fury, and each deliberate step sent a sharp click reverberating through the obsidian floor. The tension spiked as his gaze locked onto Korrath with open disdain.

"You overstep, Korrath," Drakor growled with a deep rumble of barely contained rage.

Vartharax stilled, his molten eyes flaring with sudden, seething rage, locking onto Drakor's bent frame. His claws dug into the armrests of his throne, carving deep marks into the stone. Smoke poured from his nose, thick and acrid, the air around him trembling under the force of his displeasure.

"And YOU… have failed again." Vartharax's words resounded through the room like a thunderclap, each syllable dripping with venomous disdain.

Drakor wheeled to face his master, lowering his head but refusing to avert his gaze. "My lord, I will deliver them. We have cornered the drelf. She cannot hide for long."

Vartharax studied him, his countenance giving nothing away. "And yet, here we are. Again. With no results."

The words remained suspended like a death sentence. Drakor stiffened but stood firm. "The Elven wards, my lord, protect them. They impede our reach. But the nemods—"

Drakor's voice shook as he continued, "The nemods pursued them to the woods and severely wounded her. But the elf—"

"The elf," Vartharax interrupted, his tone a venomous growl. "The elf…?"

"My lord—"

"You swore you would succeed," Vartharax added, his voice descending to a deadly whisper that sent shivers down Drakor's spine. "You begged for another chance. And this is what you deliver? Nothing?"

Drakor's wings twitched, his head lowering. "I have them within reach, my lord. The drelf's wounds are severe. The elf may have saved her, but it is only a matter of time before—”

“Enough!” Vartharax’s roar shook the chamber, the dark walls groaning under his fury. Before Drakor could react, a thick, coiling tail lashed out and wrapped around his throat.

Drakor’s eyes widened in terror as the crushing force slammed him down, his claws scrabbling at the unyielding scales. The air left his lungs in a tortured gasp, his vision flickering.

Vartharax leaned forward, his eyes blazing with icy fire. “You forget your place, Drakor. You are nothing but a creature of shadows and scheming. Your value is measured only by your results.” His voice rumbled like an earthquake, the vibrations tearing through Drakor’s chest.

“My… lord… please…” Drakor choked, the words squeezed from his windpipe as his vision darkened. His claws twitched, fighting against the inevitable, his desperation palpable.

Vartharax’s grip tightened. “Do you think I have not heard of how an elf humiliated us?”

Drakor’s panic escalated. His limbs grew numb, the pressure against his throat merciless. His pride and his ambition—both shattered beneath Vartharax’s crushing grasp. But he compelled himself to focus, clawing his way through the fog of agony to find his voice.

“I will find them. I swear it. Give me….”

The plea escaped his lips, his body trembling with the effort to speak. The darkness seemed ready to swallow him whole. Then, Vartharax's tail uncoiled, and Drakor collapsed to the floor, gasping and coughing as air flooded his lungs.

"It is too late, Drakor," Vartharax snarled, his words like shards ripping through the room. Korrath will bring me the drelf. And if you show yourself again without invitation, I will tear you apart myself and feed your worthless carcass to the shadows."

Drakor shuddered, his entire frame quaking. "As you wish, Master." The words scraped over his tongue like shattered glass; each syllable laced with humiliation and venom. His body trembled with effort as he lifted himself from the floor, his legs unsteady, his eyes fixed on the floor. His mind reeled, every nerve alight with a mixture of dread and loathing.

How dare Korrath scheme against him? How dare Vartharax entertain such insolence?

But the fact was undeniable. He had failed. And Korrath had not only witnessed his disgrace but twisted the knife deeper with his smug proposal. Worse, Vartharax had granted the crimson beast permission to act—to seize what should have been Drakor's victory.

His claws scraped against the blackened stone, the tremors running through his limbs not only from the near-death chokehold—no, it was fury. Burning, seething fury.

Vartharax's attention moved to Korrath, whose smirk gleamed like fresh blood. "Unleash the Shadow Panthers," Vartharax commanded. "But heed this warning, Korrath—should their hunger turn upon you, your screams will be the last sound you hear."

"Understood, my lord," Korrath replied, though the satisfaction in his countenance was impossible to miss.

Vartharax reclined back onto his throne. "Now, both of you—leave me. And Korrath, do not return until you have the drelf."

Korrath dropped his head with exaggerated reverence, every movement taunting. He turned and strode out of the chamber, his heavy footfalls echoing down the darkened corridor.

Drakor followed, his breath rasping against his bruised throat. His fury clung to him like a sickness, its claws burrowing deep into his soul. As they passed the doorway, Korrath's voice slithered behind him.

"So … the runt has lost his master's favor. How quaint."

Drakor's eyes burned with raw, undiluted hatred. "You would do well to remember, Korrath," he snarled his tone a rasping snarl of pure malice. "The shadows are mine. And when they consume you, it will be at my command."

Korrath's laughter was a dagger twisting between his ribs, echoing down the passage like a death knell.

Drakor's taloned wingtips curled inward, the sharp points impaling the stone floor until thin rivulets of dark blood seeped forth. His breathing was shallow, ragged bursts, his throat raw where Vartharax's crushing hold had been. Yet, despite the pain, one truth blazed like fire.

Korrath would fail.

And when he did, Drakor would be there to tear him apart, piece by miserable piece.

Chapter 12

The trees groaned as though they were breathing, their ancient branches straining under an unseen power. Shadows stretched long across the narrow path, and every rustling leaf carried a sense of a watchful presence. Eldrin squeezed Silverwind's reins, his glance shifting to Lyria, who rode beside him.

"This place..." Lyria began, her voice quiet and uneasy, "it feels..."

"It is," Eldrin replied, his voice a whisper. "The enchanted forest has always been more than just trees and soil. It protects the Elven kingdom, and... it knows something is wrong."

Ahead, a faint glow pulsed in the dense underbrush—a sickly, shifting light that sent a chill down Eldrin's spine. The Aetherstone pulsed, its warmth confirming what he already knew. "The nemods are near," he said.

Lyria straightened on her horse, wincing as the movement bumped her injured wing. "How many?"

"Too many," Eldrin muttered, his sharp ears catching the faint growls that echoed in the trees. The creatures were closing in, their numbers swelling as more joined the hunt.

Duskrunner snorted and tossed his head, sensing the tension. Lyria stroked his neck, though her nerves betrayed her attempts at calm. "Let's get out of here," she said, digging her heels into the sides of her mount as she grabbed a handful of mane.

Before Eldrin could reply, the forest reacted. The wind shrieked within the trees, carrying with it a sound like a distant roar. Branches creaked and groaned, and the earth trembled beneath their mounts. Vines slithered across the ground, moving as if guided by unseen hands.

"The forest will slow them," Eldrin said, a ray of hope breaking through his fear.

But even as he spoke, glowing eyes cut through the night, their grotesque forms emerging between the twisting roots and shifting branches. They snarled and hissed, their claws destroying the living vines that sought to ensnare them.

"We can't outrun them," Lyria said, panic edging into her voice. "Not in here."

Eldrin's mind raced. The Shrouded Vale couldn't be far. While he scanned the path before them, he caught movement from his peripheral vision. A figure emerged from the darkness, cloaked and silent, moving with purpose.

Before Eldrin could react, an arrow flew past him, striking a nemod through its chest. The creature shrieked and then collapsed to the ground.

"Move! I'll hold them off!" yelled the cloaked figure.

Eldrin wheeled Silverwind around, confusion and frustration etched into his face. His bow drawn. "Finnian? What are you doing here?"

"Saving your neck, apparently!" His voice was incisive, his double blades flashing as his eyes darted to Eldrin, then the drelf beside him.

"Explain why you're committing treason with a—" Finnian hissed, cutting down a charging nemod.

"There's no time for explanations." The creature crumpled, spilling blood onto the forest floor. More crawled out of the night, their eyes glowing like embers, their snarls resounding.

The forest erupted into chaos. Vines lashed out at the nemods, entangling their limbs and pulling them to the ground. Trees groaned as their branches swung down like clubs, smashing into the attackers. But the brutes were relentless, clawing and tearing their way forward.

"We have to leave!" screamed Lyria.

"You think?" Finnian growled, parrying a strike from another nemod. He whirled, his blades shearing through the creature's thick hide as he pressed the attack.

Eldrin lept off his horse, landing beside Finnian.

"I'm not leaving you to fight them alone."

Finnian's mouth opened to protest, but another nemod charged, forcing him to redirect his focus. "Get out of here!" He shouted between strikes.

Eldrin clenched his jaw, slashing at a nemod with his dagger. "Not without you. We do this—together!"

The two fought side by side, their movements in unspoken harmony, but the onslaught of nemods pressed harder, their numbers overwhelming. The forest trembled with the force of the battle, roots shifting beneath them as if moved by an invisible force.

"Eldrin, let's go!" Lyria's voice penetrated the chaos, her mount stamping beneath her. "Get on your horse before it's too late."

Finnian slashed through another nemod and glanced ahead, where the forest opened a path. "I'll cover you," he shouted. "Get going—now!"

Eldrin stopped for only a split second before gripping his friend's arm. "Come with us."

Finnian shook him off, his expression a mix of fury and determination. "You want me to ride with her?"

"Right now, there is no other choice," Eldrin said, scanning the forest. "I'm not leaving without you."

Finnian turned to cut down another nemod, giving them the opening they needed. "Get her out of here. I'll follow—but you'd better have answers." Finnian's voice cracked like a whip, his gaze never leaving the encroaching nemods.

Eldrin swung back onto Silverwind, his hands trembling as he gathered the reins. He hesitated, but only for a moment. "We're heading north — catch up!" he yelled, his voice strained with urgency. He kicked Silverwind into motion, Lyria's gelding thundering alongside them as they raced through the woods.

Finnian whirled to face the oncoming nemods, his bow drawn. The arrow struck true, burying itself far into a snarling creature's throat. The beast crumpled with a guttural hiss, but others surged forward, their twisted forms crashing through the bushes with relentless fury.

His arrows flew rapidly, each shot buying his friend's precious seconds. But the monsters kept coming, their howls penetrating the vapor like knives. They circled him, hunger gleaming in their ember-filled eyes. Finnian backed away, his breath catching, until his boot struck something solid. His horse. Embermane's ears lay flat against its skull, nostrils flaring with wild terror, snorting, but the steed held its ground. He flung his bow onto his back and drew his sword, its steel gleaming as he spun and slashed at the closest nemod. Its black fangs snapped inches from his face before his blade found its mark, a deluge of black splattering the ground.

Finnian lunged for the saddle. "Yaw!" he shouted, grasping the horn and swinging himself upward just as Embermane lurched into a desperate sprint. His feet scrambled for the stirrups, his legs clinging to the horse's flanks.

The ground blurred, the air filled with snarls and the thunderous pounding of hooves. Finnian's heart raced with every frantic beat of his horse's gallop. Nemods erupted from the thicket, their guttural cries clawing at their heels, but Embermane's speed was unmatched.

Finnian shifted on the horse, his knuckles pale against the reins. His free hand fumbled for his bow, nocking an arrow with a quickness born of pure desperation. He spun and loosed it without hesitation, the arrowhead embedding itself into a nemod's leering face.

"Missed me, you filthy sacks of rot!" he roared, his laughter wild and breathless.

As Embermane's hooves thundered from the carnage, the sounds of battle grew more frantic. The forest itself seemed to scream in fury. Roots surged from below, wrapping around the nemods' legs, dragging them down into the shadows. A massive tree swung a branch with the force of a battering ram, smashing one nemod flat, but two more took its place.

Finnian's gaze snapped forward, catching sight of Eldrin and Lyria's distant figures just ahead. Relief rushed over him, but the grim realization of how close he'd come to being torn apart tainted it. He urged Embermane ahead. Though his legs ached from the desperate ride, he needed to close the gap between himself and his friends. The echo of snarls and guttural roars at his back kept his pulse racing, pushing him faster.

The air was colder, heavier, and thick with decay and ancient magic. Eldrin's Aetherstone flared, its warmth a guiding light in the encroaching darkness. The light penetrated the mist ahead, revealing a faint shimmer—a barrier pulsing with ancient runes.

"This must be it!" Eldrin shouted, his voice almost drowned out by the forest's roars and the distant screams of the brutes. He reined Silverwind to a halt, his eyes locked on the shimmering barrier ahead. The air around them was thick, humming with an ancient energy that pulsed synchronously with the Aetherstone's glow. Lyria pulled Duskrunner beside him, her gaze flicking between the barrier and the chaos closing in behind them.

"Eldrin, we have to keep moving," Lyria said, her voice tight, her breath ragged.

"Not without Finnian." Eldrin's jaw clenched as he turned, eyes scouring the shadows for any sign of his friend. His heart pounded against his ribs, the consequence of his choice to leave heavy on his chest. "He's coming. I know it."

Lyria's brows drew together, a mixture of fear and frustration warring in her expression. "I can hear the nemods. They're following us."

"We're not leaving him behind," Eldrin snapped, his eyes fastened to the shadowed path. His fingers were on the

Aetherstone, its warmth seeping into his flesh as if urging him forward. "Just… a little longer."

A sudden crash through the thicket tore their attention to the trees. Eldrin readied his sword.

Finnian erupted from the tangled shadows, Embermane charging forward with all the ferocity of a beast in flight. Finnian was frantic, his eyes darting wildly, desperate for breath, but miraculously alive.

"About time you two stopped dawdling!" Finnian called, though his voice trembled with exhaustion.

Eldrin sighed with relief. "You made it."

He swung down from Silverwind, pulling the Aetherstone from his pocket. He nodded for the other two to dismount as the stone's glow intensified, resonating with the magic of the Vale. The ancient barrier flickered before them, runes shimmering like liquid starlight woven through the mist.

The trio urged their horses forward, tugging at the reins; the ground beneath them trembled as the barrier loomed closer.

"Quickly," Lyria called, glancing back at the approaching shadows. Her face was pale, her grip around Duskrunner's reins tight. "They're gaining on us!"

Eldrin hesitated for only a moment before stepping towards the barrier. A pulse emanated from the Aetherstone, and the shimmer before them rippled, parting like a curtain. A puff of cool air enveloped them, laden with the aroma of ancient magic and untold secrets.

Finnian's voice broke the moment. "Where are we?" His eyes shot to the barrier and then back to Eldrin.

"Can't explain now," Eldrin said, pointing toward the opening. "Just go."

Lyria approached first, eyes narrowing. As she moved closer, the mist spiraled around her, the runes nearest her position flaring before settling. She led Duskrunner, her steps cautious but determined as she crossed over the invisible veil. The mist closed around her like a sentinel.

"Come on," she urged, her voice strained as she gestured for the two elves to follow.

Eldrin and Finnian exchanged a frantic glance, their boots sinking into the wet, earthy ground. Eldrin felt the Aetherstone warm, its glow blazing brighter with each step, resonating with the barrier's ancient magic. They guided their horses forward, pushing through the veil just as a hulking nemod lunged at them, its claws outstretched.

A surge of radiance burst forth from the barrier, striking the creature and hurling it backwards with a deafening screech, its body crumpling into the mass of pursuing nemods.

Eldrin twisted around, his breath rapid as the creatures churned just on the other side of the shimmering veil. The runes pulsed and twisted, their shapes shifting like living script until the entire barrier vibrated with a deafening hum as it sealed behind them. Enraged howls erupted, and their furious cries, enveloped in the thick silence, were the last thing they heard.

The group halted, their breaths ragged and uneven. The Aetherstone dimmed to a soft, steady pulse. Around them, the mist thickened, swallowing sound and shadow alike. The vale's power cut off the enraged howls of the brutes, leaving only the eerie silence stretching before them.

"We made it," Lyria whispered, her voice imbued with disbelief, her legs trembling beneath her.

Eldrin fixed his eyes on the barrier. From behind the shimmering curtain, the nemods clawed and howled, their fury palpable. "We're safe—for now."

The veiled valley stretched ahead, its ethereal beauty both mesmerizing and foreboding. Ancient trees twisted together to form towering canopies, their leaves glowing. A soft, otherworldly drone permeated the atmosphere as though the Vale itself was alive.

Finnian, jaw clenched, said, "I'm not going any further until you tell me what's going on, Eldrin." His narrowing gaze fixed on Lyria. "A drelf? You've risked everything—your honor, your life—for her? Why? Do you even know what you're doing?"

Lyria stiffened. "I'm right here," she said with an icy voice. "If you have questions, ask them to my face."

Finnian's glare didn't waver as he snapped. "I wasn't speaking to you."

Eldrin positioned himself between them, his voice tense. "She's not your enemy, Finnian."

"Then, who is Eldrin? Because right now, it feels like you've turned your back on your kingdom—on everything we swore to protect!" Finnian's voice cracked with frustration, but underneath it lay a bit of uncertainty, a plea for his friend to make sense of the chaos.

Eldrin's heart twisted. He wanted to explain, to reassure Finnian, but the words wouldn't come. He looked at Lyria, who met his gaze with quiet determination. The burden of his choices pressed down on him, but there was no turning back now.

"I don't understand myself," Eldrin said, his voice low but resolute. "But for now, you'll have to trust me that this is about more than what it seems."

"Then perhaps you should enlighten me," Finnian insisted, with his arms folded across his chest. His voice was shrill.

Eldrin stiffened. "I don't owe you an explanation for every choice I make, Finnian," he snapped, his tone sharper than he intended. "But before you ask why I'm out here risking everything, maybe start by asking yourself why you followed us."

Finnian furrowed his brows. "I came after you because I thought you'd lost your way, Eldrin. Because I believed you were better than—" He stopped, his eyes flicking to Lyria. "Better than this."

Lyria's lips thinned, but she said nothing. Her gaze centered on the mist swirling near the path.

"Better than what?" Eldrin challenged, stepping forward. "Better than trying to stop whatever darkness is coming? Better than trusting that maybe—just maybe—there's more on the line here than you understand?"

The ground beneath them trembled, and a low drone infused the air. The mist surrounding them thickened, twisting into strange shapes that flickered and dissolved like smoke.

Finnian stepped back, his hand moving to the handles of his blades. "What's happening?" he asked, his voice lowering.

"The Vale," Lyria said, focusing intently. "It doesn't like this."

Eldrin's heart throbbed as the mist wound between them, forming ghostly figures that shifted in and out of focus. Faint whispers echoed, their words unintelligible but carrying an undeniable weight. The Vale's presence grew heavier, oppressive, as if it were displeased.

"We must calm down," Eldrin said, his voice tense but steady. He released the Aetherstone, his hands open in a gesture of peace. "It's responding to us."

The roiling mist sharpened, forming shadowy outlines of creatures—watchful and waiting. Finnian's clutch on his blades tightened. "What is this place?" he demanded, his earlier anger replaced with unease.

"The Shrouded Vale," Lyria replied, her voice softer now. "It tests those who enter. Anger feeds it. Division challenges it. If we don't stop, it'll consume us."

Finnian swallowed hard. "How do you know all this?" he echoed, his tone wary.

"Because, as a drelf, I know something of magic and power," Lyria answered, her voice steady despite the increasing resonance around them. She hesitated; the faint lines of her tattoo shimmered in the shifting light. "And because of the mark... It's tied to places like this. To things considerably older than ourselves."

Eldrin's eyes flashed to the tattoo, which now pulsed harmoniously with the Aetherstone. "Your mark," he said, realization dawning. "It's reacting to the Vale."

Lyria nodded, her expression unreadable. "The mark recognizes it. Or maybe the Vale recognizes me. Either way, it's why I understand this place—why I sense its magic. And why it will let us pass if we're worthy?"

Finnian's eyes narrowed. "You're saying this place judges us? Based on what?"

"It's testing us. All of us," Lyria said, her eyes flashing.

"Testing us for what?" Finnian demanded. "For survival? For loyalty?"

"For truth," she replied. "It doesn't care about our doubts or grudges. It only cares if we're true to our path."

Finnian hesitated, his disbelief clashing with the creeping unease the Vale was stirring in him. "What path is that?" he asked as if dreading the answer.

"The prophecy," Eldrin and Lyria said in unison, their voices resonating like a shared oath in the enchanted air. Lyria's tattoo shimmered brighter, its eerie light weaving into the twirling patterns of the fog as though responding to an unseen call.

"What prophecy?" Finnian demanded, his voice tight, tasting the word for the first time.

The Aetherstone beat, its glow surging with a rhythm that matched the tattoo's cadence. Eldrin experienced an almost imperceptible hum coursing through the blade of his dagger as if it, too, was waking. His chest tightened, the moment pressing against him. Swallowing hard, he touched the dagger's hilt, its warmth flowing into his fingers like a whispered promise of something greater. He opened his mouth, but no words would come.

Lyria responded. "A prophecy that binds us. With this mark," she said, her hand against her throat, her voice tinged with bitterness. Her eyes shone in the mist's light, and her tattoo shimmered synchronously with the pulsing air around them.

"Is this 'prophecy' really so important that it made you throw away everything, Eldrin? Your honor, your loyalty, the trust of your people—?" Finnian asked.

"He didn't choose this, Finnian. And neither did I," Lyria said.

"I wasn't talking to you. I was talking to my friend. At least, I thought he was my friend," Finnian spoke with a cutting voice.

Eldrin's jaw bulged. "I *am* your friend, Finnian. That hasn't changed."

"Could've fooled me," Finnian muttered, shaking his head. "You vanish during a patrol, reappear with a drelf—and think I'll just play along?"

"I didn't plan any of this," Eldrin said. "I didn't wake up one morning and decide to betray the kingdom. But when I found her... when I saw the mark—something inside me *shifted.* It's like... I've been trained since elfhood to follow orders, to do what's expected. But in that moment, I knew I couldn't."

He eyed Lyria, then turned to Finnian. "You saw what we just faced out there. Nemods. In Elven lands? The wards didn't stop them. They're after her—and that mark. Which means there's more to the prophecy than we ever believed."

Finnian folded his arms, eyes narrowing. "So, what, you're a believer now? You believe this mark is going to do … what?"

"I don't know," Eldrin admitted. "But I know that whatever this is—whatever she is—it's real. And we must protect her."

The quiet that ensued was thick with tension. The mist swirled around them, the glowing runes behind casting faint reflections in their eyes. At last, Finnian looked away, exhaling through his nose. He recoiled, his hand gripping his sword's handle so tightly his knuckles turned white.

Finnian's frown deepened as he faced Lyria. "This is on you. Were you so desperate for help that you had to drag him down with you?"

"I didn't ask for his help," Lyria snapped, the heat in her words returning. "He made his own choice."

"Maybe you wanted to get your claws on him? The son of an Elven King."

"You think I'm after… him?" she scoffed.

Eldrin's brows shot up. "Excuse me?" he said, his voice sharper than intended. He glanced between them, clearly flustered.

"You don't have to make it sound like such a ridiculous idea," he muttered.

Lyria ignored his comment but softened her voice. "You think I enjoy being hunted like an animal? To carry something, I don't even understand?" she said, weariness crossing her features. "But here I am. Here we are."

Finnian opened his mouth to respond, but the Vale itself interrupted. The mist surged inward, coiling tighter around them, and a low hum permeated the air. It vibrated in their bones, deeper and more resonant than before, as if the Vale was speaking without words.

Eldrin raised his hand to calm the brewing tension. "Enough. Both of you." He directed his attention to Finnian, his voice quieter, more measured. "She's right, Finnian. This wasn't her choice. And it wasn't mine either. But the moment I saw her mark, the moment Gantar explained even a sliver of what it means... I couldn't walk away. I didn't know what I was stepping into, but I couldn't ignore it."

Eldrin drew the dagger slowly, its faint glow returning as it caught the radiance from the mist. "This dagger... It's tied to all of this. To the mark. To the Vale. I don't know how or why, but I feel it. For now, you'll just have to trust me."

Lyria's gaze settled on the dagger at Eldrin's belt. "You didn't tell me about this."

"I wasn't sure until now," Eldrin said. "But every step we take, every time the mark reacts, so does the dagger. It's like... It's connected to something bigger."

Finnian gazed at the glowing blade, his expression flickering between distrust and unease. "And what about me? Do you think this prophecy chose me, too? Because I didn't ask to be here, Eldrin. I didn't ask to be caught up in whatever this is."

Eldrin sheathed the dagger, his shoulders sagging. "No, Finnian. It didn't choose you. You followed us. You became involved in the fight because you couldn't walk away. Just like I couldn't walk away from her." He hesitated, meeting Finnian's eyes. "And I'm sorry for that. I never wanted you to be involved in this."

Finnian's face hardened. "Then what do you expect me to do now?"

Eldrin's voice softened, heavy with guilt. "I don't know. But if you want to leave, I wouldn't blame you. This... this isn't your fight."

Finnian's eyes rested on his friend, the hurt within his expression yielding to something deeper. He didn't respond. The silence lingered between them, filled with everything neither party could say—shared memories, broken trust, the echo of a friendship strained by forces greater than both of them.

Then Finnian exhaled. A sharp breath. He put away his sword.

"Leave?" His tone was low, almost disbelieving. "After everything we've been through?" He met Eldrin's eyes. "You're a fool if you think I'd let you face this alone." However, the distrust lingered as his eyes flicked to Lyria. "But don't think for a moment I trust her. I'm here for you, Eldrin. That's it."

Eldrin cast a glance at Finnian, noting the flicker of doubt that lingered in his friend's eyes. He didn't blame him. Yet, despite everything, Finnian remained by his side, and for that, Eldrin felt a pang of gratitude he couldn't yet put into words.

The mist eased, its oppressive weight lifting, as the Vale acknowledged their unity, however fragile. Lyria's tattoo dimmed, the glow receding into her skin.

She interrupted the quiet, her voice resolute. "Then let's keep moving. We may prefer not to be part of this prophecy, but that doesn't mean we can ignore it."

Eldrin nodded. He looked into Finnian's eyes, and they reached an unspoken agreement.

Together, the trio ventured deeper into the Vale, their doubts curling behind them like mist—silent, watchful, and reluctant to be left behind.

Chapter 13

Mist swallowed their steps the moment they crossed the vale.

It coiled around their ankles and drifted like smoke, thickening with every breath. This place did not welcome travelers—it studied them. Watched them. Judged them.

Eldrin moved cautiously, the forest now silent except for the persistent hum vibrating beneath the soil. There was no path, no markers—only twisting roots, shifting shadows, and the low throb of magic permeating the atmosphere. The faint warmth of the Aetherstone remained the only constant in a place where time seemed to waver.

They walked without speaking, each step drawing them deeper into a realm that appeared to rewrite itself with every glance.

"This is impossible," Finnian muttered, his voice sharp with frustration. He snapped the reins of his horse, glancing around the dense mist. "We've passed that tree before. Twice."

Lyria frowned, her gaze darting to a group of gnarled roots protruding from the ground. "He's right. We're going in circles."

Eldrin ground his teeth. "The Vale's magic is playing tricks on us."

Lyria's tattoo glowed, catching Eldrin's attention. "The Vale knows we're here for a reason," she said. "Unless we prove ourselves worthy, we may never leave."

A faint voice carried across the mist, lilting and cheerful, breaking the eerie silence like a ripple across still water.

"Fizz-fizz, flicker and sing,
Through the mist, I spread my wings.
Lost are they, deep in the Shroud,
But I'll find them all. Oh, so proud!"

Finnian halted mid-step, his blade half-drawn. "What in the blazes was that?" he whispered, his senses sharpening as he peered into the swirling mist.

Eldrin looked at the others. "Stay sharp," he said, one hand on his weapon.

The voice grew louder; the words shifting into a humming tune, punctuated by strange mutterings. Flickers of light danced in the haze, weaving erratically like fireflies caught in a storm. The group tensed, their eyes flitting between the shifting shapes.

"Oh, fiddlesticks and frothy brew,
Who's this lot? Not one, but two... no, three!

Three little travelers, caught in the mist.
Should I greet them with a twist?"

The light surged closer, revealing a small, winged figure darting amid the fog with an erratic but confident grace as if the mist itself had woven him from light. Intricate patterns, like glowing runes, swirled across his body, adding an air of magic to his already otherworldly appearance.

His translucent wings, veined with delicate gold filigree, fluttered with a soft crackling sound, scattering tiny sparks of glittering gold with each movement. They gave him an almost dragonfly-like quality, though their elegant span suggested something far older, far wiser. Large, expressive green eyes dominated his rounded face, shining with both curiosity and mischief, and his grin stretched wide, revealing small, pearly teeth that gave him an impish charm.

A long, slender tail trailed behind him, ending in a tuft of luminous, wispy filaments that glowed, pulsing in rhythm with his wings.

"Greetings, travelers!" the figure called out with a dramatic flourish, his tone a bright melody that broke the tension. He swooped low, bowing midair, his grin wide. "Fizzlewing, at your service!"

While he hung suspended, his wings faltered, and with a startled yelp, he dropped out of the air in a heap of shimmering scales. "Oh, blast it all!" he cried, leaping up and brushing dust from his body with exaggerated indignation. A quick snap of his fingers reignited his wings, their golden sparks sputtering back to life. "Nothing to worry about, perfectly normal!" he chirped, spinning midair with renewed enthusiasm.

"Well, I see how you got your name," Finnian said, a slight smile gracing his lips as he sheathed his blade. "Do your wings always fizzle out, or is this just for our entertainment?"

Fizzlewing gasped, clutching his chest in mock offense. "How dare you! My wings are a masterpiece of magical engineering! A rare marvel of the Vale's finest craftsmanship. Why, they—"

"They fizzled out," Eldrin interrupted, his tone dry as he moved forward, his look intensifying, his sword drawn, pointed at the little creature. "Enough theatrics. Who—or what—are you?"

Fizzlewing huffed, straightening mid-hover with a defiant tilt of his chin. "I am Fizzlewing! Keeper of whispers, finder of paths, and unmatched singer of songs!" He spun midair, his glowing wings crackling. "And I've come to guide you, oh wayward travelers."

"Guide us to what, exactly?" Lyria asked, skeptical but calm.

Fizzlewing darted closer, his eyes glinting with mischief. "Why, to answers, of course! You've come seeking answers, have you not?"

Lyria frowned, her voice even yet cautious. "We came for refuge, nothing more."

"Did you?" Fizzlewing replied, his tone lilting with skepticism. He twirled midair, sending faint sparks of light across the mist. "The Vale rarely offers refuge without reason. Surely you sensed it? The pull? The nudge that brought you here?"

Finnian rested his hands on his waist, his voice marked by a hint of doubt. "And if we did? What then?"

Fizzlewing stopped mid-flight, his wings humming as his grin melted into something more thoughtful. "Then it's clear this place has plans for you. Refuge, yes, but there's always more to it. The Revealing Pool lies ahead—a place where truths become clear. If you are bold enough to look."

Finnian frowned, crossing his arms. "What truths?" His voice was edged with caution but also intrigue. "And what makes this pool so special?"

Fizzlewing's eyes gleamed, and his voice fell to a reverent tone. "The pool isn't just water, my skeptical elf. It's the Vale's mirror, reflecting not just what is, but what was... and what might be. For those courageous enough to see, it offers clarity. Answers. Perhaps even a glimpse at destiny."

Finnian's eyes moved toward Eldrin and Lyria, his wariness deepening. "And you think we'll find these... truths there?"

Fizzlewing's grin returned, mischievous and teasing. "Oh, I don't think. I know. But are you brave enough to face it? That's another matter entirely."

Finnian cocked his head, a flicker of pride lighting his features. "Brave enough? You think elves aren't brave enough?"

Fizzlewing's grin widened, his wings sparking as he spun in midair. "Oh, I don't doubt your bravery, dear elf. But bravery is not always the same as readiness. The Vale has a means of testing even the strongest of wills."

Eldrin's expression tightened. "And if we fail?"

Fizzlewing stopped, his wings dimming before sparking back to life. "Then the truths will remain hidden, and the Vale might just keep you wandering until it decides you're ready... or not."

The trio exchanged uneasy glances, his words hanging over them like the mist itself.

Fizzlewing clapped his legs together, the light in his wings sparking anew, shattering the tension with his usual exuberance. "The mystical pool awaits, and it doesn't like to be kept waiting!"

He twirled backwards mid-flight, flying upside down for a few beats.

"Well? Don't just stand there like moss on a rock. Follow me." Then he shot ahead, a whirl of motion disappearing into the maze.

They followed Fizzlewing further into the vale; the mist growing denser as they went. The hum that had lingered around now resonated louder, pulsating through the ground and into their bones. He flitted ahead, his wings flashing with bursts of light that guided their path, though the way seemed no clearer than before.

Lyria kept close to Duskrunner, her hand stroking the horse's mane as if grounding herself. "How much farther?" she asked, her tone clipped but steady.

Fizzlewing darted back, hovering with an impish grin. "Farther? My dear, distance is relative to the Vale. It's not about how far you travel, but how ready you are to arrive."

Lyria frowned, her expression hardening. "That's not an answer."

"You're right," Fizzlewing said, fluttering to right himself. "But you won't find the pool by rushing. It will appear when it's meant to."

Chapter 14

As if on cue, the mist shifted, dividing like a curtain. The tangled roots and foliage yielded to smooth, moss-covered earth, damp and springy like the forest's heartbeat. A faint glow emerged ahead, soft at first but growing more intense with every stride, drawing their eyes to a wide clearing bathed in ethereal light.

The group moved cautiously, their footsteps muted against the mossy ground. An energy that jiggled their bones charged the atmosphere. In the clearing's center lay an unusual pool, unlike anything they had ever seen. Its surface shimmered like liquid glass, reflecting not only the surrounding trees but also the shapes and lights that flickered and danced beneath, as if the pool itself were alive.

Lyria paused, as her tattoo beat in time with the pool's hum, as if answering its call. "This is it," she breathed.

Eldrin scanned the clearing. "At last," he murmured.

Fizzlewing swooped into view, his wings twinkling as he pointed to the water with an exaggerated motion. "Indeed! I give you…The Pool of Revelation," he declared, his voice hovering between reverence and excitement. "Where the truths of past, present, and future entwine. Magnificent, isn't it?"

Lyria moved closer, her gaze fixed on the pool's surface. The lights beneath it shifted like whispers, drawing her in with their fluid, hypnotic motion. "What are we supposed to do?" she asked, her tone steady but tinged with unease.

Fizzlewing hovered nearby, his tone subdued. "You approach it slowly, one at a time, and the pool reveals truths—not the ones you want, but the ones you need."

Eldrin asked. "And if we cannot face those truths?"

Fizzlewing's grin faded into something almost contemplative. "Then the pool remains silent, and the answers you seek stay hidden." He tweaked his head, the crackle of his wings breaking the quiet. "But let's not dwell on failure, hmm? Think of it as an opportunity—a glimpse into what binds you to your future."

A heavy stillness descended upon the clearing, interrupted by the pool's steady hum, which grew louder with every passing moment. Lyria glanced at her companions; the tension between them was softened by their shared uncertainty. Without a word, she handed Duskrunner's reins to Eldrin. Her expression hardened with quiet resolve.

"I'll go first," she stated, her voice calm.

Eldrin stepped toward her, his worry clear. "Lyria, you don't have to—"

"Yes, I do," she said, focusing on the pool. "This mark... this curse... It's mine to face."

Her spiraling band brightened as she approached the water, the light coiling about her throat as if it were alive. The pool responded in kind, its luminescence intensifying and casting shimmering patterns upon her features and around the surrounding clearing. She crouched at the water's edge, her reflection rippling with unseen magic. Her heart pounded, and her throat went dry.

Doubt passed through her mind, but she pushed it aside. She leaned forward, her reflection blurring and shifting as if the pool were reaching back toward her. The moment her fingertips touched the surface, the water came alive, swirling with light and shadow that pulled her into its depths.

As she bent closer, her surroundings seemed to fade away, overtaken by a vast expanse of darkness and brightness. The pool's drone intensified, vibrating through her very being as if pulling her deeper into its grasp.

The water stilled, and an image took shape—a vision so vivid it was as if she were there.

She saw a great gathering of white dragons, their opalescent scales gleaming like stars, their massive wings casting shimmering reflections across a pristine lake surrounded by towering trees. Among them stood elves, their hands raised in unison, their magic intertwining with the dragons' glowing breath to form a radiant sigil in the heavens—a mark of unity, the Great Covenant. The dragons roared in harmony, their voices harmonizing with the elves' chants, a perfect balance of power and purpose.

But the vision darkened.

The white dragons' scales dulled, and their radiant eyes turned cold and shadowed. Among their ranks, darker figures emerged—dragons with scales as black as midnight, their eyes brimming with greed and malice. The elves' magic faltered as whispers of forbidden knowledge corrupted their ranks. The sigil fractured, the once-brilliant light shattering into shards of shadow that fell from the heavens.

And then the scene shifted, plunging Lyria into blackness.

She stood alone, her tattoo burning with an unbearable heat. From the night emerged grotesque figures—nemods, their claws glinting and their snarls echoing in the void. She tried to move, but her body remained rooted, her legs unable to obey her desperate commands. A sudden roar broke the silence, and from the obscurity leapt a massive panther-like beast, its fur rippling with the same blackness that possessed the nemods. It lunged for her throat, and she flinched—

Only to see her body collapse on the earth, the tattoo extinguished. The nemods swarmed her fallen form, their claws piercing the glowing mark as it faded. Above them, a figure loomed: An immense dragon with an obsidian-scaled body, its wings casting a shadow so vast it blotted out the light. Its eyes—pits of impenetrable darkness—seemed to drink in the very life around it.

Her vision sharpened, the dragon's jagged teeth gleaming as it exhaled a plume of black fire that consumed the surrounding trees. The once-pristine white dragons lay shattered and broken at its feet, their silvery blood staining the ground like spilt moonlight. Raw power coursed through the scene, the air vibrating as the dragon roared—a sound that reverberated deep within Lyria.

The ground beneath the scene shifted, and her lifeless face stared back at her, pale and frozen in death. Above her, the dragon's claws curled around the extinguished brand upon her skin, its inky darkness spreading like poison through the land. The forests withered, mountains crumbled, and the skies turned crimson, echoing the calamity of a world fallen to darkness.

Suddenly, the dragon's massive wings unfurled, and it turned its piercing gaze at her as though aware of her presence beyond the vision. A guttural voice, deep and venomous, filled her mind.

"You cannot stop what is already written."

As the voice faded, the vision burned away into smoke and darkness, leaving only a single word etched in black blood at her feet: **Vartharax**.

The vision wrenched her forward again.

She saw glimpses of her companions—Eldrin, standing on a battlefield, his glowing dagger raised against a tide of darkness. Finnian was bloodied and surrounded, but his blades were unwavering as he fought beside his friend. And then, a dragon—its scales gleaming white but streaked with black, struggling against chains of shadow that seemed about to swallow it.

The last image was burned into her memory: herself, standing at the cusp of a precipice, the band around her neck glowing in the darkness, holding back the tide with a blinding light. The mark wasn't just hers—it was a key, a source of immense power that balanced on the razor's edge between salvation and destruction.

And with that realization came the final, chilling truth.

If she fell, the mark would not die with her. It would shift, corrupted, to him—to darkness itself. Her death would not end the prophecy—it would destroy it, twisting its purpose into a weapon for his dominion. The harmony of the realms would tip irreversibly into shadow.

The image dissolved as Lyria withdrew from the pool's edge, her face pale and drawn as if the vision had drained the very breath from her. Eldrin and Finnian watched her, their unease thickening in the heavy silence.

"What did you see?" Eldrin asked, his voice low, as if afraid to disturb the surrounding tautness.

Lyria wavered, her eyes glancing from one to the other. "It showed me..." She faltered, clutching the reins of Duskrunner as if to anchor herself. "It showed what will happen if they destroy me." Her voice reduced to a whisper.

"Evil itself will take the mark. The balance will break, and the dragon..."

Her words floated, unfinished but laden with dread.

Finnian's jaw tightened, his expression hard to read. "You're saying your life—that mark—? That if you fall, we fall with you?"

Lyria nodded, swallowing hard. "Yes. I saw a horrible black dragon... it wants more than destruction. It seeks... absolute power. Darkness swallows the realms. I think... I think the mark's power, whatever that is, would go to it..."

Her voice cracked, and she looked away, unable to finish.

Finnian whistled softly. "That's... serious," he muttered, lost in thought. Then he glanced at her, his voice softening. "And you're sure about this? About what it showed you?"

"It wasn't just a vision," Lyria said, her voice measured. "It felt real. Like… like a long-hidden secret was attempting to rise."

Eldrin advanced, concern etched across his features. "You said you saw the dragon's name?"

Lyria hesitated. Her lips parted, but no sound came. The encircling mist seemed to tighten, pressing in about her as if waiting expectantly.

Her voice dropped to a whisper. "Vartharax."

The name landed like a bombshell below the surface—silent but deadly. The mist quivered, pulsing once before falling still again. Both elves froze. Their eyes connected for a heartbeat, a spark of recognition—and fear—passing silently between them.

"You've heard it?" Lyria said, looking from one to the other. "You know the name?"

Eldrin's mouth tightened. "It's a name from ancient history. A dragon whispered in war songs and warnings. Elves never speak it. Not even in lore."

Finnian whispered. "They say it was him. That he broke the Covenant and turned against his kind... against everyone, they say…he is… darkness—."

Lyria's gaze dropped, her mark pulsing like a heartbeat. Alive—shimmering like moonlight beneath water, each beat echoing from the name, still echoing.

No one spoke.

Finnian glanced at Eldrin; his skepticism dimmed by Lyria's revelation. "Well," he said, his voice forced into something resembling lightness, "sounds like we're in for a proper fight, doesn't it?"

Eldrin just stood there. His eyes stayed glued to the pool. Finally, he sighed. "If we're going to stop this, we need to know more. I'll go next."

Lyria looked at him. "Are you ready?"

"No," Eldrin admitted. "But if this prophecy ties me to it, if what you saw is true, then I must understand what we're up against."

Finnian came forward, his usual bravado replaced by quiet concern. "Be careful, Eldrin," he said, his swords shifting as though even they sensed the importance of the situation. "You've got enough on your shoulders without whatever that thing's about to show you."

Eldrin grinned slightly. "Thanks, Finnian. But I must confront my truth, whatever that is."

Finnian watched as his friend drew near the water, the stiffness in his posture unspoken but undeniable.

"Whatever you see…"

Eldrin halted on the shore. Turning to Lyria, he put a finger to his lips.

She fell silent.

His gaze scanned the shimmering surface, where lights and shadows swirled in hypnotic patterns. The drone emanating from below resonated through the clearing, matching the pulse of his heartbeat. He knelt, his fingers brushing his dagger. The faint buzz of the blade met the pool's rhythm, and he drew a deep breath, composing himself.

The water rippled, his reflection distorting in the pool's magic. Behind him, Lyria stood, Duskrunner's reins still clutched in her grip, her gaze locked on him. Finnian lingered a few steps back, his blue eyes flicking between Eldrin and the pool.

“Let’s see what truths you have for me,” Eldrin murmured, leaning forward while the mist churned below. The pool’s light brightened, pulling him into its heart.

As Eldrin leaned over the pool’s shimmering surface, everything around him seemed to dissolve. Soft hums from the water intensified, flowing through his body until his soul was attuned to its ancient magic. Beneath the surface, shifting lights brightened, twisting into mesmerizing patterns that beckoned him forward.

He sensed a pull, like something at the bottom of the pool was calling to him. Then, the lights burst outward, enveloping him in a sudden flood of blinding radiance.

When his vision cleared, Eldrin stood in a place both familiar and alien. The tall trees of the Elven realm stretched upward, their silver leaves shimmering in a perpetual twilight. Yet shadows flickered at their edges, twisting and encroaching as if the light was losing its battle with the darkness.

Before him stood a figure: his mother, Thariel.

Her silver hair caught the faint light, and her vibrant green eyes held the same intensity he remembered from childhood. She wore battle armor, the intricate etchings glowing with Elven symbols. In her hand, she had a dagger—the same dagger Eldrin carried, though it gleamed with a supernatural luminescence as if newly forged.

"Mother?" Eldrin's voice pierced the stillness, trembling with disbelief.

Thariel didn't respond. Instead, she turned, her eyes focused on a distant horizon where storm clouds roiled, creating uneven shadows over the land. Within the chaos, a great dragon loomed, its obsidian scales glinting with malice. The surrounding space appeared to warp, the trees bowing as though in submission to its presence.

Thariel spoke, her voice low and resonant. "Eldrin… the blade you carry was forged for a single purpose. It is not merely a weapon—it is a key."

Eldrin inched a slow step forward, heart pounding. "A key to what—?"

"To overcome the darkness."

"How?"

"You must discover that on your own. The path is not mine to give." She paused, her gaze falling to the knife sheathed at his belt. "But know this—the dagger… was once mine."

Eldrin stifled a gasp. "But I thought… Father gave it to me."

"He did," she breathed. "Yes, but it was I who left it for you."

"Why was I never told?" His voice wavered. "Why didn't you—or Father—say anything?"

Thariel's eyes softened, the edges of her expression threaded with sorrow. "Because you were not ready." She stepped closer, her voice lower now, full of quiet intensity. "You were born into this, my son. The prophecy flows through you as surely as your blood."

Eldrin's grip tightened around the dagger. "What does that mean? What am I supposed to do?"

Her image flickered like a flame battling the wind. "You must unite the realms. They cannot stand alone—they must be bound once more, as they were under the Great Covenant."

The scene changed abruptly, and Eldrin was no longer standing beside his mother. Instead, he was on a battlefield, the atmosphere thick with smoke and the cries of war. Nemods swarmed from every direction, their clawed hands reaching for him. He fought them off, wielding his dagger, its blade glowing with an intense, fiery light that repelled the creatures.

But he was not alone.

Beside him stood Lyria, her mark shining like a beacon, and Finnian, his swords flashing with precision as he held the line. They fought together, their movements instinctive, as if they had been born for this moment. And beyond them, a dragon emerged—its scales shimmering with both white and black as if caught between light and shadow.

The battlefield shifted again, and Eldrin saw himself alone, standing before the great black dragon. Its dark fire roared, consuming everything in its path. His dagger felt heavy, its glow dimming as the dragon's shadow engulfed him.

"You cannot defeat it alone," his mother whispered. "That requires the strength of all three realms to unlock its true power. Only together can the balance be restored."

The dragon lunged, its fangs bared, and Eldrin raised the dagger in desperation. The image vanished just as its jaws closed around him.

Eldrin gasped, recoiling back from the water as though burned. His face flushed as sweat beaded his brow. The vision still burned in his memory—the shadows, the dragon, his mother's words echoing like a forgotten melody.

"Eldrin!" Lyria's voice was sharp with concern. She reached out for him, her hand hovering near his arm but not quite touching. Uncertainty reflected in her eyes.

His breathing was uneven as he tried to steady himself. "I saw... her. My mother. She told me the dagger—it's part of the prophecy. It's connected to your tattoo, to the covenant between the realms."

Lyria touched the luminous band encircling her neck, and her expression tightened. "What does it all mean?"

Finnian's brow furrowed, his light demeanor shadowed by unease. "What else did she say?"

Eldrin fixated on the water as its surface returned to a quiet shimmer. "She said the dagger is a key, but it can't unlock anything on its own. The three realms... they have to work together." He swallowed hard, the vision pressing down on him. "And… she told me that the knife was once hers."

Silence lay between them, weighty and oppressive, the pool's soft hum the only sound.

Finally, Finnian broke it, his tone sober. "How would we ever work together with our enemies?" His hand hovered near his blades as if the thought of an alliance required a defense.

Lyria's gaze darted to him, her glare sharp. "It's not impossible. We're standing here together, aren't we?"

Finnian arched an eyebrow but said nothing. The flicker of skepticism remained.

Eldrin gave a faint, humorless smile. "I think that's what we have to figure out. Before it's too late."

Finnian's eyes scanned Eldrin's face. "You alright?"

"No," Eldrin admitted. "But I will be."

Lyria moved toward him, her expression softening when their eyes met.

Eldrin exhaled and faced Finnian, his tone calm but weighted. "Finnian," he said, meeting his friend's gaze. "It's your turn."

Finnian blinked, his gaze darting toward the pool. His fingers flexed in front of his body, releasing the tension he'd been holding. A quick smirk crossed his face. "Great. Let's see what nightmare the pool has for me," he quipped, though his tone betrayed the nerves hiding behind his humor.

"I have every confidence that you will succeed," Eldrin said.

Finnian offered him a lopsided grin, some of his confidence returning. "I'd better. Otherwise, you'll be down one ridiculously talented friend."

Eldrin laughed softly, shaking his head. "We can't have that."

As Finnian stepped forward, brushing past Eldrin with a fleeting glance, he concentrated on the pool, its surface rippling as though expecting him. "If I end up fighting shadow beasts, or worse, you two owe me a drink," he added, his smile broadening.

Lyria crossed her arms, the hint of a smile tugging at her lips. "We'll make it a strong one."

Finnian knelt before the pool, the humor leaving his expression supplanted by a seriousness rarely seen. He eyed his companions again—Eldrin's quiet encouragement and Lyria's steady gaze provided him a moment's pause before he turned to face the shimmering water.

"Alright," Finnian murmured, his voice just above a whisper. "Let's see what's in store for me."

As Finnian leaned closer, the shimmering surface rippled, drawing him in. The light beneath the water twisted like a writhing serpent, pulling him down into nothingness. The hum swelled, vibrating through him until his surroundings dissolved.

Finnian found himself in a familiar place—a training ground he hadn't seen in years. The clash of blades and the barked orders of his instructors pervaded the air. He recognized himself as a younger elf, his twin swords clumsy in his hands as he sparred with an opponent who seemed effortlessly skilled.

"You're too slow!" the instructor barked, his voice cutting through Finnian's concentration. The younger version of himself stumbled, dropping one sword as his opponent knocked him down. Laughter spread through the watching crowd, sharp and unforgiving.

"Always the joker," the instructor murmured with a slight frown. "Maybe if you took this seriously, you'd actually be worth something."

The words stung even years later. Finnian clenched his fists as he watched the scene, his younger self-standing and forcing a grin to mask the humiliation. "It's just a scratch," the younger Finnian joked, picking up his sword. "Wouldn't want to make the others look bad, would I?"

The view changed, plunging him into darkness. When the scene cleared, he found himself on a battlefield. Eldrin was in the thick of it, his dagger blazing with light as nemods swarmed around him. Lyria stood nearby, her mark glowing as she battled shadowy beasts, her movements precise yet strained.

Finnian scanned the scene, searching for himself, but he was nowhere to be found.

Panic gripped him, and his voice choked. "Eldrin!" he shouted, but the din of battle overwhelmed his words. He tried again, louder, but it was like he didn't exist at that moment.

Eldrin faltered, the nemods pressing closer, their claws inches from his throat. Finnian's heart pounded upon seeing his friend struggle, his own helplessness gripping tight like a vise.

"You weren't there," a voice whispered, cold and accusatory. "You weren't there when he needed you."

The battlefield dissolved, leaving Finnian standing in a vast void. A single figure materialized out of the night—himself, older and scarred, his swords bloodied. The older Finnian's eyes flared with resentment and self-loathing.

"You hide behind your jokes, your charm," the older version sneered. "But when it matters, you falter. You let them down. You let *him* down."

"I wouldn't," Finnian snapped, his voice shaking but firm. "I wouldn't leave him."

"Then prove it," the older Finnian hissed, stepping closer. "Prove it when the time comes. Because if you fail..." He pointed towards the void, and the battlefield reappeared, darker and more desolate than it had been before. Eldrin lay motionless, his dagger extinguished, while the black dragon loomed above, its shadow consuming everything.

The vision's weight bore down on Finnian, suffocating him. He clenched his fists, his sharp wit and bravado stripped away, leaving only raw determination. "I won't fail him," he said, his voice firm despite the tempest raging inside him.

The older Finnian smirked. "Then fight. Not just with your blades but with your heart. Trust them in the same measure that they will come to trust you."

Finnian staggered back as the scene melted away, his breath coming in short, uneven gasps. He clutched his swords with white knuckles as the memories of the vision lingered.

Eldrin moved toward his friend, concern etched into his expression. "What did you see?"

Finnian hesitated. The usual smirk that so often played on his lips was gone. He stood up, his grip on his double blades loosening. "I saw what happens if I fail you," he said, his voice stripped of bravado.

He blinked hard, his stance unsteady—less the bold swordsman, more a shadow of someone haunted. His face had gone pale, his jaw set tight. The blades he once carried with pride now looked more like burdens. His eyes shifted between the pool and his companions as if grounding himself in the present.

"You would never—" Eldrin began.

Finnian raised a hand, cutting him off. He drew in a slow breath. When he spoke again, his voice was quieter than they'd ever heard it. "I saw... you. Worn down. Bleeding. Losing ground."

He looked up, meeting Eldrin's eyes. "You were standing alone." His voice caught. "Against something… something vast. Bigger than all of us. And I wasn't there to help."

Finnian continued, his voice tinged with vulnerability. "You're at the core of all this. I'm unsure why, but the vision made it clear—you're the one holding everything together. If you fall... we all fall."

Lyria shifted, her eyes narrowing as she studied him. "And me?" she asked. "Did you see me?"

Finnian locked eyes with her, a glimmer of his distrust tempered by what he'd just seen. "Yeah. You were there, fighting." His voice grew quieter. "But it wasn't enough. Not without him."

Eldrin's eyes darkened. "And what if I can't do what's expected of me?"

Finnian shook his head. "That's not an option, Eldrin. You don't get to fail. Or give up. I won't let you... because if you do…." He trailed off, the vision flashing through his thoughts—the shadows, the cries of the battlefield, and the overwhelming weight of hopelessness. "Then everything goes to hell."

Quiet fell upon the group, the gravity of Finnian's words palpable like the fog.

Lyria broke the stillness, her voice quiet but resolute. "None of us can afford to fail—not me, not you, not any of us."

Finnian let out a brief, mirthless laugh. "No pressure, right?"

Eldrin drew nearer, placing a hand on Finnian's shoulder. "We've made it this far, Finnian. Whatever lies ahead, we'll face it the same way. Together."

Finnian smirked, though the pain behind his eyes lingered as he regarded Eldrin. "Guess I'll just have to make sure you stay alive, won't I?"

Lyria's expression softened as she regarded him. "You're not just here for him anymore," she breathed. "Whether you like it or not, this prophecy... involves you, too."

Finnian and she exchanged glances, his usual sharp retort absent. Instead, he nodded. "Yeah. I figured that much out." His voice became more constant, and a hint of his familiar humor resurfaced.

"So, what's the plan? Charge headfirst into the next disaster, or take a breather first?"

Eldrin and Lyria looked at each other, and Eldrin smiled. "Let's take a reprieve. I have a feeling the Vale isn't finished with us yet."

As they regrouped, settling their horses and themselves, the mysterious pool shimmered behind them, its light dimming as if satisfied. The drone of the vale grew fainter, replaced by the gentle rustling of mist and the quiet snap of Fizzlewing's tail as he floated nearby, watching them with a subdued expression.

"You've seen what you needed to see," Fizzlewing said, his voice softer than usual. "Now it's time to decide what to do with it."

Chapter 15

Dusk cloaked the Dragon Realm in an eerie glow as volcanic winds howled across the sharp peaks, carrying with them the acrid scent of molten rock and ash. An onyx plateau extended like a blackened scar, its obsidian surface cracked and steaming from the fiery rivers beneath. The flow shimmered like ribbons of flame, their golden-red reflections illuminating the barren expanse and casting restless shadows that danced like phantoms across the fractured ground.

In the very core of the plateau, a ceremonial fire roared, its flames bright, twisting, and surging as though alive with purpose. Ancient carvings encircled the fire pit, their once-pristine etchings blackened and scarred by centuries of flames and neglect. The carvings depicted dragons in their prime—majestic and unified, their wings outstretched beneath the radiant sigil of the Great Covenant. Now, erosion marred the sigil's edges, fragmenting the story and mirroring the dragons' lost unity.

Korrath stood near the fire, his scales catching the fiery light and glinting like freshly spilt blood. His presence dominated the gathering, his massive frame towering over the others. His wings were folded against his back, but the tension in his body was palpable, as if a tempest were about to be unleashed. Nearby, a dozen dragons of varying sizes and colors formed a loose circle. Their glances darted between each other as they waited for someone to speak.

Korrath stepped forward, the embers glowing on his scales reflecting the fire in his eyes as his deep voice rumbled like distant thunder. "Drakor has failed again," Korrath began, his voice a low rumble that grew sharper with each word. His gaze swept across the assembly, daring anyone to challenge him. "The mark-bearer eludes capture, and the nemods falter against the vale's magic. The moment has arrived to unleash the shadows."

A sense of unease swept through the circle. One dragon, his bronze scales dull and pitted, shifted his weight nervously. "Drakor has forbidden it," he said, his voice hesitant. "He leads with the Dark One's blessing—"

"Drakor has lost favor with the dark lord," Korrath interjected with a snarl. "I am your leader now."

A green-scaled dragon breathed fire, smoke billowing from her nostrils. Zyressa, her name known for carrying weight among the ranks, stepped into the light, her movements deliberate and her claws curling slightly beneath her. "And does Vartharax command us to follow you?" Her voice was laced with the unspoken accusation of overreach. "Or do you presume to act in his name without his blessing?"

Korrath's attention shifted to her, his tail striking the surface with a crack that sent tremors through the cavern. "Vartharax demands results!" Korrath growled, his tone unwavering, though the nuances behind his words hinted at something more profound—a fear he dared not name. His wings twitched briefly, betraying the stress in his coiled form before he stilled himself with deliberate control. "The drelves will learn what happens when they defy us, and the branded one will fall."

Zyressa didn't flinch, but stood her ground, with a challenging glint in her eyes. "Boldness without caution is folly, Korrath. If you overstep, it will be your scales that burn." Her wings unfurled slightly, their dark green edges catching the firelight as her challenge ignited the air.

Korrath's lips formed a dangerous smile, his tone softening but infused with steel. "Let my scales bear the burden of action, then. If Vartharax demands a sacrifice, I will gladly offer it—after I deliver him the drelf."

Smoke curled from Zyressa's fiery nostrils. Her sharp stare was directed at Korrath, challenging. "Even the darkness cannot breach the Vale. The magic is too strong."

Korrath's eyes narrowed, his gaze drifting toward the molten river winding through the crater. Its surface bubbled and hissed, responding to the turmoil within him.

"Yes, Zyressa," he said, his tone low and deliberate. "We cannot breach the Vale," he said. But perhaps it doesn't need to be."

Zyressa's tail flicked, the sharp movement revealing her unease. "Go on…"

Korrath straightened, his wings stretching, their edges glinting in the firelight. "The drelf lands lie exposed. Vulnerable." His voice grew stronger, laced with conviction as the plan took shape. "Attacking their stronghold will force the marked one to emerge. She will not abandon her kind to slaughter."

The assembled dragons exchanged nervous glances as the weight of Korrath's words settled over them. Some nodded, emboldened by his conviction, while others remained silent, their doubt etched across their faces.

"You know we cannot wage war without Vartharax's blessing," Zyressa insisted, her voice sharp and unyielding.

Korrath's talons curled upon the stone, deepening the already carved furrows as his talons dug in with restrained frustration. His wings twitched as he imagined himself standing before the dark ruler, the drelf crushed beneath his claws. If he succeeded, he would cement his place as the ruler's true right hand, and Drakor would bow to him. If he failed... He forced the thought aside, his eyes focusing with determination. The time to act was now.

"We can't attack. But the shadows can," Korrath sneered, his lips curling to reveal jagged teeth.

A hush descended upon the circle, the fire's crackle now a faint backdrop to Korrath's words. Some dragons shared apprehensive looks, their tails twitching, while others fixed their gazes on the fire as though searching for answers in its depths.

"Vartharax must give us permission to summon such darkness," hissed Zyressa.

"He already has," Korrath breathed, the fire's reflection shining in his pupils as he approached the flames. The fire crackled, sending sparks aloft as the murmurs grew louder. A split formed within the group—some were eager for action, while others were wary.

"You gamble with chaos, Korrath," Zyressa said, her voice subdued, but no less cutting.

Korrath's claws flexed as doubt whispered at the edges of his mind. Failure was unthinkable—not with Vartharax's gaze so close and unyielding. If this gamble failed... No. He shook that thought away, a steely glint appearing behind his eyes with renewed determination. Victory was the only path.

"No one can control those elusive black panthers. Once they appear, they can't be called back," the bronze dragon said, as he shifted and coiled his tail around his legs like a shield. Across the circle, a younger dragon with silvery scales flicked his wings, his gaze darting between Korrath and the others. The air felt heavy, charged with unspoken fears that hung over the assembly like smoke from a fire.

"The panthers follow one thing—fear," Korrath growled. "If they sense weakness, they strike. They are not mere beasts," he said, his voice dropping to a near-whisper that carried over the crackle of the fire. "They are nightmares given form, forged from the darkest recesses of magic. Yes… once summoned, they will hunt without mercy. The drelves will tremble in fear once we release them, and thus, they will be powerless to stop the beasts. The drelf who bears the mark will come to their aid, and when she does…there will be nowhere to hide."

Korrath's eyes lit up with imagined triumph. He envisioned it now: the drelf kingdom reduced to ash, its defenders scattered, their screams echoing across the ruins. The marked one crushed before him, her light extinguished. And when he returned to Vartharax with her body, he would take his rightful place as leader of all dragons.

The murmurs from the other dragons swelled, a discordant chorus of fear, doubt, and reluctant approval. Some nodded, their eyes bright with the fire's reflection, emboldened by Korrath's sinister plan. Others shifted, their tails flicking in protest against the heat of his ambition. High aloft, the fiery gales rose to a howling crescendo, whipping through the rugged crags as if the realm itself cried out in warning. Yet Korrath stood unmoved, his wings unfurled as he gazed into the fire's heart, where sparks danced like heralds of the chaos to come.

"Set up the summoning circle," Korrath ordered, his tone leaving no room for dissent. "The panthers will soon satisfy their hunger with the flesh of drelves."

"You're playing with fire, Korrath," Zyressa hissed, her eyes blazing defiance. "And fire does not discriminate."

Korrath's wings snapped open with a resounding crack, the movement sending a rush of heat through the gathering. His voice dropped, each word laced with venom. "Then stand aside. Let those with vision act, while the timid cling to their doubts."

Zyressa's wings shifted. "And when the panthers turn on us?" she asked, her voice quieter now, almost obliterated by the fire's roar. Beside her, the others exchanged hesitant glances, their tails flicking. The bronze dragon took a partial step back, his wings folding as though bracing for Korrath's retort.

As Korrath faced the fire, the flames surged higher, as shadows twisted and danced like demons across the plateau. From the summit, the fiery blasts stilled, replaced by an unnatural silence that pressed against the ears like a held breath. The others watched, their unease etched in the fire's glow, as Korrath's words broke the stillness.

"Tonight, we unleash the panthers—and with them, the very first scream of a world that will remember what it is to fear our fire."

Zyressa squinted but said no more. Other dragons shifted, wings twitching, their murmurs rising like smoke. Doubt infiltrated the ranks, coiling through the firelight like a second, unseen flame.

Volcanic gusts howled as something moved overhead—a ripple across the jagged rock. A shadow among shadows. Hidden in the crags, mottled scales became one with the stone, and yellow eyes gleamed with cunning.

Drakor watched with keen interest.

Korrath's speech had stirred them, yes—but not all flames served the same fire.

A smile ghosted across Drakor's maw, crooked and cold. "Reckless fool," he murmured. "I'll let you light the blaze... then choke you with the smoke."

He retreated into the night, his presence slipping away like ash on the wind. Below, the fire roared, casting a fleeting silhouette across the rocks—wings outstretched, spine jagged, vengeance coiled like smoke in his wake.

And then he disappeared.

The cavern below pulsed with heat, the molten veins within the rock walls glowing like embers of a dying fire. Shadows shimmered and moved, twisting in the heavy, stagnant air. A smell of sulfur and scorched rock permeated the chamber as Korrath stood amidst an ancient summoning circle—a jagged formation of Draconic runes etched deep within the volcanic rock.

Low, guttural chants in the ancient tongue rumbled from within him, the words vibrating with an unsettling power. His wings, marked by old battle scars, stretched wide as he lifted a claw toward the circle.

The runes pulsed once—twice—before they burst alight with a crimson glow. A sickly shadow, thick and writhing, seeped from the fissures in the rock while the ground trembled beneath them.

A gust of unnatural wind coursed within the cavern, howling like a distant wail. Next came the first guttural growl.

Deep and predatory.

A tremor of anxiety swept through the onlookers like a ripple when the darkness within the circle shuddered, then split open.

Out of nothingness emerged panther-like creatures, their forms sleek and ethereal, shifting between physical and spectral. Their eyes burned like molten embers, unblinking, calculating. They moved with unnatural grace, silent despite their size, their muscles flexing beneath dark, spectral pelts.

One stepped forward, its glowing eyes fixed on Korrath.

Korrath grinned. "Hunt the marked one," he commanded. "And leave nothing in your path."

Those shadowy cats did not roar, nor snarl in answer. Instead, they vanished, one by one, melting into the night like smoke.

Gone—carried on the breeze, spreading like a plague far and wide.

The ritual chamber fell silent again, but a deep, lingering chill hung in the air. Korrath's smile widened, feeling the thrill of what was to come.

The hunt had begun!

Chapter 16

The mists of the Shrouded Vale wove an ethereal web around the weary trio as they trudged onwards. Their footsteps echoed in the silence, a rhythmic cadence that matched the Vale's quiet hum. The weight of their visions was palpable, and an unusual stillness tempered even Finnian's usual quips. He led Embermane by the reins, his gaze scanning the shifting fog as though he expected it to part and reveal some new enigma.

Lyria walked alongside Duskrunner, her fingers trailing along the horse's side. The ink at her nape pulsed, no longer burning but still an ever-present testament of her burden. She cast occasional glances toward Eldrin, who trailed a few paces behind, his thoughts elsewhere.

Finnian broke the silence. "Well, I don't know about you two, but if this place wants to whisper more cryptic warnings, it could at least throw in a hot meal. Mystical wisdom is hungry work."

Eldrin couldn't help but smirk. "You're insufferable, you know that?"

"I like to think I'm resourceful," Finnian replied with a mock bow, the faint clink of his swords punctuating the movement. "And let's face it—we could all use some cheering up."

"You're the one who said you couldn't wait to explore the Vale," Lyria quipped, her lips twitching.

"I said that before this place started humming in my chest like it's alive," Finnian countered, his tone light but his posture betraying his unease. His eyes glanced at the shifting shadows, ever watchful. "Where's our fearless guide, anyway? Did Fizzlewing decide we're not worth the effort?"

A beam of light zipped into the haze, accompanied by the familiar crackle of wings. Fizzlewing darted into view, his iridescent scales reflecting the illumination from the Vale's shifting radiance. He paused mid-hover and grinned. "Me? Abandon you? Perish the thought!" he declared, spinning in midair. "I've been scouting ahead. I found a delightful spot for you to rest. Oh, and food. You're welcome."

Finnian lifted one eyebrow. "Food?"

"You're all tired, edgy, and, frankly, not much fun to be around. A meal will do wonders for your mood," Fizzlewing said as he gestured dramatically. "This way."

Despite himself, Finnian chuckled. "He's got a point there." He tugged on Embermane's reins and followed the small creature. Behind him, Eldrin and Lyria exchanged glances, the faintest hints of their earlier tension melting away.

Fizzlewing darted ahead, his compact form navigating the fog like a glowing ember. He paused at a break in the trees, spreading his tiny arms. "Behold! Your humble guide has found you the finest resting spot in the valley! Food, water, ambiance, and some mystery—everything a weary traveler could desire."

When the group stepped forward, the mist thinned, revealing a narrow creek that wound its way through the gnarled trees. The glowing water reflected the Vale's soft light, casting ripples of gold and silver against the mossy banks.

Silverwind snorted, eager to quench his thirst. Embermane plunged his muzzle into the stream, drinking, while Duskrunner pawed at the water before bending to drink. Eldrin crouched beside Silverwind, the horse's silvery coat gleaming in the strange light. He filled his flask, watching his horse drink with a contented stillness.

"They needed this," Lyria said, running her fingers along Duskrunner's mane as she knelt beside him. She glanced toward the water, tracing the pattern of the glow as it shifted with each ripple. "We all did."

Finnian wiped his face with his sleeve after splashing water over it, droplets clinging to his hair and dripping onto the verdant soil. With a dramatic toss of his head, he sent a cascade of water flying in every direction.

Lyria flinched as the cold droplets spattered her arm and neck. A frown creased her face, and she brushed the water from her skin with sharp, deliberate movements. "Really?" she said, her tone laced with annoyance. "You couldn't keep that to yourself?"

Finnian flashed a grin, unapologetic. "Sharing is caring, Lyria. Besides, you seemed like you could use some cooling off."

"The next time you act like a dog," Lyria said, "I will treat you like one."

Finnian froze mid-motion, mock offense washing over his features. "Careful, Lyria. That almost sounded like a threat."

"Try me," she replied, flat and unwavering, her tail flicking behind her.

Eldrin, crouched by Silverwind, sighed. "Finnian, maybe don't test her right now," he said, his voice weary but firm. "We're all tired."

Finnian raised his hands in playful defeat, his grin creeping back as if the tension had never touched him. "Fine, fine. No more spraying water." His tone, however, betrayed him, as there was no genuine remorse. Running a hand through his damp hair, he looked at Eldrin, giving a sly smirk. "Alright, that's one problem solved. Now, what about food? I'm starving here."

Fizzlewing, sitting on a mossy stone near the creek, flicked his tail. "Ah, I thought you might say that." With a sweep of his arm, he pointed toward a cluster of bushes nearby.

"Behold! The berries of the vale — sweet and filling. Gather away, my ravenous friends."

Finnian arched a brow but didn't wait for further encouragement. He plucked some of the bright blue berries, inspecting them before popping one into his mouth. His eyes widened. "Alright, these are... superb."

Lyria reached for a few herself, offering a delicate smile. "Fizzlewing may actually be useful after all."

"I resent the 'may,'" Fizzlewing replied with mock indignation, wings sparking while hovering above the group.

As Finnian handed berries to the others, Eldrin opened his pack and pulled out a wrapped bundle of dried meat and flatbread. He ran his fingers over the carefully tied strings momentarily, his thoughts drifting. "Gantar packed this before we left," he said, unwrapping the bundle and setting it between them. "He thought of everything, didn't he?"

Lyria glanced up at him, her face softening. "You miss him."

Eldrin nodded, his jaw tightening. "I wonder how he's holding up. With everything going on in the kingdom..." He trailed off, shaking his head as if to dispel the thought. "We should eat. There's no telling when we'll have the chance again."

As the trio shared the meal, Finnian tore into a piece of meat with enthusiasm. Eldrin ate more methodically, his movements deliberate as he divided the flatbread and offered it the others.

Lyria sat quietly, her claws curling around the strip of meat as she inspected it with clinical precision. Her eyes glanced at Duskrunner, who nibbled at the grass near the creek, then again at the food in her hands. She didn't tear into it as the others had; instead, her claws slid through the meat, slicing it into clean, even strips.

Finnian was watching her with mild curiosity. "What, not good enough for drelves? You're not about to tell me you only eat gemstones or something, are you?"

Lyria raised an eyebrow, but didn't rise to his teasing. "We don't eat gemstones," she replied, her tone dry. "Though some dragon kind do."

Finnian grinned. "I knew it."

Ignoring him, Lyria brought a strip of meat to her mouth. Her sharp canines gleamed as she took a slow, deliberate bite. Instead of chewing, she seemed to hold the meat briefly before swallowing, her movements precise, almost instinctual.

Eldrin's gaze lingered, curiosity apparent in his expression. "Do drelves eat like dragons?" he asked, his tone careful.

Lyria finished another strip, licking her lips. "Sometimes," she admitted, her tone steady. "We don't consume in the quantity of dragons, but... There are instincts. Ways we prepare food that is different. We're more sensitive to the raw elements in what we eat—it's energy."

Finnian raised both brows. "Energy? Like... magic?"

"Sort of," she replied. "It's more about balance. Certain foods nourish not only the body but also the mind. Raw meat has more energy than cooked meat. The taste isn't always the point."

Finnian popped another berry into his mouth and shrugged. "I think taste is the whole point. But hey, whatever works."

Lyria glanced at him, a faint smirk gracing her lips. "I'd imagine you have eaten nothing without tasting it first."

Finnian grinned. "Guilty."

Eldrin chuckled, shrugging his shoulders, the animosity between them easing. "We all have our habits."

As they continued their meal, Lyria's quiet, methodical approach dissolved into the flow of their shared moment. Yet, it remained a subtle but poignant symbol of her dual nature—a drelf caught between two worlds. But in that fleeting silence, it felt as if the rift between them had narrowed, if only by a step.

The noises of the horses grazing, as the quiet murmur of the vale was almost ethereal, the mist curling along the ground was nearly hypnotic. As they ate, the world shifted subtly. Bright bursts of color appeared between the trees—glowing flowers unfurling their petals in response to the group's presence. Tiny winged creatures flitted in the misty air, their translucent forms shimmering, leaving trails of light in their wake. The creek itself deepened in color, its glow intensifying to reflect shades of gold and sapphire.

Finnian, mid-bite, watched a winged creature dart past him. "Okay, this is officially strange," he mumbled, yet his tone held more awe than apprehension.

Lyria tilted her head, her gaze drawn to the vibrant flowers sprouting along the creek's edge. "It's... interesting," she murmured, brushing her fingers against a glowing petal. The flower responded with a slight shimmer, as though recognizing her touch.

"It's the Vale," Eldrin said, his voice thoughtful. "Alive in ways we can't understand."

Fizzlewing grinned, alight with mischief and pride. "And aren't you lucky to be here under my expert guidance?"

Eldrin grinned but didn't reply, his attention lingering on how the vale appeared to breathe around them. The moment was calm, even serene, but beneath it lay an undercurrent of something more—something that hinted this place had more secrets yet to be revealed.

The three companions lingered by the creek until their bellies were full, the simplicity of the meal easing some of the day's tension. Fizzlewing darted among the trees. "I've found you a cozy little nook for the night," he announced, speaking softly. "The Vale is uneasy... Best not to linger out in the open."

He guided them to a sheltered grove where the trees arched overhead, their gnarled branches forming a natural canopy. The air, cool and damp, carried the faint scent of earth and water. Soft moss blanketed the ground, its radiance casting a soothing glow.

Eldrin cleared a patch of ground near the moss, laying out the bedrolls Gantar had provided him before their journey. The worn but sturdy material smelled of the herbs and sage he often used. "Not exactly luxurious," he remarked, testing the earth with a hand, "but it'll do."

Finnian dropped his pack onto the mossy floor with a groan, stretching out. "Not bad," he admitted, lacing his fingers behind his head. "Could almost call it comfortable. Almost."

Lyria settled Duskrunner nearby, brushing a hand along his flank before unrolling her blanket. She lowered herself onto the grass with practiced ease, tucking her legs to the side to accommodate the long, tapering curve of her tail. Her claws traced patterns on the soft earth, her gaze distant as the vale's resonance deepened, vibrating inside her like a reflection of her mark's pulse.

The three sat in relative silence, the sighing from the mist and the subtle hiss of unseen energy the only sounds. The quiet was almost peaceful, but a tension lingered beneath it, a weight none of them could ignore.

Lyria spoke first. "We can't stay here forever. Eventually, I'll have to confront what's waiting for me out there."

Eldrin, who had been tracing the handle of his dagger, looked up, his brow furrowing. "You mean *we'll* have to confront it," he said, his tone subdued yet firm.

Her eyes turned towards him, and something sharp crossed her expression—pride, or perhaps defiance. "I didn't ask for your help," she replied. "This... is not your fight."

Finnian, reclining against his pack, emitted a soft snort. "Funny. From where I'm sitting, it looks like we're already in the middle of it."

Lyria's jaw tightened, and she glanced away, her fingers curling. "You don't have to be," she muttered. "I'm not your responsibility."

Eldrin sat forward, a frown furrowing his brow. "You think that's why we're here? Because we feel responsible?"

"I don't know why you're here," she shot back, her voice sharper now, although it quivered at the fringes. "But if anything, bad happens to you, I don't want it to be because of me."

"Lyria—" Eldrin started, but she cut him off with a look.

"No." She shook her head, her tail brushing against the ground. "You've seen the visions. You know what's coming. And if you — because of me..." Her voice faltered, the words trailing into silence as her eyes dropped.

Eldrin's gaze softened, and he leaned back, his tone gentler. "It's not because of you. It's because of the prophecy. We're all tied to it now."

Finnian added, in a lighter tone, "Prophecies don't choose volunteers," even though his eyes contained a more profound shadow. "They just sweep you up and toss you in."

Lyria released a soft, bitter laugh, her shoulders sagging. "And what if that's the worst part? That everyone around me suffers for the curse I bear? I need to do this alone."

Finnian straightened, leaning his elbows against his knees. "I hate to break it to you, but no one does anything alone—not really. Even dragons stick together when it matters. Mostly."

Eldrin's lips curved into the slightest hint of amusement. "You can't do this alone, Lyria. None of us can. Remember our visions. The prophecy has involved every one of us."

She glanced at him, her demeanor unreadable, before exhaling a soft breath. "I'll try to remember that," she said, though the tightness in her posture didn't ease.

Eldrin nodded, his shoulders relaxing as he stretched out his bedroll. "Good. Now, we all need to rest."

Finnian smiled, reclining against his backpack with a touch of theatrics. "Finally, some common sense. Wake me when the next life-changing vision shows up."

Lyria's gaze lingered on her companions as they settled. Guilt churned within her, an unwelcome, bitter weight. She hated this—needing their help, their protection. But with a damaged wing plus the mark burning like an unspoken promise, she had to accept it. For now.

Her eyes drifted to the soft glow emanating from her neck, and she gulped. *Then I'll find a way to protect them from me.*

Eldrin shifted onto his bedroll, adjusting his position until he felt comfortable. His fingers wrapped around the

Aetherstone as his thoughts drifted to Gantar, to the elf kingdom, and to the shadowy threats that lay ahead. The rhythmic drone from the Vale echoed his unease, lulling him reluctantly toward sleep.

Beside him, Finnian's breathing had already evened out, his chest rising and falling rhythmically as sleep claimed him.

Lyria, however, could not sleep. She lay still, her eyes fixed on the misty canopy above. Her mark vibrated, its warmth neither painful nor comforting, but undeniably present—a reminder of its weight and purpose.

Quietly, she rose, careful not to disturb the others. Her movements were fluid, her feet silent against the soft moss as she moved past the circle of resting companions. Duskrunner stirred but did not protest, his eyes following her before he resumed his grazing.

Lyria stood in the cool mist at the verge of the grove, her arms crossed as she gazed into the shifting fog. Her tail swished back and forth. The mist coiled closer around her, as if listening, its gentle luminescence deepening into a faint golden hue. The reverberation of the vale thrummed within her, steady and unyielding, with a rhythmic pulse.

Fizzlewing perched nearby on a gnarled branch, his iridescent wings sparkling in the Vale's muted light. His eyes regarded her with quiet curiosity. "You're restless," he said, his voice softer than usual.

Lyria didn't look at him right away. "The Vale hums like it's alive. As if it knows more about me than I know about myself."

Fizzlewing turned to speak. "The Vale shows what needs to be seen," he replied. "But not everything. Some truths are for you to uncover." His tone shifted, gentle but probing. "What's keeping you awake?"

She sighed, her gaze falling to the ground below. "I didn't say goodbye." Her voice was hushed, almost to herself.

Fizzlewing's wings buzzed as he adjusted his perch. "Goodbye? To whom?"

"To Kaelis," she said, her throat tightening as she spoke the name aloud. "Kaelis Skythorn. She's been my best friend since we were hatchlings. I just... disappeared without telling her why. She's like family." Her voice softened. "The last time I saw her, she was standing in the training circle, her laugh echoing through the mountains after I missed my target. She told me 'You're too focused. Relax… and trust your instincts."

Fizzlewing's eyes gleamed with interest. "Best friends have a way of understanding us better than we understand ourselves."

"She deserved better," Lyria said, her voice heavy with guilt. "Kaelis always stood by me, even when others didn't. She would have fought for me, but I couldn't bring her into this." Her talons brushed against her tattoo, the faint pulse matching the ache in her heart. "It's my mark. My burden. Not hers."

Fizzlewing regarded her, his expression unreadable. Then he spoke with a serious tone. "Lyria Ironwing, you carry a name as strong as your spirit, but even iron bends when it carries too much alone."

Lyria's glance shot to him, her gaze narrowing. "How do you know my full name?"

Fizzlewing tilted his head, his antennae twitching. "The Vale whispers many things," he said. "Perhaps it told me. Or perhaps I've heard it before." The mist swirled faintly, as though punctuating his words, its golden hues flickering with shades of violet. He managed a weak smile, his wings crackling. "Does it matter?"

"It does if you're hiding something," she countered, her tone sharp.

"Relax, Lyria," Fizzlewing said. "Your secrets are safe. I know more than I say, and I say more than I should. Let's leave it at that."

Lyria frowned, but didn't press further. Her tail flipped from side to side. "I don't like keeping secrets."

"And yet, you're in the Shrouded Vale," Fizzlewing quipped, his tone regaining some of its usual playfulness. "This place thrives on them."

A suggestion of a smile touched her lips, but her eyes remained distant. "If I ever get back to my kingdom... I'll explain everything to Kaelis. Maybe she'll understand."

Fizzlewing's golden eyes softened, as though reading the emotions she didn't voice. "Something tells me Kaelis Skythorn is a lot tougher than you give her credit for. And if she's anything like you, she knows you had a valid reason."

A swirling mist reappeared, and faint whispers seemed to rise from its core—soft, indistinct murmurs that sent tingles down her spine. The Vale's hum intensified, almost as though it, too, sensed the significance of her words.

"That... does sound like her," Lyria said, her eyes lighting up.

The two fell into a companionable silence. The Vale's drone intensified, and a faint rustle among the fog seemed to mimic their unspoken thoughts.

Fizzlewing disturbed the stillness, his voice quiet and reassuring. "I'll keep watch. Go rest. Whatever the Vale offers next, you'll face it better after some sleep."

Lyria hesitated, glancing back toward the grove where Eldrin and Finnian rested. Finally, she nodded. "Wake me if anything happens."

"Of course," Fizzlewing replied as he settled on his perch. "But you've earned a bit of peace tonight."

Lyria went back to the grove, her steps lighter, but her thoughts were still heavy.

Eldrin stirred on his bedroll but did not awaken as Lyria approached. His hand twitched, brushing against his side. Finnian slept not far away, his brow creased, though he seemed captive to his dreams.

When Lyria lay down, sleep came slowly, until the Vale disappeared from her consciousness, and the familiar landscape of her kingdom unfolded around her, cloaked in the dusky hues of an overcast sky. Jagged mountains framed the horizon, their sharp peaks silhouetted against a backdrop of swirling clouds. Ancient stone structures, etched with Draconic carvings, stood as silent witnesses to an age-old legacy, their surfaces worn smooth by the passage of time.

Kaelis Skythorn walked among them, her figure vivid against the muted backdrop. Her slender frame moved with a blend of purpose and frustration, her purple-streaked braids catching faint glimmers of an unseen light. She faltered, her gaze flickering around the space. Her shoulders tensed, as if she sensed something unseen. 'Lyria?' she whispered, a thread of uncertainty underlying her words. Her fingers clenched around a leather bracelet.

Lyria tore at the barrier between them, desperation rising. "Kaelis, I'm here!" But the void swallowed her voice.

Kaelis paused, spinning slowly as if looking for an unseen person. Her voice lowered to nearly a whisper. "What happened, Lyria? Why did you leave?"

The words landed like a blow, and Lyria's chest tightened. She tried once more to claw through the barrier, but her movements were sluggish, as if the air itself resisted her. "Kaelis," she tried to answer, her lips forming the name, but no sound emerged.

A heartbeat later, the shadows surged, swallowing Kaelis whole.

A white dragon, the same one that warned her of the nemods, ascended from the brilliance, its immense form majestic. Its scales shimmered with an ethereal glow, and its eyes radiated ancient wisdom. The dragon's voice resonated, low and commanding, as it addressed her. "Your kingdom faces a darkness. It cannot fight alone. The darkness moves—your people will not stand for long. Return, Lyria Ironwing, and bring those who would stand beside you."

The imagery transformed, flashing glimpses of the drelf kingdom: barricaded gates struggling to hold against an unseen force, fires burning, and drelves fighting. Among them, Kaelis was at the forefront, her sword gleaming as she faced the encroaching shadows with unyielding determination.

The dragon's voice rang out once more, the words echoing through Lyria's mind. "Strength lies in unity. Alone, even the strongest will fall."

As the light dimmed, the dream began to unravel. The last image lingered in Lyria's mind—Kaelis turning toward her, her expression resolute but shadowed with sorrow. Her lips moved, forming words Lyria couldn't hear before the scene dissolved into darkness.

Lyria awoke abruptly, her chest heaving as if she'd been running. She sat up, her claws piercing the soft earth as she struggled to calm her breathing.

Her thoughts churned, the dragon's words and Kaelis's voice echoing in her mind. *Return to your kingdom. Bring those who would stand beside you.*

A lump formed in her throat, her gaze flickering towards the shifting mist. Her kind—her home—is in danger. And Kaelis… Kaelis was there, ready to fight, while Lyria fled. A bitter knot tightened in her stomach. She had abandoned Kaelis, saying nothing before leaving. Had she thought Lyria had abandoned her? The thought stung worse than any wound.

Her claws pressed against the moss, her breath uneven as the significance of her dream began to sink in. The Vale had shown her what was coming, but the choice was hers.

I must go back. The realization permeated her being, solid and unshakable. But how? How could she fight for her kingdom when she wasn't even whole? She didn't yet know what the mark meant, or what the prophecy demanded of her. And she couldn't even fly. Her tail swished behind her, agitated. Ever since she'd received the symbol, she felt trapped, but this was suffocating.

A low hum drifted through the Vale, as if a ghost from another time. It was soft at first, almost indistinct, but it carried a rhythm—steady, haunting, and old.

Lyria's ears twitched at the sound, her focus shifting.

Eldrin.

She shifted her gaze, watching as he lay still in sleep, his lips moving as the unfamiliar melody passed through them. The notes were of Elven origin—of that she was certain. But there was something heavier about them, something ancient and distant, as if pulled from the recesses rather than conscious thought.

She shifted, leaning toward Fizzlewing, who had perched nearby, his eyes glimmering under the cover of night.

"Fizzlewing," she whispered, her voice barely audible over the melody. "Are you awake?"

The small creature answered. "Of course, I'm awake," he murmured. "I'm keeping watch, remember?"

Lyria glanced back at Eldrin, her voice lowering. "What's he humming?"

Fizzlewing's gaze darkened, his antennae twitching as if he, too, felt the song's pull. "A war song," he whispered. "An old one."

Lyria's tail stilled. "Where would he have learned that?"

Fizzlewing didn't answer right away. His wings flickered, sending tiny sparks into the air. "Sometimes, dreams carry what the waking world forgets," he said. His voice, though quiet, carried the meaning of something profound.

Lyria hesitated. Should she wake him? Should she share her vision with him? Finnian stirred, his brow creased; his dreams seemed intense, and his body twitched. Lyria sat up slightly, her tail wrapping around her.

She reached out toward Eldrin as his humming grew more intense. But before her hand could brush his shoulder, Fizzlewing's voice stopped her.

"No," he said. "Let him be. He might need to recall the tune one day soon."

Lyria withdrew her hand as Eldrin's song faded into silence, his breathing evening out once more.

She exhaled, forcing herself to lie back down, but sleep eluded her. The words from the dragon still resonated within her, a warning wrapped in an undeniable truth.

She had to return.

But she couldn't do it alone.

Her thoughts ended suddenly as the horses stirred, their ears flicking and nostrils flaring. Silverwind whinnied, his body tense and alert. Duskrunner stamped on the ground, his eyes wide with unease.

"What's wrong?" Eldrin murmured, sitting up and gripping his dagger.

The Vale's ever-present hum wavered, faltering into an unnatural silence. Even the glowing flora seemed to dim, as if in suspense. Then a distant growl pierced the air, low and resonant, carrying a primal weight that silenced even the Vale's hum. The group froze, their eyes darting toward the source of the sound.

Finnian straightened, his swords already in hand. His grip was too tight, his breath uneven. He feigned a smirk; however, his voice gave him away. "Fantastic. That's definitely not something friendly."

Fizzlewing landed between them, his wings crackling with tension. "We must move," he said, his tone grim. "Now!"

Chapter 17

The air in the Elven chamber was thick with tension, the flickering candlelight casting long streaks throughout the chamber. King Eldermyst sat at the head of the long, intricately carved table, his posture rigid and his gaze sweeping over the gathered council members. He projected the image of an unshaken ruler, but beneath the mask of composure, a storm raged.

His son was missing.

Reports flooded in from every area of the kingdom. Eldrin, first, and then Finnian, had vanished without explanation. The nemods attacked Elven patrols in the forest and surrounding lands, forcing warriors into relentless skirmishes. Many of the creatures were slain by the warriors; however, the increased numbers and aggression were troubling.

And now, a greater danger had emerged—one that had infiltrated their sanctuary.

Gantar stood before the council, his weathered face unreadable. The flickering torches along the walls cast deep lines across his worn features, yet his eyes stayed steady, unwavering. Questions swirled around him like vultures circling, each voice layering over the other in sharp inquiry.

He had faced storms before, but none like this.

Lady Alariel, Mistress of Lore, was the first to speak, her voice measured but pressing. "You were the last to see Eldrin before his disappearance, were you not?"

Gantar tilted his head slightly. "I was."

Lord Thalion, Commander of the Elven Guard, braced his arms on the table, his gaze flinty. "And yet you did not think to report his absence immediately?"

"I had other concerns," Gantar replied. "Caelith's grievous wounds demanded my immediate attention."

Elder Faelorn, the Master of Nature, leaned forward, his gnarled fingers drumming lightly on the table. "And what about the disturbance in the woods? The unnatural storms? The trees whisper unease, Gantar. Something unnatural is at work. Is it possible that's connected to Eldrin's disappearance?"

Gantar looked into his eyes. "I think such things indicate a shift in our realm. That darkness is closing in, and it's all connected."

Lady Seraphina, Ambassador of Alliances, tilted her head. "What does that mean?"

Gantar exhaled. "The very essence of the land twisting, as though something—someone is trying to unravel it. The prophecy has begun…"

A murmur swept through the room, but it was Elder Sylthir, the Shadow Watcher, who silenced the noise. "We have heard such claims before. Visions, signs, warnings. But proof? What does Eldrin's leaving have to do with the prophecy?"

Gantar hesitated. He could not lie, entirely, but neither could he betray Eldrin's trust.

"I know only that he is following a path greater than our understanding," Gantar said, his voice calm but firm.

King Eldermyst's fingers curled into fists at his sides. "Then you must know why he left."

"He left because he believed he had no other choice."

Lord Thalion narrowed his eyes. "That is not an answer."

"It is the only one I will give."

Silence fell over the chamber like a shroud. King Eldermyst stood up and pushed back his chair, his voice a low, controlled rumble.

"You have long been a trusted friend to this kingdom, Gantar. And to my family." His voice dipped lower. "To Thariel."

Gantar's expression did not change, but something shone behind his eyes at the mention of Eldrin's mother.

The king stepped closer. "I have tolerated much from you over the years, and I consider you a friend. But do not mistake that for patience without end. Where is my son, Gantar?"

Gantar gazed into the king's eyes. "He is safe, Lord. You have my word."

The king focused his gaze, his brows furrowed as he peered into the old sage's soul. "Are you aware that Finnian has also disappeared?"

The seriousness of the words settled like a heavy stone.

For the first time, Gantar's composure faltered.

"Finnian?" he echoed, his brows knitting together.

Lord Thalion nodded. "No word, no trace. He vanished mere hours after Eldrin."

Gantar exhaled. *Of course he did.*

It was so like Finnian to throw himself into the fire unannounced, with a smile on his face and a reckless spirit. Finnian was loyal to the core. He would stand with Eldrin. Even at his demise, Gantar was sure of this.

"And your horse, Gantar? Gone. While you remain…" King Eldermyst pressed the sage further. "I'm sure that Eldrin took Silverwind, and Finnian took his horse, but why would your mount be missing?"

Gantar's jaw tightened slightly, but he remained silent.

A gentle murmur disturbed the stillness.

Elder Sylthir, his tone sharp and knowing, gestured. “Please, elaborate. Why would they need a third horse?” His words slithered forth, more accusation than question.

The council fell silent. A fresh ripple of doubt spread among them.

"Silverwind is a fine horse, but even he cannot carry both a rider and extra provisions for an extended journey,” he said. “Duskrunner was the best choice.”

Lady Elowyn, Mistress of Healing, spoke gently, though her gaze was keen. “You aided Eldrin in his departure, didn’t you?”

Gantar refused to look away but did not speak.

Silence filled the room.

“Didn’t you!” Lady Elowyn demanded, slamming a fist on the table.

“I did.”

The admission sent a tremor of tension through the council.

The king leaned forward slowly, with calculation.

Silence grew dense like smoke.

King Eldermyst’s voice dropped low. “Finally, you speak some truth.” His eyes darkened, and his patience was thinning. “Now I want the full details and the real reason for your actions, Gantar.”

The effect of his words permeated the space.

A chill settled within the room. A sentence unspoken, yet understood.

The other council members stiffened, their gazes darting between their king and the healer. Even Gantar was not above the law of the Elves.

A long pause.

Gantar held the king's gaze.

He spoke with a calm demeanor, stating, "I have served this kingdom all my life. I have protected its warriors, healed its wounded, and stood by its elves when others turned away."

What he said next struck with a swift blow.

"But I cannot turn my back on the prophecy. It must be fulfilled, no matter the cost."

A heartbeat passed. The hush was deafening.

Lady Alariel's voice was razor sharp.

"We searched your cabin, Gantar."

Gantar remained still.

"And found traces of blue blood."

Silence descended on the chamber, deeper than before.

No elf bled blue.

The council's comprehension came like the strike of a war drum.

A drelf. A creature of exile. And a shadow of betrayal.

A sudden gasp rippled through the room. Whispers stirred like dry leaves—hushed, urgent, and tinged with something colder.

Lord Thalion's fingers clenched into a fist. "Tell us the truth, Gantar. Did you shelter a drelf within our kingdom?"

The moment stretched; Gantar could feel every gaze upon him. The silence pressed like a knife against his throat.

He then met the king's gaze and spoke the words that could not be undone.

"Yes."

King Eldermyst's face gave nothing away; however, his eyes focused on Gantar like a tempest on the horizon. "And does the drelf remain?"

Gantar hesitated for a fraction too long. That hesitation was answered enough.

Lord Thalion's voice, when it came, resembled a blade striking stone. "So, Duskrunner was not used to carry supplies, was he?"

Gantar stayed quiet.

Lord Thalion said, gritting his teeth, "You lent your horse to aid Eldrin in the drelf's escape. Didn't you?"

A heavier hush draped over the room.

Elder Sylthir, ever the watchful hunter, leaned in, his silver eyes gleaming with cold certainty. "Then it is not only you who has committed treason, Gantar." He let the words settle like poison before turning his gaze to the king. "Your son has as well."

The impact was immediate.

The chamber burst into action.

Voices clashed, accusations flew, and the repercussions of his confession spread throughout the room.

Through it all, Gantar remained steadfast.

But one voice had still not spoken.

King Eldermyst.

The ruler of the elves glared at the sage whom he had once trusted beyond measure.

And the hush was far heavier than any accusation present.

The tightness in King Eldermyst's jaw betrayed his attempt to stifle all emotion.

"Enough! You have placed this kingdom in danger," he said, his voice like the distant rumble of thunder. "My son's involvement remains to be seen. But do you realize what this means for you?"

The room fell into silence, the import of his question pressing down on them all. The fate of the kingdom, of Eldrin, and the seer dangled at the threshold of the unknown.

Gantar's expression remained impassive, though his eyes darkened. "I do."

Chapter 18

The growl rumbled again through the Vale, causing every hair on their necks to bristle.

"What, was that?" Eldrin asked, as a rush of energy surged beneath his palm at the dagger. The sound had come from outside the Vale's protective shroud, low and guttural, but unmistakably near.

Finnian sat up, rubbing the sleep from his eyes; his usual light-hearted demeanor was absent. "That… was not my stomach," he muttered, though his voice lacked humor.

Lyria's breath hitched. Her mark pulsed, not with pain, but with a quiet, insistent warning. She looked into the mist, her eyes scanning the shifting veil that separated them from whatever lay beyond.

The Vale had been eerily still after the sound. There were no answering calls, no rustling of unseen creatures; only silence, thick and unnatural.

Fizzlewing, perched upon a low-hanging branch, clicked his tongue. "They know you're here," he murmured. "And they're waiting."

Eldrin turned and asked, "What is waiting?"

The small creature's iridescent wings flickered. "The things beyond the mist," Fizzlewing said cryptically.

Eldrin approached Fizzlewing. "That doesn't answer the question."

The tiny beast held eye contact with him for a considerable time, then shrugged, his usual mischief absent. "No, it doesn't."

Finnian exhaled slowly as he rose. "Fantastic. Cryptic warnings at the crack of dawn. "Alright, let's hear it then. What exactly is out there?"

Fizzlewing's usual smirk did not return. "I'll say this—beware the silence between the growls."

A shiver crept down Lyria's spine.

Eldrin took a measured breath, scanning the Vale. "The mist is thinning."

It was true—the thick, protective fog that had cocooned them was shifting. It was not retreating but rolling forward in slow waves, curling around their feet and nudging at their limbs like an insistent hand. It coiled and stretched, pressing outward and urging them onward.

Lyria fidgeted, her tail twining around her legs. "It wants us to leave."

Finnian furrowed his brow. "Why do I feel like that's not a good thing?"

Fizzlewing dropped from his perch, landing on a moss-covered stone. He studied them before speaking. "The Vale kept you safe. But you don't belong here. And it knows that. It is time to move on."

Lyria forced herself to swallow. Her dream still clung to her thoughts. She had hoped for more time to think, to plan. But there was no more time.

"My kingdom is at risk," she finally said, voice firm but raw with urgency. "They will be under attack soon. The white dragon revisited me last night to warn me. I must return."

Silence hung heavy between them. Finnian shifted, and Eldrin's gaze turned toward his friend.

Eldrin slowly released his breath, his jaw rigidly set. "You're asking me, us, to turn our backs on the elves," he said, voice quiet but sharp. "To commit treason."

Lyria faced his gaze, her own unwavering. "I'm not asking you to do anything. I'm telling you what I must do."

She continued. "You don't owe me anything. And I won't ask you to risk yourselves for my kingdom. But I must leave," she stated, as she carried her bedroll and gear toward Duskrunner.

A low whistle escaped Finnian's lips. "You sure have a way of making a guy feel useless."

Eldrin remained quiet, though the Aetherstone warmed and glowed at his side. He looked away and sighed heavily. "You expect us to let you ride off alone?"

Lyria hesitated. "It's not your fight."

Eldrin's lips pressed into a thin line. "This is true. But perhaps it is my destiny."

Her brows knit in confusion. "What?"

"The prophecy," he said at last. "You said it yourself. This isn't just about you or the drelves. It is about all the realms; our choices will shape the future, whether good or bad. I can feel it, in the dagger, and the stone."

Lyria pursed her lips, hesitating before speaking, "You were humming in your sleep. A song. Fizzlewing said it was a war song. Where did you learn it?"

Eldrin stilled, his eyes remained fixed on hers, but his mind drifted inward, beyond the present—beyond the Vale, beyond the prophecy—to something hidden deep within him. He caught his breath, and a sudden weight pressed on his chest.

The melody hovered at the periphery of his mind, aching, familiar. Not forgotten—buried.

Then the memory unraveled. His mother's voice, soft yet firm, whispered the words as she held him close. The comforting presence of her arms, the steady rhythm of her heartbeat against his ear. She had sung the melody to him, over and over, her fingers combing his hair, her voice soothing and strong. He had clung to the song as a child. Then, somewhere along the years, he had let it fade.

His grip tightened around the dagger, the cool metal grounding him. The prophecy. The dagger. The song. They were all connected.

He forced down the lump lodged in his throat and said, "My mother, Thariel, taught me the song when I was very young. I hadn't thought about it for years. Until now."

Finnian crossed his arms, glancing between them. "Ah, perfect. Ancient war songs, cryptic prophecies, and an enemy we can't see. Sure. Why not? Sounds like a solid plan."

Eldrin faced him and grinned. "You're with us, then?"

Finnian sighed, shrugging his shoulders like he was shaking off the weight of the moment. Then, with a smile that fell short of his eyes, he clapped Eldrin on the shoulder. "Wasn't planning on letting you two have all the fun." He looked toward Lyria. "Besides, someone's gotta keep her from flying off alone."

Lyria arched a brow. "I can't fly."

Finnian winked. "Not yet."

Lyria huffed and shook her head at Finnian's remark, but a hint of something enigmatic crossed her face. Not yet. The words lingered longer than they should have.

She paused... A part of her still wanted to resist—to insist this was her fight alone. But she knew better.

She raised her eyes to Eldrin and then to Finnian. A quiet sense of relief steadied her as she realized she wasn't standing alone in this fight.

She nodded. "Then let's go."

A sudden clearing of the throat interrupted the moment.

Fizzlewing hovered in front of them, arms crossed. "Much as I love watching your inspiring group solidarity, there's the minor issue of actually *leaving* the Vale." He gestured to the shifting mist. "The exit will not roll out a welcome mat."

Eldrin turned, his brow furrowing. The mist was moving—coiling, twisting. Urgent. Purposeful. The Vale was shifting again.

Finnian squinted. "I don't like how it's doing that."

Lyria's mark pulsed, an echo of something unseen. "Neither do I."

Eldrin adjusted his cloak, his shoulders set with renewed resolve. He addressed Fizzlewing. "Ok, fearless guide. Will you show us the way out?"

For once, the little creature hesitated. Something mysterious passed through his eyes.

Then, with an exaggerated sigh, he squared his tiny shoulders. "Fine. But don't say I didn't warn you about what was waiting out there."

Lyria glanced back, an unshakable sense of finality seeping into her very being. The Vale had protected them, but now… now it was urging them to leave.

As if it knew.

As if it sensed they must leave.

The trio quickly mounted their horses. Finnian tightened the strap on Embermane's saddle, muttering about bad omens and mist that moved on its own. Lyria adjusted Duskrunner's reins, turned her head and flexed her shoulders, her bound wing an oppressive testament to her situation. Her claws skimmed over the bandages, grating against the rough fabric.

Flight.

She longed for it.

The wind against her scales, the freedom of the skies instead of the land beneath her feet. Yet, as her hand drifted back to Duskrunner's mane, she knew she had grown attached to the steady, earthbound companion who had carried her through the unknown.

The saddle would have to do for now.

Eldrin secured Silverwind's stirrups, his movements methodical, but his thoughts elsewhere—on the dagger, the stone warming in its pouch, the war song that had surfaced.

Fizzlewing watched them intently, wings flickering. When Lyria caught his gaze, he snapped back into his typical swagger, clapping his front legs together.

"Right, inspiring. Very inspiring. But if you're all done making your horses comfortable, we should leave before the Vale changes its mind."

Finnian swung into his saddle, a smirk curving his lips. "Why do I sense you know something you're not telling us?"

Fizzlewing grinned. "Because I do."

He took off without another word, darting ahead — as if in a rush to be rid of them. The whirling fog glowed in odd, uneasy pulses, whispering against their skin as they followed him closer to the Vale's edge.

The trees thinned, and the mist stretched out before them, forming a swirling boundary where the Vale ended and the unknown began.

Fizzlewing hovered just beyond it, his wings slower now as the air grew heavier around him. The moment of departure had arrived.

Lyria cast a last glance at him, something clenching within her breast. "Come with us."

For once, Fizzlewing looked truly sad. "I can't."

Finnian frowned. "Can't? Or won't?"

Fizzlewing's eyes flickered. "Both. The Vale is part of me. I can't just walk away."

Lyria's throat tightened. "Then this is goodbye."

The small creature's wings crackled. "For now. But, you never know when we might meet again."

He hesitated, then darted toward her, landing on Duskrunner's saddle. From the pouch on his hip, he pulled out a small, shimmering stone in the shape of a flower—no larger than a coin, its surface shifting between violet and silver hues.

"Here," he said, pressing it into her palm. "This is for you."

Lyria frowned, studying the stone. "What is it?"

Fizzlewing's eyes softened. "Call it a token of friendship," he said, then tapped a leg against it. "And maybe a little luck. Just don't lose it."

She narrowed her eyes. "Fizzlewing—"

But the creature lifted off her saddle, hovering just out of reach. "If you ever need me, just call my name. Now, you've got your own mess to deal with. Get moving."

A breeze swept past them—a breath of something beyond the Vale. The comfort of the hidden sanctuary faded, leaving the cold bite of the real world pressing in.

Finnian shifted in his saddle. "Well, that's not ominous at all."

Lyria held the gift in her palm, feeling its warmth against her touch. She hesitated, then dropped it in the leather pouch attached to her waist. A faint pulse echoed at her neck—the mark responding, though, to what she could not say.

Eldrin moved through the thinning mist, hand on his saddle and exhaled. No turning back. No more hesitation. He tightened his jaw, gripped the reins, and rode forward. Lyria and Finnian followed, their steps steady despite the uncertainty of what awaited them.

The moment they crossed the mist, silence greeted them.

Then—

A growl. Low. Lingering. And just past the trees, two eyes glowed in the darkness…

Chapter 19

The elf council chamber was in chaos. Voices clashed like swords in battle, rising and falling, accusations flying from every direction.

"He harbored a drelf!" Lord Thalion's voice sliced through the uproar, his fists slamming against the table. "A crime punishable by exile, if not death!"

"This is treason of the highest order!" Elder Sylthir's sharp tone followed.

Lady Alariel folded her hands on the table, her piercing gaze fixed on Gantar. "The law is clear, Your Majesty. We cannot allow such betrayal to go unpunished-"

"Enough!"

The word from King Eldermyst struck like an arrow amidst the chaos as he arose from his chair, his cloak billowing as he stepped forward. The chamber fell into stunned silence.

For the longest time, he said nothing.

Then—his eyes surveyed the room, slow and deliberate.

His speech was hushed, yet it carried enough weight to shift the council. He turned, locking eyes with each of them. "Have you forgotten who you serve? Who rules these lands?"

No one dared answer.

King Eldermyst's voice hardened. "You are advisors—nothing more. I alone decide the fate of traitors." His ultimate words rang with an undeniable command.

The council hesitated, glancing at one another.

"Leave us."

The hesitation deepened.

His voice rose. "I said—leave us. Now!"

The power of his fury broke their resolve. One by one, the council members rose, bowing before departing from the chamber.

Lady Elowyn paused before the door, her gaze flickering with an enigmatic expression. But as King Eldermyst's piercing stare settled on her, she dipped her head and followed the others in silence.

Only Gantar remained.

The doors closed.

Silence settled between them.

The massive doors shut with a loud thud, sealing the two elves inside. The silence that followed was suffocating, thick with years of unspoken words and buried pain.

"I trusted you."

The words were low measured, but the anger beneath them was barely restrained. The king moved toward Gantar, his unwavering gaze burning into the sage he had once considered an ally—a friend.

Gantar stayed motionless, his expression calm but watchful as the king paced. The consequence of betrayal lingered in the void between them, implicit yet suffocating.

"You have been loyal to this realm longer than most sitting on that council. You have healed our warriors, stood beside my family—beside my wife—" His voice faltered just a fraction, but it returned like a honed sword. "And yet, you betray me."

Gantar released a slow and steady breath. "I did what was right."

"You aided a drelf! You led my son—" His voice cracked into something far more threatening. "My heir—into treason!!"

Gantar met the king's furious gaze, unflinching. "I did not lead him, my king. He chose his path."

A beat of silence. The air between them was thick, brimming with everything that had not been said.

"You speak as if this was fate."

"It was."

The king remained silent. His Elven features were sharp and unyielding as years of pain etched themselves across his face.

"Enough of such talk." He turned away, pacing several times before whirling back to face Gantar. "I forbade you from ever mentioning the prophecy again. And yet, not only do you still cling to this madness—you have dragged my son into it!"

Gantar stood, unwavering. "The prophecy has come to Eldrin, my king. Not by my words nor my will, but by what must be. You cannot stop it, however much you may wish to."

The king's countenance hardened, his fury deepening into something darker. "You would have me believe this madness—that a cursed prophecy, the same foolishness that took Thariel from me—is destiny?"

"She sought the truth. And the truth remains, regardless of how long you ignore it."

"The truth?" His laughter was bitter, humorless. "She died for nothing. And now, my son—" King Eldermyst said, his teeth clenching so tightly his jaw trembled. "You were supposed to protect him, Gantar."

Gantar's expression flickered—not with fear nor defiance, but something quieter, heavier. Regret. Not for his actions but for the weight they placed upon a king who had already lost too much.

His voice, when it arrived, was unwavering. "I did, my Lord." A pause, softer now but no less confident. "And I still am."

The king's breath came in shallow bursts, his shoulders rigid, oppressed by the weight placed upon them as years of suffering and frustration were reflected in his eyes. He was a king, but the pain of being a father threatened to consume him.

"Then you will protect him from the confines of a cell."

The words were like a hammer's blow, but Gantar remained unmoved.

"I will keep you imprisoned until I decide your fate." Though he spoke evenly, it carried an undeniable finality. A sentence not just spoken but felt.

"This disloyalty stops now."

The words he spoke next were loud enough to shake the dead.

"Guards! Take him."

The command broke through the thick silence. The guards hesitated only for a fraction of a second before stepping into the chamber. Their heavy boots echoed against the polished stone, each step a hammer striking against what little remained of trust.

Gantar offered no resistance.

His expression remained impassive and unreadable as their hands closed around his arms, gripping tightly. He was a healer, not a warrior. And yet, he stood with more resolve than any soldier.

He did not look at the guards. Only at the king.

The accumulation of all their years—of friendship, of trust—lay between them like an invisible specter. And yet, there was nothing left to say.

Gantar bowed his head—just slightly. A last act of respect. A farewell, though neither spoke it.

King Eldermyst's jaw tightened, his hands curling into fists at his sides. He did not return the gesture. Could not.

The heavy doors groaned open, the rush of cool air from the corridor beyond pressing in like an unwelcome visitor. The guards pulled Gantar toward the exit. He did not struggle.

And then—precisely when the doors were swinging shut—Gantar glanced back.

It was brief, a glimpse of movement, but something surfaced in his eyes. Something the king could not name. Not defiance nor regret, but something more profound.

The doors shut with a resounding thud.

King Eldermyst did not move. Did not breathe.

His fingers unclenched, only to find his palm aching; nails had dug into his skin without his notice. He exhaled, but it did not steady him.

The chamber was empty now. And the surrounding silence was suffocating.

For the first time in many moons, it was not rage that gripped him. Not duty. Not grief.

It was fear.

Chapter 20

Lyria halted first, her pulse thrumming against her eardrums. She didn't see them. But she sensed they were there.

The forest hushed. Even the wind dared not stir the leaves. A thickness settled over them—not just darkness, but something alive.

Lyria forced herself to swallow. The feeling of unseen eyes pricked at her scales.

Then—movement. Not a sound, but a shift. Like the night itself was breathing.

They were definitely being watched.

Finnian tightened his grip at the reins, his easygoing nature stripped away by the surrounding tension. Embermane snorted, moving under him.

"Tell me someone else feels that," Finnian muttered.

But before anyone could answer, the Aetherstone burned in Eldrin's pouch. A pulse—frantic. His stomach twisted as he felt the stone's heat against his body. "They're not just moving. They're closing in."

Then—

A growl. Low. Lingering within the trees like a whispered omen.

Immediately past the trees, a pair of eyes gleamed.

Eldrin gripped his knife as it began to glow. His heartbeat fell into rhythm with the ancient power thrumming through him.

Another growl. Then another. This time, it didn't come from the same direction.

Shadows slipped between the trunks, sleek and deliberate. The creatures did not charge. They did not prowl. They stalked. Watching. Waiting.

A terrible, sinking weight settled in Eldrin's chest.

No. That's not possible.

Then he saw them. The shifting forms. The molten eyes. The living darkness.

His entire elfhood slammed against him like a crashing wave—the whispered stories, the crackling firelight, the hushed warnings that made his skin prickle. Thalendir's smirk. His voice was teasing and sharp. *Chasing shadows again, little brother?*

Eldrin's throat tightened.

Mere stories. Legends. That's all they were.

But the glowing eyes said otherwise.

They were real.

His tone was barely audible, yet it carried like a portent of doom.

"Shadow Panthers."

Finnian inhaled, his bow quivering in his grip. "No. No, that's not… they're not…" He swallowed hard. "They're not real."

But they were.

Lyria shot them both a sharp look, her confusion cutting through their shock. "Shadow Panthers?"

A rustle—fast, sharp.

A current of darkness moved among the trees. Then another.

Finnian's voice dropped tight with fear. "This might be a bad time to ask, but does anyone have a plan?"

Lyria moved towards the motion, heart hammering. "They're moving."

Eldrin remained silent. His hand had already gone for the bow slung on his back. Another pulse.

Not just from the dagger — but from something deeper, something ancient. His breath hitched as warmth flowed through his body. His dagger was glowing brighter.

Then, beside him, a second light flared.

Eldrin tightened his legs around Silverwind, and his other hand held his bow. Lyria stiffened as the golden band of her tattoo shimmered to life, its intricate designs sparkling in the moonlight.

A dark shape lunged.

Eldrin reacted on instinct. He twisted in the saddle, drawing his bow in one fluid motion. The string thrummed, and the arrow loosed. It struck true—but passed through the panther as if through smoke.

"Damn it!" Finnian cursed, already notching another arrow from Embermane's back.

"They shift between the shadows!" Lyria shouted, turning Duskrunner sharply.

Another panther darted forward, its molten eyes locked on Silverwind's flank. The mare reared back, sensing the unnatural threat.

Eldrin barely kept his seat as the beast leapt toward them.

His dagger flared into life.

A beam of searing light shot from the blade the instant a panther closed in. The energy surged through the atmosphere in a wave, forcing the creature to solidify for just a moment—

"Now!" Eldrin bellowed.

Lyria was already moving. She leapt off Duskrunner, curled into a roll, and slid beneath the panther as it took form. Her twin blades sang as they sliced upward, meeting the beast's chest where it was now fully tangible.

The panther howled as it collapsed into a shadowy mist.

But there was no time to celebrate.

Three more circled.

Finnian loosed an arrow, striking one in the shoulder as it materialized mid-lunge. The creature snarled but didn't fall to the ground.

Another leapt at Eldrin, faster this time. He barely had time to parry before it struck him, sending him crashing into the dirt. His dagger flickered—reacting. Surging.

Power coiled at the cusp of his senses, desperate to be released.

As a tempest trapped beneath his skin.

The energy gathered in the recesses of his consciousness, pressing, twisting, whispering. It was a storm in his blood, surging toward his fingertips, aching to be freed.

Let go.

The utterance wasn't his own. *Or was it?* The thought rattled him.

His hold on reality wavered. The storm swelled. He stood on the cusp of something vast, something beyond him.

The hesitation cost him.

Pain. Claws raked across his arm.

Finnian's next arrow thudded into the panther's chest.

The horses shifted, sensing the danger their riders could only glimpse

A trickle of dread settled in Lyria's gut. If they ran, the creatures would chase after them. But if they stayed still—

A third growl, deep and guttural, shattered the fragile stillness.

The shadows lunged again.

Eldrin reacted right before a panther-like form lept out of the night, its body twisting between corporeal and shadow, its claws slashing at the air. He yanked his dagger free, the glow intensifying as he raised it in the nick of time. The creature's strike met the blade — and light exploded outward.

The impact sent the beast skidding back, a snarl breaking the silence as golden embers crackled where Eldrin's dagger had touched it. His breath hitched as his dagger burned with power.

Lyria's mark flared in response.

She gasped as energy surged through her, the same golden fire sparking over her skin, matching the glow of Eldrin's blade.

The panthers hesitated. Their crimson eyes flicked, sensing the shift. But then, more shadows rushed forward.

Finnian ducked low as one beast lunged, his blades a blur of movement. The creature recoiled, its form shifting into smoke before reforming behind him.

"They cheat!" Finnian barked, ducking at the last moment.

A deep, rippling growl vibrated the air. Their shadows circled faster now.

Lyria didn't wait. When a second beast pounced, she pivoted — fast, sharp. Her hands came up, and power flared from her mark. A golden arc of energy lashed out, slamming into the creature mid-strike. The force sent it reeling, its form flickering between shadow and flesh, snarling as it struggled to regain shape.

Eldrin's chest constricted. He felt it. Her power. His power. Working together.

Another beast came for him. He didn't hesitate. He slashed forward with his dagger, but now something different happened.

His blade reached outward — toward Lyria.

At the exact moment, Lyria swung her arm toward him.

The golden energy flared between them, crackling — not magic as Eldrin knew it, but more significantly, something intrinsic in the marrow of his bones.

He sensed it before he saw it. A pull. A thread of warmth stretched toward Lyria's mark.

And then—a sudden rush, like two rivers colliding.

Her eyes widened. She experienced it as well. Not just energy, but reflex.

Then—light erupted, searing and relentless, a shockwave of energy shredding through the forest. The force rippled outward, rustling branches scattering leaves like a sudden storm.

The panthers screeched, their shadows convulsing, writhing as if the very fabric of their existence was unraveling.

Heat lanced through Eldrin's palm. He gasped, fingers locking around the dagger's hilt as it flared brightly. It burned. But something beyond instinct kept him from letting go.

Lyria staggered from the force of it.

What was this?

Finnian took the opening, striking low and fast, forcing one creature back. "I don't know what you two just did—" He dodged a snapping jaw. "—but do it again."

The panthers snarled, regrouping. The shadows rippled around them, restless, shifting.

And in their molten eyes—recognition.

Lyria's heart pounded. She recognized what this was. She didn't understand it, but one thing was clear…

"We're stronger together," she whispered.

Eldrin met her gaze, his eyes flashing.

"Then let's end this."

And this time, when they moved, they moved as one—two threads of the same fate, entwined in fire and shadow.

The light faded, leaving only smoldering embers in its wake.

In a flash, everything stilled.

The sleek black felines stayed near the trees, their molten eyes afire with something new—hesitation. Their elegant forms flickered between darkness and light, rippling with unease.

Eldrin steadied his breath, his dagger still pulsing, his veins humming with the energy they had unleashed.

The largest of the creatures—a beast taller than the rest, its form darker, its stare colder—stepped forward. It did not attack. It did not lunge.

It simply watched.

Lyria's pulse thrummed.

It held their gaze for one agonizing heartbeat, then another.

With a slow, deliberate motion, it turned. The others followed, returning to the trees.

The silence following them seemed more significant than the battle itself.

Lyria exhaled, her limbs trembling from spent energy. She looked to Eldrin, searching his face, searching for an explanation.

He had none.

A breathy laugh escaped Finnian's lips, though there was little humor in it. "So…" He ran a hand over his face. "Just to be clear—those were actual Shadow Panthers? Like, the ones from the stories?"

Eldrin forced a swallow, nodding. "They were real."

Finnian gave a low whistle. "Right. Okay. Great. What else from childhood nightmares is waiting for us?"

Neither Eldrin nor Lyria answered, but they were wondering the same thing.

Finnian exhaled. "Alright, but just so we're covering everything—" he gestured between them, a steely glint in his eyes, "—what was that thing?"

Eldrin hesitated. He knew precisely what Finnian meant.

The light. The connection. The way their powers had fused—not separate forces, but two pieces of the same whole.

Lyria shifted, glancing at Eldrin, then at her own hands—still tingling with the remnants of that golden fire. "I… don't know."

Finnian crossed his swords. "Well, watching you two glow like twin stars while vaporizing childhood nightmares? Yeah, that's… something."

He paused, gaze flicking between them.

Eldrin met Lyria's gaze, something unspoken passing between them.

Lyria gulped nervously. "The prophecy. It links us."

Eldrin strengthened his grasp on his dagger. There was no denying it.

Whatever the future held, they were in this together.

Chapter 21

The darkness of the cell was unfamiliar to Gantar. The silence was not. It carried something else. Something waiting.

The distant torchlight flickered, its glow reaching the ancient stones. He sat unmoving, palms on his knees, his mind replaying the king's last words.

"Your betrayal ends here."

The words stuck with him like a hammer.

Betrayal.

Was that truly what this was?

He had been loyal to the throne longer than the king had worn his crown, stood beside Thariel when the king still called her his heart and held Eldrin as a child. He'd whispered healing words over Eldrin's scraped knees and watched him grow from a quiet boy into a warrior with his mother's fire.

Had a single choice undone all of that?

Gantar exhaled slowly and measuredly, but the weight did not leave his chest.

He had known what he was risking when he sheltered Lyria. Knew the law. Knew the hatred for her kind.

But he had seen her mark.

And he had known.

The prophecy was unfolding, whether the king willed it or not.

And now, the young elf whom he had once soothed to sleep was out there, walking towards a fate that neither of them fully understood.

Gantar closed his eyes, not in regret, but in resolve.

His duty had only just begun.

There was a shift in the environment.

A presence.

Gantar did not raise his head; he sensed someone was there.

Footsteps. Quiet but deliberate. A measured breath. The faintest rustle of fabric. Whoever stood beyond the iron bars was no mere guard.

A moment passed. Then another.

Finally, he spoke.

"I was wondering when you'd come."

A pause. A slow exhale. Then—a voice, familiar yet imbued with something new.

"You expected me?"

Gantar lifted his head. The shadows played across the silhouette beyond the bars, but the stance, the presence—it was unmistakable.

"Prince Thalendir."

The Elven throne's successor stood rigid, his typical demeanor infused with an enigmatic element. Uncertainty? Annoyance? Regret?

Gantar studied him—the furrow in his brow, the way his hands clenched. And he understood.

Thalendir had made a decision. One he was still grappling with.

The young prince exhaled sharply. "We're wasting time." His voice was soft, lacking its usual mocking lilt as the key scraped against the iron, turning with quiet finality.

"We don't have long."

A fleeting expression crossed Gantar's face—not quite surprise, not quite satisfaction. A knowing.

"You're here to release me?"

Thalendir's jaw became rigid. "Yes, but I have no interest in discussing it."

But Gantar only angled his head slightly. "And yet, I suspect you're not doing this for me."

The prince stood rigid. He did not answer immediately.

Then, finally, he said, "Eldrin has doomed himself. Or maybe he's finally awake. Either way, he's drowning."

Gantar waited.

Thalendir's gaze was sharp, his voice infused with something almost involuntary—an admiration he didn't wish to admit. A slow grin spread over his mouth.

"He defied the council. The king. Our father." He shook his head. "It's so unlike him. But I'm certain that whatever he's gotten himself into, he's going to need our help."

Gantar raised a thick brow. "Our help?"

Thalendir's next words were quieter.

"I made a promise. Many years ago. To protect Eldrin if ever the time arose."

He exhaled, his hand tightening beside him before he forced himself to stillness. He'd spent years overshadowing his younger brother, belittling him, besting him.

Yet now, he was here, undoing the chains of fate.

Their gazes locked.

They both knew whom he'd made that promise to.

Gantar's voice was soft but certain. "Your mother would be proud."

Thalendir flinched—but it was quick, controlled. He turned, already reaching for the door.

"Don't waste words, healer." His tone was harsh, but it lacked venom.

He exhaled, clicking the lock free.

"We leave. Now."

The iron door swung open.

Gantar stepped forward, rolling his shoulders as if shedding the burden of confinement. He glanced at Thalendir—not just assessing, but truly seeing him.

Perhaps there was more to the young prince than he thought.

"You came prepared," he noted, eyes dropping to the sword at Thalendir's hip and the confident set of his shoulders.

Thalendir's lips twitched, but the usual arrogance wasn't there. "I hate to waste time. Our horses are waiting in the stable. If you're up for the adventure?"

Gantar said nothing, arching a brow before matching his stride.

They hurried through the corridors, boots silent on the polished stone. The dim torches flickered, casting shifting shadows along the passageway.

At the first set of guards, Thalendir didn't hesitate.

"Stand aside."

The nearest elf straightened, glancing between Thalendir and Gantar. His brow furrowed. "Prince Thalendir, I have received no orders—"

Thalendir's gaze was ice. "You dare question me?"

The guard faltered. "But—"

"The king sent me to fetch the prisoner," the words rang through the corridor. "Shall I tell him you refused his command?"

The two guards exchanged uneasy glances.

"Of course not, my prince," one said, stepping aside.

Thalendir ended the discussion as he strode forward, Gantar following silently.

Once they were out of earshot, Gantar murmured, "That was convincing."

Thalendir smirked, but it was hollow. "It should be. I've been lying my whole life."

Gantar gave him a sidelong glance but remained silent.

They moved through the lower halls, avoiding unnecessary eyes. The tension in Gantar's chest remained. He wasn't used to being part of a deception.

Thalendir was not bound by duty like Eldrin.

He bent the rules when it suited him. Broke them when it didn't.

But yet, here he was, breaking the law not for himself but for his brother.

Gantar's lips formed a thin line. Thariel must have had quite the conversation with him before she passed.

The sage had never witnessed this aspect of Thalendir before.

And yet—he wished to believe it was real.

The distant hum of voices forced them to halt.

Gantar tensed, his sharp eyes glancing toward Thalendir. The prince raised a hand—wait.

Another set of guards.

They stood stationed in the eastern corridor, blocking the way; two armored sentries with silver helmets reflecting in the torchlight.

The sage's voice was low. "We won't get through unseen."

Thalendir paused before answering. His fingers twitched beside him, his mind already working through possibilities.

Another bluff?

No. These were royal guards, handpicked by his father, less likely to fall for mere words.

The healer shifted beside him, expectant. "Well, prince?"

A flash of annoyance crossed Thalendir's face before he breathed out heavily.

"There's another way."

Gantar lifted an eyebrow. "And it didn't occur to you to mention this before?"

Thalendir scowled at him. "It's been years. I almost forgot it existed." He pivoted. "Come on."

The sage followed without argument, though curiosity stirred beneath his usual calm. Something unknown within the palace? That was rare.

The corridor twisted deeper within the palace, where the torches burned lower, flickering against walls smoothed by age. Time-worn stone—nearly forgotten.

And then, they reached it.

A small, arched opening, hidden behind a column, its frame carved with delicate Elven runes.

Gantar narrowed his eyes. "A servant's passage?"

Thalendir's smirk was fleeting. "A tunnel. One Eldrin and I often used to escape our tutors when we were young." He exhaled. "No one ever thought to seal it."

The sage eyed the prince, but his skepticism softened. There was truth behind his words, a quiet weight beneath it all.

Thalendir brushed his fingers along the old stone, finding the hidden groove at its center. The moment his palm met the surface—a whisper of magic stirred.

The passage groaned, dust shaking loose as the stone gave way, revealing a darkened tunnel that descended beneath the palace.

Cool, damp air rushed out to greet them—earth and memory.

Thalendir hesitated.

A shadow flickered through his head.

Not the past he had expected.

Not Eldrin.

A glimpse of golden hair—a stream of light, tumbling like sunfire. Blue eyes, wide with laughter. A voice—soft, distant, and fading even as it called out.

"Thalendir—wait!"

A chill skated up his spine.

His breath hitched. Where had that come from?

He didn't remember.

No, he couldn't.

Still, the image remained with him, reminiscent of something elusive.

A name he should know.

A face lost to time.

Gantar examined him. "Prince?"

Thalendir's jaw tensed. He pushed the thought away. Now was not the time to revisit the past.

In silence, he stepped inside, followed by Gantar.

The passage closed behind them, swallowing them in darkness.

They reached the stables just as dusk settled over the kingdom, the sky bleeding into deep purples and blues. Two horses stood waiting, saddled and ready. Thalendir had loaded the saddlebags with supplies and tied a bedroll with leather strings behind each seat. One mount was a sleek black stallion, its braided mane a dead giveaway of royal breeding. Steel was Thalendir's personal horse.

The other, a powerful chestnut gelding, bore the crest of King Eldermyst's stables.

Gantar sighed. "You stole from the king?"

Thalendir mounted without hesitation. A wide grin crossed his face. "Borrowed," he corrected. "It's only stealing if we don't return it."

Gantar climbed onto the chestnut, casting Thalendir another careful glance. "For someone who has spent his life avoiding responsibility, you seem awfully determined."

Thalendir's jaw flexed as he reined in his horse.

Then—his voice dropped, almost an afterthought.

"I don't break my promises."

Gantar's hold strengthened on the reins. He'd never witnessed this part of Thalendir. Perhaps Thariel had influenced him more than anyone realized.

But time didn't allow him to dwell on it.

The last rays of the sun's light faded as they reined their horses into the dense underbrush.

"We'll head for the eastern border," Thalendir said. "Once we clear the portal, we ride all night."

Gantar didn't answer. Instead, he veered his horse left toward the densest section of the woods.

Thalendir frowned. "You're going the wrong way!"

Gantar didn't slow. "We can't use the portal."

Thalendir's stallion pranced beneath him, sensing the sudden energy shift. "What?"

"The sentries will watch the roads." Gantar turned in the saddle. "I know a better way."

Thalendir exhaled sharply, but before he could argue…

"There! Stop them!"

A shrill voice pierced the night.

Thalendir's head snapped toward the main gates. A squad of Elven sentries had just come out of the barracks, their armor capturing the moonlight.

One of them pointed. "The prince—he has the prisoner! After them!"

Thalendir didn't hesitate. "Ride!"

Gantar was already ahead, spurring his mount forward. The sound of galloping horses erupted behind them as the guards leapt onto their horses in pursuit.

The forest rushed past in a torrent of silver-lit leaves as they crashed through the underbrush, branches snapping as their mounts leapt over roots and ducked beneath low-hanging limbs.

"How long until we reach this 'better way' of yours?" Thalendir shouted, gripping the reins as Steel surged forward.

Gantar didn't look back. "Not long. Keep going!"

"Halt! On behalf of King Eldermyst!" one sentry bellowed behind them.

Thalendir cast a quick look backwards. A dozen riders. Gaining.

One guard maneuvered ahead, trying to cut them off.

Thalendir's jaw clenched. They won't harm me. But they might hurt Gantar.

A second guard veered sharply to the left, trying to cut across Gantar's path.

Thalendir jerked his reins, driving Steel into the narrowing gap. The powerful mount barreled forward, slamming shoulder-first into the lead rider. The force sent the guard sprawling, knocking him into his companion. Both tumbled in a mass of limbs and armor, hitting the ground with a jarring thud.

"Prince Thalendir, stop!" another guard shouted. "Turn back! Your father will—"

Too late.

They were already past them, surging deeper into the woods.

Thalendir turned toward Gantar. "Tell me we're close."

Gantar's voice was tight. "Almost there."

The trees thinned—a clearing.

A steep rock wall rose before them, covered in thick ivy.

Thalendir reined in. "A dead end?"

Gantar didn't slow. He leaped from his horse, running toward the ivy-covered stone. "Not quite."

His fingers traced over hidden runes beneath the foliage, whispering an incantation.

The ivy shuddered.

Then, it parted, revealing the dark gateway to the tunnel.

"Inside! Now!"

Thalendir hesitated. The guards were almost upon them.

"Prince Thalendir, you do not have to do this!" one sentry pleaded. "You are not a traitor!"

Thalendir's grasp tightened.

No. He wasn't a traitor.

But he would not abandon his brother either.

His stallion snorted, fidgeting beneath him.

The guards closed in.

A decision.

Thalendir made it.

With a swift motion, he swung from the saddle and dashed into the tunnel, pulling his horse with him.

The stone door slammed shut behind them.

Thalendir stiffened, eyes narrowing.

"What is this?"

"A concealed path," Gantar said. "Older than your father's crown."

Thalendir exhaled, tilting his head. His eyes flicked over the cleared stone. Some recent footprints shone in the evening light. His gaze snapped back to Gantar.

"Someone's been through here recently. Eldrin?"

Gantar didn't confirm it, but he didn't deny it, either.

Thalendir studied him intently. Then, with a scoff, he dismounted. "And here I thought you were just a healer."

Gantar raised his grey brows. "I guess we're both full of surprises."

The dark tunnel extended ahead in calm obscurity, the clatter of hooves reverberating against the damp stone.

"Which way did he go?" Thalendir frowned.

"I know which way they were headed," Gantar replied. "When he followed this trail."

Thalendir frowned. "Where is that?"

"I sent him to the Shrouded Vale. For protection," Gantar admitted.

"The Shrouded Vale?" Thalendir barked a laugh—sharp, humorless. "You sent him chasing myths?"

Gantar offered no reply, but a smile crossed his wrinkled face.

They rode in silence for another beat before Thalendir scoffed. "You mean we're tracking my fugitive brother on a hunch? To a place that may not exist?"

Gantar smiled. "It exists."

"Then where is it?" Thalendir glared at him, then exhaled through his nostrils.

"You have no idea, do you?"

Gantar feigned insult as Thalendir gave him a look.

The sage sighed. "Fine. I know the general direction."

Thalendir's expression was dry. "Which way is the 'general direction?"

"This way…" Gantar murmured as he prodded his horse and took the lead.

Thalendir muttered something, but despite himself, he almost smiled.

Silence hung between the two for a while.

Then, abruptly, Thalendir spoke. "Tell me…"

Gantar's gaze remained focused on the path ahead. "Tell you what?"

Thalendir exhaled sharply. "Don't play the old sage routine with me." His voice was curt. "I want the truth."

Gantar gave a slow exhale as if he had expected this.

"Are you wondering if the rumors are true?"

Thalendir squeezed the reins tighter. "I need to know what my brother has done. And why?"

Gantar was quiet, carefully contemplating his words.

"Eldrin made a choice. One that went against everything he was raised to believe."

Thalendir scoffed, "So it's true? He didn't just break the law—he shattered it by harboring a drelf?"

Gantar turned his gaze; his tone was unwavering. "He saved a life and chose mercy."

Silence filled the space, heavier than the granite blocks around them.

Thalendir exhaled, his thoughts unraveling. "Why would he show mercy to a drelf? He's not reckless," he muttered, almost to himself. "Not like this. Not unless—"

His eyes flickered toward Gantar.

The sage raised a brow. "Unless?"

Thalendir's jaw worked, the pieces shifting through his brain. "Unless there was a good reason."

A slow smile tugged at Gantar's lips. "Perhaps."

Thalendir's patience snapped. "Spare me the riddles. Tell me what you know."

Gantar kept a steady gaze. "What is it you already suspect?"

Thalendir's eyes narrowed. His fingers tapped against his saddle, the sound sharp against the quiet. "The night he returned from patrol, his tunic was torn, his hands were stained blue." He paused, letting the words hang. "There's just one being in these lands that bleeds blue, Gantar."

His voice lowered, barely above a breath. "And his eyes… they were hollow. Haunted. As if he'd seen a ghost—and couldn't forget it."

Gantar just stared ahead, following the bobbing of his horse's head as they moved along the path.

Thalendir's breath left him in a slow, measured exhale. "It's true, then. He abandoned everything—our father, the kingdom, his very heritage. For a drelf?" His eyes bore into the sage's back, demanding an answer.

Gantar remained quiet. Then, he exhaled, weighing his words.

"What are you not telling me?" Thalendir's voice dropped, infused with something more than frustration—something dangerously close to fury. "Eldrin wouldn't commit treason unless he had a damn good reason."

Gantar finally said, "He is being pulled toward something."

Thalendir's eyes darkened as his frustration boiled over. "Pulled? By what? If you know something about my brother's fate, you'll tell me now."

Gantar exhaled. "It has already begun."

Thalendir's pulse hastened. "What has?"

"The prophecy. The one your mother foresaw."

Silence fell between them.

Thalendir's breath caught, his fingers tightening on the leather reins.

"...What?"

Gantar ignored his stare, but his voice held weight. "She spoke of a crack in the realms. A fracture in what once was whole. And she knew—" He hesitated. "That your brother would be the key."

The sage's gaze sharpened, looking back at Thalendir—as if seeing something even he had yet to understand.

A beat.

Another piece of the puzzle fell into place.

Then—quiet, steady, unshakable—

"It's why she entrusted you with his life."

Thalendir mulled over Gantar's words, his mind turning over the importance of his mother's request and the choices that had led Eldrin down this path—and now his role in it.

He couldn't decide which unsettled him more.

The prophecy—the one his mother had whispered about, though never fully explained.

Or the promise he'd made to her.

The tunnel walls narrowed, the air thick with damp earth and timeworn magic. The only sounds were the constant beat of hooves against stone and the faint breath of wind filtering through unseen cracks in the cavern walls.

Had she known this would happen? Thalendir wondered.

A shard of moonlight slipped through a crack overhead, casting pale silver onto the tunnel floor. As it shifted across Gantar's chest, something caught the light—not merely reflecting it, but refracting it, sending a faint shimmer of deep azure and yellow across the tunnel walls, as if the stone itself breathed with unseen energy.

Thalendir caught the movement. "That's no ordinary talisman."

The sage's fingers grazed the amulet hanging from his neck—a smooth, darkened stone worn from years of touch. He glanced down at the stone, his voice calm. "No. It was once part of a larger whole."

Thalendir's eyes narrowed. The way the light caught the pendant — the way it seemed to breathe with a life of its own—stirred something buried deep within the depths of his soul.

A slice of moonlight spilt across the smooth stone. The glimmer of power beneath delicate fingers. His mother's hands brushed over a gem that glowed with the same quiet pulse.

She had worn something like this. Held it. Cherished it.

A chill slipped down his spine.

Thalendir's jaw tensed. "Is that the Aetherstone?"

Gantar nodded slightly. "A fragment. A tether. To the original." He held the reins loosely, but Thalendir could see the moment Gantar's shoulders stiffened—the way his breath stilled as if sensing something unseen.

Then, just for a split second, the stone pulsed.

A faint, barely perceptible hum close to his heart.

"What was that?" asked Thalendir.

Gantar's gaze sharpened. His fingers brushed over the pendant as if reaching for something unseen. "Eldrin," he murmured. "He is not as alone as you think."

Thalendir pulled his horse to a stop. "Where is he?"

"Headed for trouble."

Chapter 22

The evening air carried a biting chill, threading through the cliffs of the Drelf Kingdom. The jagged peaks stretched endlessly, their shadows resembling sleeping beasts under the silver glow of the twin moons. A lone scout soared above them, his wings gliding soundlessly through the sky, tail flicking for balance as his sharp, reptilian eyes surveyed the ravine below.

Something wasn't right.

Soryx had patrolled this stretch for years—he knew the shape of every peak, the rhythm of every wind current. However, the silence tonight felt unnatural. No night birds stirred from their roosts, no breeze rustled around the cliffs. The darkness pressed too close, thick and waiting.

The drelf adjusted his altitude, his taloned claws flexing against the chill as he dipped lower, scanning the valley below.

Then—movement.

Soryx banked sharply, his gaze focusing intently. A ripple along the rocks, barely noticeable in the darkness.

There.

Something was down there. Watching.

He sent a signal cry to the others when a sharp gust of wind tore past him.

Instinct screamed.

He twisted mid-air, in time to glimpse the winged shadow descending upon him.

Too fast.

Too silent.

The last thing he saw was burning crimson eyes—then talons struck.

His screech carried across the night.

Then—nothing.

The wind swallowed the sound.

And Soryx was gone.

Kaelis Skythorn lifted her head.

She had been preparing the evening watch, briefing the younger scouts on their patrol routes when the cry resounded through the night. Since Lyria's disappearance, they had increased patrols. The sound was distant, muffled by the gale, but the moment it reached her ears, her scaled tail flicked in agitation.

The others heard it, too.

"That was Soryx," one scout whispered, shifting, his scales glinting under the torchlight. "He was on first watch."

Kaelis paused before answering. Instead, she looked skyward. Nothing. Not even an inkling of movement in the clouded sky. Her sharp instincts warned her—something was wrong.

"Take positions," she ordered her voice firm despite her inner turmoil. "I want eyes on every outpost. No one flies alone."

A few hesitant nods. Then the drelves dispersed, each taking to the air, wings unfurling as they moved to their stations.

Kaelis exhaled. The evening had grown too still.

Then, just a breath—

The wind shifted.

Her golden eyes darted toward the valley below.

A strong wind blew along the cliffs. The darkness had deepened, but the usual sounds-the distant rush of wings, the calls of sentries—lay subdued beneath an unspoken tension.

Kaelis remained still.

The scouts had taken their positions. The watchfires were burning. Still, the unease within her did not settle.

Soryx had not returned.

She clenched her jaw. He was one of their finest scouts—disciplined, sharp-eyed, and trained for survival. If something had taken him, it had done so quickly.

That was the part that disturbed her most.

Wyverns.

The thought flitted across her mind, unbidden and unwelcome. The only winged predators capable of moving unseen in the black of night.

Kaelis inhaled. The wind carried the aroma of damp earth and another acrid scent—something unnatural. Above, the stars had vanished, swallowed by a creeping veil of storm clouds that had not been there moments before. As the wind stilled, the night pressed in as if sentient.

A shiver traced down her spine. It had been decades since the nemods last unleashed wyverns against them. The drelves had fought them off before, but the cost had been devastating. Years of recovery.

If wyverns were here… the nemods would not be far behind.

A low, distant rumble vibrated through the mountains—not thunder, but something more ominous.

This was not a raid.

This was a prelude to war.

Kaelis' fingers grazed the hilts of her twin blades. If Soryx had fallen, the enemy would not stop there.

She exhaled, forcing the chill from her bones.

She needed answers, not assumptions.

Her eyes moved toward the jagged peaks above—the hidden entrance that led to Nyxari's dwelling.

She despised asking the seer for guidance. But tonight, she had no choice.

Without another word, she turned from the outpost and took to the sky, her wings tearing through the cold air as she climbed toward the higher cliffs.

The air inside Nyxari's dwelling smelled of burning herbs, the acrid smoke curling in lazy patterns toward the cavern's ceiling. A single brazier flickered in the middle of the room, casting long shadows on the stone floor.

Kaelis hesitated. Not because she feared Nyxari the Veilkeeper, but because she feared what the seer might say.

She hesitated at the threshold, her tail flicking in agitation.

"I know why you've come," Nyxari's voice resonated within the room.

Kaelis stiffened. "Then tell me."

The old seer did not turn around right away. She sat cross-legged before the brazier, her long hair, streaked with deep indigo and silver, tumbled over her shoulders in multiple braids, each woven with tiny obsidian charms that clinked with every movement, like whispered omens during the night. The firelight gleamed against the metallic strands, giving them the illusion of shifting between the hues of twilight. Her wings, veined and translucent on the rims with age, folded against her back, their once-powerful span now tempered by time. The flames' glow played over her scaled skin, making her appear carved from the mountain itself—ancient, enduring, and as tied to the prophecy as the stone she stood upon.

She looked up—eyes glazed, lost somewhere between here and the beyond.

Kaelis stepped forward. "Soryx has disappeared while on watch. We heard his cry, but there was nothing-no trace of him, no struggle. Just silence. I fear it's wyverns…and that the nemods are getting ready to attack."

Nyxari didn't move. Didn't blink.

Then she whispered, "The mark beckons the abyss."

Kaelis felt the chill of those words slip beneath her armor.

"What mark?" Kaelis demanded.

The mystic exhaled, her fingers twitching as she pressed her palms to the floor. Flames dimmed from the brazier, a low wind whispering inside the chamber, though no entrance was open to the evening air.

"The one that has chosen Lyria."

Kaelis froze.

Briefly, she forgot the cold, the smell of smoke and burning herbs.

The words struck her like a physical blow.

Her breath escaped in a sharp exhale, her wings snapping slightly at her sides.

Kaelis' heart pounded. "She's alive?" The words escaped her before she could temper them, raw and disbelieving. "You can see her?"

Nyxari's silver-threaded braids clinked softly when she glanced at the brazier. The firelight cast shifting shadows across her face, but her expression remained unreadable.

"Yes."

Kaelis's breath caught, a sharp mix of relief and anger twisting inside her. "Then where is she? And why hasn't she come back?"

Nyxari exhaled, her wings shifting slightly as if she carried a burden far older than herself. "Because she could not."

Kaelis moved forward. "What do you mean, she 'could not'? Did something happen to her? Was she taken?"

The seer lowered her gaze. "No. She left."

Kaelis staggered back a half step, wings tensing. "Then… then she really abandoned us?" The words tasted bitter on her tongue.

"No." Nyxari's voice was firm, unshaken. "She left to protect us."

Kaelis frowned, struggling to understand. "From what?"

Nyxari's voice lowered, heavy with meaning.

"From the mark she now bears."

Kaelis's tail flicked, her patience fraying. "What mark? You speak in riddles, Veilkeeper. Explain."

Nyxari traced a slow circle along the floor, her clawed fingertips grazing the stone. The brazier's glow flickered, deepening the shadows in the chamber.

"A prophecy older than the mountains we stand upon."

Kaelis folded her arms, her frustration mounting. "I don't care for myths, Nyxari. I care about my people. And I care about Lyria." She stepped forward, golden eyes burning. "You're telling me she left because of some ancient curse? That she abandoned everything because of a mark?"

Nyxari lifted her gaze, her expression clouded and unreadable. "Not a curse. A calling."

Kaelis scoffed. "You expect me to believe that?"

The seer sighed, shifting her weight. "Would you rather believe she left because she did not care for us?"

Kaelis parted her lips, but the words would not come.

She had fought for moons against the whispers—the doubt creeping into their people's hearts. She had stood against the accusations that Lyria had turned her back on them. And yet, standing here now, she realized she had never allowed herself to ask why.

Nyxari's voice softened, though it felt heavy as stone.

"She bears a tattoo. A mark not of her choosing. It is both a beacon and a brand. And it has awakened the dark forces that have long slumbered."

Kaelis's tail flicked. "You knew?"

A pause.

"I suspected."

Kaelis's breath sharpened. "And you said nothing? You let us think she was dead? Or worse—that she betrayed us?"

Nyxari's face remained impassive, but her wings folded tighter against her back. "Would you have believed me?"

The words hit harder than Kaelis expected.

Would she?

She had dismissed the old stories for years, calling them relics of another time and foolish superstitions. And yet, standing in this chamber with the fire casting eerie shapes against the walls, she wasn't so sure anymore.

The wind in the cavern shifted—colder now, tainted with something unseen.

Kaelis clenched her fists.

"Then tell me, seer," she said, voice steady despite the unease crawling beneath her skin. "What does this mark mean? Why Lyria?"

Nyxari stared deep into the flames. The embers reflected in her silver-threaded braids, glowing like trapped starlight.

"Forces beyond our understanding chose her," the seer murmured.

Kaelis's jaw tightened. "That's not a satisfactory answer."

Nyxari hesitated.

"No," she admitted, voice just a murmur. "It is not."

And then, the firelight dimmed.

The room lurched, the surrounding air thickening as if the cavern itself was listening.

Nyxari inhaled—as if drowning. Then her eyes snapped open.

And when she spoke, her voice was not her own.

"The tattoo burns like a brand against armored skin. A flickering glow in the night. But it is not alone. The abyss seethes, reaching, coiling, waiting. Nemods move like ink upon water, spilling through the cracks of the realms. But behind them, larger shadows stir—beasts of fangs and fury."

"A great maw opens—a dragon's roar shatters the stars. And then—A whisper, curling through the vision like a serpent."

Nyxari's body tensed, her breath rattling like dry leaves tossed by a gale.

Kaelis inched forward, her heart hammering.

The seer's lips moved, but the name did not come at first. As if something unseen resisted it. As if it did not wish to be spoken aloud.

Then—a single exhale. A single whisper.

"...Vartharax."

The flames in the fire guttered.

A chill slithered inside the room.

Nyxari gasped.

Kaelis froze.

She knew that name. Every drelf did.

A name carved into nightmares. The black dragon lord. The abyss itself given form.

She made fists with her talons. "You're telling me the mark-the thing Lyria bears—has drawn him to us?"

Nyxari's shoulders shook as she exhaled. "It has begun."

Nyxari gasped.

Kaelis lunged forward, but the seer lifted a trembling hand. "No. I am unharmed."

Kaelis exhaled, watching as Nyxari gathered herself. The faraway look in her gaze remained, but there was urgency now.

"The nemods are coming," Nyxari murmured. "But they are not the worst that follows."

Kaelis' wings tensed. "What about Lyria and the mark?"

Nyxari pushed herself upright, gripping her staff as if to steady the storm within. "Lyria is coming back. She means to help us fight—but the dark one moves through us to reach her. He's drawing her in. She is in danger."

Kaelis's breath caught. The seer's words landed like stone, anchoring a truth she hadn't wanted to face. This wasn't just a siege. Not just another war.

This was a trap.

Her speech was quieter, tinged with bitter clarity. "We're not the target."

She stood before the shadowed horizon, her eyes sharp with realization.

"We're the bait."

Chapter 23

The wind shifted as Lyria faltered mid-step, her wings twitching as a sudden wave of heat pulsed across her skin. The mark hummed, weak, but insistent, as though something distant was reaching for her—pulling her.

Eldrin slowed beside her. "You feel it too."

It wasn't a question.

His hand went to his side, where the Aetherstone beat in warning. The energy thrumming against his fingertips, warming to his touch, like an unspoken command.

Go faster. You are running out of time.

Finnian, who had been riding ahead, looked back. "Alright, that's the second time you two have stopped. Do I get to know what's going on?"

Lyria didn't answer because she heard it.

A whisper—not in her head, but in her very being.

Not words, not exactly. But a voice. A presence. One that was familiar to her.

"The abyss stirs as the mark burns. And your kingdom will fall if you don't get there soon."

She gasped. It was the white dragon.

She looked at the mountains ahead and froze.

A tempest was brewing over them. But it was more than a storm.

It was alive.

Dark clouds churned, creeping along the cliffs like ink spilt over the heavens. Flashes of sickly green lightning flickered deep within, illuminating the shifting shadows. The air had thickened, heavy with an eerie stillness.

Darkness threatened her people.

Eldrin's hold on the Aetherstone grew firmer. "We're too far. We won't reach them in time."

Finnian cursed under his breath. "Then we pick up the pace."

But Lyria wasn't moving.

Her gaze had shifted—not to the storm, but to the craggy, winding cliffs that reached for the northern pass. She knew Eldrin was right. They wouldn't make it in time. Unless... they took the shortcut.

A place she had sworn never to go.

Finnian followed Lyria's stare, his expression darkening as realization set in. "It would be faster."

Eldrin frowned. "What would be faster?"

Finnian exhaled. "There is a shortcut."

Eldrin's gaze flicked between them. "There's another way?"

Lyria's jaw stiffened. "Yes. But we're not taking it."

Finnian scoffed. "The Dragon Graves," he said. "Ancient burial grounds for fallen dragons. Cursed. Haunted. Whatever word you choose, it's considered sacred and dangerous. To those who believe in such things."

Eldrin, undeterred, turned to Lyria. "But it is faster?"

Lyria's wings bristled. "It's not an option."

Eldrin's patience thinned. "Lyria, your people are under attack."

Her eyes flared. "And you think I don't know that?"

The wind roared around them. She knew the danger her kingdom was in. But she also knew what lay among the dragon's remains.

"I will not disturb the dead," she hissed.

Eldrin exhaled. "Even if it saves the living?"

Lyria's claws curled into tight balls. "You don't understand."

Finnian crossed his arms. "Then explain it to us."

She hesitated.

The storm rumbled, casting an eerie glow upon the landscape.

Finally, she spoke. "You may see a shortcut." She took a deep breath. "But the dead do not sleep in those graves, Eldrin. They watch. They remember. And if we step into their domain uninvited, they may not let us leave."

Eldrin's gaze remained steady. "But if we don't, we might not reach your kingdom until it's too late."

Lyria took a deep gulp.

Finnian cut in, his tone softer than it had been before. "Lyria, you see, they've already unleashed the storm. You know the nemods don't travel alone. The wyverns, or something worse, are probably already there." His eyes followed the darkening sky. "If we wait and take the long way, they will leave no kingdom to save."

A deep ache coiled in Lyria's chest.

She knew better than to trespass into the Dragon Graveyard.

But she had also sworn to protect her people.

Her talons curled against her palms.

They had one choice. And if she made the wrong one...

Lyria took one final, shuddering breath—then headed for the forsaken ground.

The gale howled behind them, a rolling tide of darkness spilling over the cliffs. With determination, she squared her shoulders, dug in her clawed toes, and locked her eyes on what lay before her.

They were going through the dragon burial grounds.

She sensed Eldrin's gaze on her, measuring, questioning, yet she didn't hesitate. They didn't have time for hesitation.

She exhaled, turning to them.

"Cut the bandages."

The words hung between them.

Eldrin frowned. "What?"

"My wing," Lyria said, her voice tranquil despite the churning in her gut. "Cut it free."

Finnian's brows shot up. "You can't be serious."

She flicked her tail in irritation. "We're running out of time. I can fly ahead. I can warn them and help fight the wyverns."

Eldrin moved nearer, his expression unreadable. "No."

Lyria clenched her taloned fingers. "Eldrin—"

"No." The harshness of his tone stopped her in her tracks. Gantar said your wing might be permanently damaged. That if you push it too soon, it could break completely."

Lyria dug in her claws. "I don't care."

Eldrin's eyes flashed. "Well, I do."

Silence.

"Besides, we need you to lead us through the graveyard," Eldrin added.

A gale whipped about them, the storm closing in.

Finnian let out a breath. "Lyria… you haven't used your wing since the injury." His voice held no anger—only concern. "What if it fails? What if you can't stay aloft?"

Lyria turned to him, wings bristling. "What if my people fall?"

Finnian hesitated.

Eldrin's eyes pierced through Lyria. "And what if you never fly again?"

Lyria's heart clenched, but she didn't back down. "Then at least I'll have tried."

The Aetherstone throbbed in Eldrin's pocket, heat searing against his fingertips. His instincts shouted — don't let her do this.

But Lyria was already grabbing her knife.

Eldrin caught her wrist. Their gazes locked, but neither of them spoke.

Finally, Eldrin said, "Please don't do this."

Lyria gulped. Her damaged wing ached, as if sensing the gravity of the decision.

Her breath was unsteady now, doubt creeping into her resolve.

Could she fly? Could she even stay airborne?

She had to. But not yet.

Not in this way.

Lyria pulled her wrist free. "Fine," she muttered.

Eldrin exhaled, some of the tension leaving his shoulders.

Finnian chuckled, giving a brief bob of his head, he said under his breath, "That's a first. Lyria actually listening to reason."

She shot him a glare, but the corner of his lips twitched, easing the weight between them, just for a moment.

Then the storm rumbled again, lightning flaring on the horizon.

They were headed to the graveyard. For now, she would walk.

The night was restless.

A gale coursed through the grove of trees. Somewhere far off, an owl called once, then fell silent—too silent. The woods had been uneasy for miles now, and though Thalendir hadn't spoken of it.

Something was wrong.

He pulled his cloak tighter around his shoulders, while Gantar rode beside him, his usual calm unshaken. But Thalendir wasn't fooled. The old sage noticed it, too. The land itself appeared unsettled.

Thalendir exhaled, gaze flicking toward the darkened road ahead. They had been riding for hours, weaving through old Elven patrol routes to avoid detection. Even now, he was unsure whether his father had sent riders after them or if the Council was debating their next move.

But they would come.

His fingers contracted. He was the king's son, heir to the throne. A prince. Yet here he was, fleeing like a traitor in the dead of night.

For Eldrin. For the brother he had spent years resenting.

A spark of annoyance stirred within him, but the gravity of what he had learned muted it. His mother, the Aetherstone, the prophecy—truths buried for years. And now, with every mile they traveled, he had to confront the reality that he was a traitor, alongside his little brother.

"Deep thoughts for a rider at midnight."

Thalendir spared Gantar a glance. "I have plenty to think about."

The sage hummed in agreement, his fingers touching the pendant at his chest. The fragment of Aetherstone.

Thalendir's eyes glanced at it. The stone had glowed beneath the moonlight earlier, for a moment.

The thought sent an unexpected pang through him.

"Tell me something," Thalendir said, voice tight. "The stone around your neck—" he nodded toward the pendant "—does it call to my brother?"

Gantar didn't respond immediately. The firelight from his torch flickered against his weathered features, casting deep shadows in the hollows of his face.

"In a way," he murmured. "It does not speak, but it listens."

Thalendir scoffed. "That makes no sense."

Gantar offered him a knowing smile. "Then you are beginning to understand."

Before Thalendir could snap a retort, the air currents altered.

A sharp gust tore through the woods, cold and sudden, as if nature itself had drawn a breath. The horses tensed, their ears flicking back.

Gantar sat straighter.

Thalendir stilled.

And then—

The Aetherstone pulsed.

It was faint, barely perceptible, but Thalendir saw it. A touch of blue and gold shimmered against the old pendant.

Gantar's fingers fidgeted against the pendant. His expression darkened.

Thalendir's pulse raced. "What is it?"

Gantar exhaled. "Your brother moves toward the storm."

Thalendir frowned. "What storm?"

Then he turned.

And saw it.

A great darkness was spreading across the land.

Beyond the rolling hills, past the dense woodlands and distant peaks, dark clouds were forming. It churned, thick and unnatural, swallowing the stars as it crept toward the north. Lightning flashed within its depths, but not with the golden glow of natural light.

Sickly green.

Wrong.

This was not merely a storm. "The Drelf Kingdom," Thalendir said hoarsely, his stomach churning. "That's where it's heading."

Gantar nodded, his jaw set. "Yes."

Thalendir's mind spun. The storm was anomalous, as it wasn't a storm at all.

His instincts stirred, warning him of something he could not yet name. "What is within the tempest?"

Gantar held the pendant between his fingers, his lips compressing into a thin line. As he spoke, his tone was low and steady.

"A war."

Thalendir's stomach twisted. "You're certain?"

Gantar turned to face him. "I know it, just as I know your brother is already heading toward it."

Thalendir moved his head from side to side, attempting to grasp the full weight of what Gantar was saying. "No—Eldrin was in the Vale. That's where you said he was. Why would he go to the drelves?"

Gantar's demeanor remained steady. "Because the path of the marked drelf leads them there. He does not yet understand his role—but the mark pulls her toward the core of the storm."

Thalendir's brow furrowed. His jaw dropped. *Her?*

The word lodged in his head like a jagged stone.

His gaze snapped to Gantar, sharp with suspicion. "***Her?***" His voice was softer now, but edged with tension. "The marked drelf is a, *she*?"

The word struck a deep chord in his mind.

A whisper of a voice—his mother's voice.

He had been young, barely more than an elfling, when he'd crept into her chambers late one night. He had often done so when his father was away, when the halls of the palace felt too vast, too cold. His mother had never scolded him for sneaking in. She would pull him close, brushing her fingers through his hair as she hummed soft lullabies of the old world.

But that night… she had not been singing.

She had been whispering.

Standing alone by the window, her fingers feeling the pendant that hung around her neck—the same one Gantar now wore. He had almost turned back when he'd heard the strain in her voice, the sorrow woven between the words.

"When she comes, the balance will shift."

He hadn't understood what she meant. Not then.

But now—

Thalendir's pulse hastened.

His gaze shifted towards Gantar, who was watching him, as if measuring how much he knew. Then the old sage slowly nodded.

Thalendir swallowed hard, his mind spinning. "Tell me her name."

A pause.

Gantar exhaled.

"Lyria."

The name settled in Thalendir's mind like a stone dropped into deep water. The ripples reached the surface, stirring something distant, something half-formed.

Familiar, but not enough.

Not until—

His tone was subdued but unwavering. "Lyria, what? What is her full name?"

Gantar held his stare for a moment longer. Then, with a weight that pressed upon the space between them, he spoke.

"Ironwing. Lyria Ironwing."

The name struck like a shard, cold and sharp.

Chapter 24

The gale roared behind them, its blackened clouds swallowing the stars and flashing with an unnatural green lightning. But Lyria barely noticed.

The graveyard lay ahead.

A sprawling expanse of jagged cliffs and silent sentinels of bone—great, towering skeletons of dragons long gone. Their bleached remains jutted from the earth like ivory monoliths, half-buried in time and shadow. The air within the boundary was heavy, charged and humming with something unseen. It was not the absence of sound that unsettled her, but the presence of something else.

Something watched. Waited.

Lyria's wings twitched, the injured one straining against the bandages she'd sworn not to cut free. Instinct screamed at her to turn back. Her kind did not tread here. No, drelf did.

She inhaled deeply, forcing herself to take a step forward. Duskrunner reared slightly, eyes widened, as if aware of the vestiges of ancient death buried in the earth.

"Shhh," Lyria whispered, placing a calming hand against his trembling neck. Her fingers brushed through his mane, slow and steady. "It's just stone and silence now. Nothing here but shadows."

The horse shifted beneath her touch, uncertain but obedient, his ears still flicking at every phantom sound.

Behind her, Eldrin and Finnian followed close, their boots crunching over brittle bones and ash-dusted stone. They led their horses, but the animals resisted every step they took. Silverwind's ears were pinned flat, her nostrils flaring as she snorted and sidestepped. Embermane pawed at the ground with anxious hooves, his muscles trembling with barely leashed panic. Finnian tugged at the gelding's reins. "Easy," he muttered, although his voice lacked conviction, "We're not staying long."

The wind moved strangely here, low, curling, and cold as if the graveyard itself breathed.

Eldrin's hand brushed against his dagger while his other hand gripped Silverwind's bridle tightly. "They don't want us to be here," he breathed.

"Neither do I," Lyria whispered.

"Doesn't feel like a graveyard," Finnian muttered, glancing at the bones that rose around them. "Feels like something else."

Lyria's throat tightened. "That's because it is."

The Dragon graves were not merely a burial site; they were a sanctuary, a sacred place where relics of dragons were still believed to hold power. Even in death, the dragons moved.

And now, as she crossed their domain, she felt it.

A pulse.

A breath.

Something stirred.

Lyria stopped, as if the atmosphere itself recognized her presence.

Then, Eldrin held his breath when the stone flared to life again. A soft glow seeped from his fingertips in shades of blue and gold. The moment he pulled the stone free, its warmth diffused in the air, illuminating the ancient remains around them.

The bones shifted.

Not because of the wind. Not by any force she could see.

But by something older. Something awakening.

A deep tremor ran over the graveyard.

Lyria stiffened. Eldrin and Finnian stopped beside her, instinct pulling their hands to their weapons.

The ground beneath them… shifted.

Not the tremble of thunder. Not the crash of the storm.

It was deeper. Older. A pulse that rose through stone and bone.

A low rumble rippled through the graveyard — not above, but below.

The Earth quivered.

Bones creaked.

Dust whispered into the air as something stirred—vast and coiled—within the ribcage of a long-dead leviathan.

Eldrin gripped the Aetherstone. His voice was quiet, but strained. "Tell me that's the wind."

It wasn't.

The presence pressed against them—immense, ancient, unknowable. The force that didn't seek permission to exist.

Then—eyes.

Two of them.

Luminous. Ageless. White as moon fire, blazing from the shadows of the fallen skeleton.

Lyria's breath caught.

She knew those eyes.

Eldrin stumbled back a step, dragging his sword free with a hiss. "What in the—?"

Finnian's hand trembled as he drew both blades, his breath shallow. "That's not bones shifting."

The light in the graveyard changed. The shadows leaned toward the presence, like even the darkness bowed to its will.

And from deep within the wreckage of dragons' past, something alive rose.

Then, the voice came…

Not spoken aloud, but within her; threaded into her bones, her blood, her very soul.

"You tread where none have walked in a dragon's age."

Beyond the cliffs, beyond the edge of the graveyard, something else had arrived…

They moved like liquid darkness, hunger gnawing at them. But they did not enter the graveyard.

The black shadows paced and snarled. Their sleek, muscular forms prowled at the border—stalking, circling, but never crossing their boundary.

They could not.

The white dragon's magic still lingered here.

But it was fading.

And if they waited—if the balance tipped—the panthers would no longer be bound.

Lyria exhaled slowly, her gaze locked with the luminous eyes before her.

A low hum pulsed through the ground.

Eldrin and Finnian stood tense at her sides, swords drawn, every muscle tight with the instinct to fight.

But Lyria didn't move toward the threat.

Instead, she lifted one hand—a subtle, steady gesture—and shook her head.

"Put them down," she murmured. "She's not here to harm us."

Eldrin hesitated. "How can you be sure?"

"Because I know her."

She stepped forward, voice softer now. "From my dreams."

Then she whispered the name.

A name she had never been taught, never heard—but had always known.

"Seralyth."

The dragon's eyes narrowed — not in suspicion, but recognition. Ancient intelligence shimmered behind the glow.

"You remember."

Lyria's voice caught. "I don't—I mean, I don't know how I know your name."

Seralyth tilted her massive head. The weight of eons seemed to settle in the air between them. Then the dragon spoke, its voice barely more than a breath over stone. "Not all knowledge is given. Some is merely… known."

A hush fell across the graveyard.

Bones groaned beneath the earth.

The air trembled, thick with power.

"This place…" Eldrin said quietly, his blade lowering. "It's still alive."

Seralyth turned her gaze to him, observing him with an intensity that made Lyria's breath hitch. "No. It is dying."

A shiver ran through Lyria. "The power here—it's fading."

The dragon inclined her head. "And when it is gone, they will destroy everything."

A low, rumbling growl from beyond the graveyard seeped in like fog, their red eyes flickering in the dark. The elusive creatures lingered beyond the threshold, waiting.

Finnian exhaled. "That's fantastic. Really comforting."

Seralyth ignored him, her focus locked on Lyria. "This storm didn't come to destroy the drelves."

Lyria's wings tensed. "Then why is it here?"

A pause. Then: "To destroy you."

The force of those words hit like a stone.

Lyria's talons curled at her sides. "They… they are attacking my people to get to me?"

Seralyth did not blink. "The mark is a beacon. It calls to both light… and darkness."

Guilt and fury burned in Lyria's chest. The drelves were suffering because of her.

Eldrin approached, his voice controlled but edged. "If this place is failing, what's stopping the panthers? Why haven't they attacked yet?"

Seralyth's silver pupils narrowed. "Because I still stand guard."

Silence.

Eldrin's digits fidgeted against the Aetherstone.

Finnian held his breath.

Lyria made herself speak. "Seralyth… what should I do?"

The dragon scrutinized her intently. "You must choose."

The great white dragon's gaze bore into Lyria's soul, her luminous eyes unreadable yet ancient, as if they had witnessed the beginning and end of countless ages.

"You stand at the threshold." Seralyth's voice was not loud, yet it filled the vast graveyard as if it was alive. "The winds shift, the balance trembles…and you must decide."

Lyria inhaled, her fingers grasping her sword. "Decide what?"

Seralyth blinked. Her gaze shifted toward the swirling dark expanse above the graveyard.

Thunder rumbled.

A shudder ran through Lyria. A feeling deep within her chest ached, like an unseen thread of fate pulling taut.

"What must I choose?" she whispered.

The mist around Seralyth thickened, coiling like silver tendrils of moonlight, swallowing her towering form inch by inch. Lyria edged forward, her throat tightening.

"You will know—"

The storm let out a loud cry. The moment shattered as the mist collapsed inward, a final swirl of silver light curling around Seralyth's fading form. And then—

She disappeared.

The graveyard felt emptier, colder, and darker. The shadow of her presence had vanished, as if she had never been there. But her words remained.

You must choose.

Lyria felt the air change around them. She felt it in her soul the moment Seralyth vanished. The graveyard had been still before—sacred and silent. But now…

Now it was empty. The wave of ancient power that had wrapped around them, that had held the darkness at bay, was gone. And with it, the last veil of protection had been stripped away.

A puff of wind slithered through the dragon bones.

Finnian exhaled. "I really don't like this."

"We need to move. Now." Eldrin said.

Lyria turned—

And froze.

Beyond the graveyard's edge, where the mist had thickened, shadows moved.

First one. Then another.

And another.

Lyria's blood raced in her chest. The mist wasn't mist anymore. It was shifting, darkening—alive.

Then, eyes with slitted pupils.

Hundreds of them.

Glowing, watching from the swirling fog.

A deep, guttural growl that sent ice lancing down Lyria's spine emerged from the fog.

The dark panthers had arrived.

They prowled, their sleek, muscular bodies blending into the gloom. Their movements were unnatural, fluid as oil, their claws leaving no imprint upon the earth.

They had been watching. Waiting for the guardian to leave.

A dark streak shot out of the mist.

Lyria barely had time to dodge before talons ripped through where she'd stood. She twisted, drawing her blade, the silver steel gleaming against the storm's faint light.

Eldrin was already in motion, his weapon drawn as he intercepted the next attack, steel meeting claw with a shriek of sparks.

Finnian yelled. "Not you guys, again!"

Another shape sprang from the night, and Finnian ducked just in time. He rolled, coming up with a sword in each hand, his typically relaxed demeanor vanished.

Lyria turned as the panthers started regrouping. Circling.

Testing their prey.

The alpha of the pack appeared — monstrous, an obsidian beast with jagged spines along its shoulders and crimson eyes that locked onto Lyria.

It growled.

The others growled in return and attacked as one.

Lyria reacted before the first shadow lunged, its monstrous form a bolt of black ripping through the air. She twisted, her blade meeting the panther's claws in mid-air, the force rattling up her arm. The creature snarled and recoiled, its eyes an unnatural fire.

To her right, Eldrin's dagger flared. The silver runes along the hilt ignited, reacting to something unseen—the same force that pulsed against her mark. He struck, steel meeting shadow, his dagger carving through the beasts as they closed in.

Finnian was already mid-air, both blades slashing as he weaved between the snarling creatures, ducking, rolling, fighting to keep them from enveloping them.

The pack leader stalked toward Lyria, singling her out. Its lip curled back, revealing serrated fangs slick with black ichor.

It lunged.

Lyria pivoted, her blade cutting in a clean arc—but the creature was faster. It feinted left, then struck low, its massive form barreling into her. Pain exploded through her ribs as the impact sent her skidding across the dust-covered bones. The beast was upon her in one leap, looming over her, shadows curling from its body like smoke, moving in for the kill.

Then—the dagger.

Eldrin appeared in a flash. His blade slashed across the panther's side, sending it recoiling with an unnatural screech. He stepped between her and the beast, dagger raised, eyes full of determination.

Lyria's mark flared — a sudden burst of silver light. The dagger in Eldrin's hand blazed blue in answer.

For one suspended heartbeat, their powers collided in a radiant pulse—light meeting light, threads of energy spiraling through the air in a vortex of silver and flame.

The lead panther shrieked, recoiling as the force struck it full in the chest. It staggered, claws raking furrows into the bone-littered ground, jaws split in a soundless roar.

And then, its head snapped toward Eldrin.

Not in retreat.

In vengeance.

Eyes like dying embers locked onto him, low and burning with ancient hatred. Its lips peeled back, revealing long, dripping fangs.

With deliberate, stalking steps, it advanced.

One step.

Then another.

Eldrin took a step back, boots sliding on shattered bone, the dagger trembling in his hand.

Lyria's breath caught — sharp, unsteady.

Not in fear.

Not in relief.

In horror.

He was unaware that the edge was so close— until his heel suddenly slipped into emptiness.

The world tilted.

The ground vanished beneath him.

"Eldrin!" Lyria's voice ripped through the storm.

Too late.

He slipped, boots scrabbling against wet stone—grasping, slipping—

Then—impact.

His chest slammed the cliff's rim.

Fingers clawed for purchase, scrambling over moss-slick rock.

For one breathless second, he hung there—
Half over the void, his arms trembling, his body swinging against the jagged wall.

Lyria's heart stopped. His fingers scraped the cliff's brink. For one breathless second, he caught himself—his arms straining, body swinging against the jagged rock.

Lyria moved. Her legs burned as she sprinted, her padded feet barely touching the brittle earth. The cliff and Eldrin were too far, as though she was slogging through mud.

He gripped the edge, his fingers straining, and muscles trembling from the effort. But the pack leader wasn't done. The beast loomed above Eldrin, a shadow given form, its spined shoulders rising, claws scraping the ground, death on its breath. Eldrin tried to haul himself up, but the panther had already opened its jaws…

Lyria screamed.

She didn't think. She acted as the tattoo flared. The dagger in Eldrin's grip pulsed in answer. Their power met in a searing collision—beams of light erupting between them, laced with something older, deeper.

Lyria's blade whistled through the atmosphere, the power exploding through her in a final, desperate strike.

The cat howled as the explosion tore through its body, light engulfing it in a violent surge. Shadow met steel, met magic, met fate. An unnatural, ear-splitting wail echoed off the cliff walls and rattled the graveyard. Then—nothing.

The body disintegrated. Gone.

But the impact of the kill shook the earth below.

And Eldrin slipped further.

Lyria lunged.

Their hands met—her talons locking around his wrist just as his hand slipped from its hold. Rocks tumbled past him, vanishing into the abyss.

She had him. But just barely.

His weight yanked her forward with brutal force. Her knees slammed into the stone, breath tearing from her lungs.

Don't let go.

She gritted her teeth and pulled, muscles straining, her heart pounding like war drums. Rain slicked her grip, her claws digging into his skin for a hold.

Her feet skidded. One heel slipped, and for a heartbeat, they both hovered on the brink.

No.

With a grunt, she drove her legs back under her, her good wing flaring wide against the wind, her tail whipping behind her in a frantic search for balance, desperate to anchor herself to something, anything.

Above them, the storm screamed.

Below, the chasm waited.

Eldrin's breath came in harsh, uneven gasps. "Lyria—"

She tightened her grip. "Don't you dare."

He tried to pull himself up. She struggled to hold on, tried to pull him up.

But he was slipping.

Her arms trembled. The strain burned in her muscles and her bones. Her talons scraped the stone, scratching for a hold.

Her injured wing throbbed.

She couldn't pull him up.

His fingers were sliding as their eyes met.

And in one terrible, heartbreaking moment—

He fell.

Lyria grasped at thin air, screaming his name. The wind roared, swallowing her voice as Eldrin plummeted, his body disappearing into the abyss below.

No. No, no, NO!

Her mark blazed—a searing heat against her skin. Her heart pounded in her chest as she reached behind, fingers slick with sweat and trembling with fury.

She slashed frantically. Steel met fabric. Met armor. Met flesh.

A sharp pain tore through her back as her blade sliced through everything it touched, until it found the thick bandages and severed the layers that had caged her, that had kept her grounded.

Her wing jerked, spasming and fighting against the bonds—not fully healed, not entirely whole.

But she didn't care.

Eldrin was falling. And she would not let him fall alone.

With a final, desperate slash, the remaining bindings gave way—

And Lyria jumped.

Chapter 25

The wind whistled past the graveyard as the last panthers fled, sensing the power surging between elf and drelf.

Finnian was near the edge of the cliff, breath ragged, heart pounding. Dust and shattered rock still crumbled from where Eldrin had slipped, where Lyria had jumped.

The storm raged above, a relentless, churning mass of black and green flashing with eerie veins of lightning. The battle had ended in a flash, the world tilting sideways before Finnian could stop it. One second, he had been cutting down the remaining panthers, driving them back, keeping them at bay—the next, his best friend had vanished over the edge.

His chest burned. His hands shook.

He staggered forward, skidding on his knees at the ledge. His fingers dug into the fractured earth, his pulse racing as he stared into the void, straining against the tempest, against the darkness, against the cruel silence that answered him.

His voice tore from his throat, raw and desperate.

"ELDRIN!"

Nothing.

Only the wind, howling like a tormented beast, swept past him with cruel indifference.

Finnian staggered forward, pebbles scattering beneath his boots as he reached the edge. The void gaped below. No sign of movement. No echo of a cry.

"LYRIA!" he bellowed, his voice breaking, shattering in disbelief.

Silence answered him.

Not even the whisper of wings.

He stood trembling, swords clenched uselessly in his hands. Then he swore and shoved them into their sheaths with unsteady fingers.

Eldrin… his mind screamed. Lyria…

But the words never escaped his lips; his chest heaved, and his legs buckled. He knelt, fingers pale against the stone at the edge of the cliff.

It couldn't be real.

It couldn't have happened that fast.

One moment, they were there.
Fighting. Running. Alive.

The next—gone.

Swallowed by shadow and wind.

It was her fault…

The drelf.

If she hadn't come along—if she hadn't dragged them into this—none of this would've happened.

A violent tremor shot through his hands. His heart hammered against his eardrums.

He turned, fury rising through the grief that burned like acid in his throat.

"LYRIA!" he bellowed into the emptiness again, his voice ragged, hoarse with rage. With loss.

Still nothing.

Finnian's jaw locked. His throat clenched.

She was supposed to be their guide among the graves. Instead, she had led Eldrin to his death.

He slammed his fist into the ground, pain jolting up his arm. No.

No, he refused to believe this was how it ended.

Eldrin couldn't be dead, not like this.
Not because of her.

Not because of a prophecy he never even asked for.

His hands curled into fists, nails biting into skin as his chest rose and fell in ragged heaves.

"Eldrin!" he roared once more, the name torn from his soul.

The wind screamed back, cold and merciless. A mockery.

Finnian dropped to the ground, his fists pounding against his chest.

He wanted to break something, tear something and undo it all.

They were gone.

His body shook.

His mind rebelled.

But the abyss before him gave nothing.
Only silence.
Only shadow.

No voice called back.

No hand emerged from the shadows.

Nothing.

Finnian squeezed his eyes shut as tears streamed down his cheeks.

Gone.

The tempest swirled, unsettled.

An icy wind tore through the darkened peaks where Drakor stood, his dull armor almost gleaming beneath the flickering storm. His eyes narrowed, his taloned feet curling as the surrounding air shifted—subtle but undeniable.

A split in the abyss.

He had felt it the moment it happened. A shift—not just in the weather, but in power. The balance he had worked to keep in darkness had wavered.

Drakor exhaled, his breath coiling in the frigid air. The nemods below him stirred, a rippling wave of unease slithering through their ranks. They felt it, too. The tether that bound them to the abyss had trembled.

That should have been impossible unless...

A deep rumble built within his chest.

The mark.

Something had happened.

Drakor gazed at the dragon's burial ground. That was where the abyss was opening. That was where it had taken place.

His talons flexed. Something had changed.

The storm flickered, the green lightning flashing erratically as if uncertain and fighting against something unseen. Dark clouds moving above did not churn with the same unnatural weight. The abyss was pulling, yet something pushed back against it.

It was faint. A fracture, a splintering in the threads of fate.

But it was there.

Drakor's lips curled back in a snarl.

"She is near. And I will find her."

Finnian hadn't moved. He was still on his knees, looking into the depths; his breathing was labored and shallow. The wind howled across the cliffs like a mourning wail.

The grief of loss bore down on him, sinking into his bones, heavy as stone.

Gone.

The word echoed in his thoughts, relentless and cruel like the storm.

His breath hitched.

He lifted his head, blinking against the harsh wind as the darkened sky shuddered. The lightning, once thick with eerie green veins, staggered—its glow pulsing erratically, faltering.

Finnian's pointed ears twitched. There was a different feeling in the air as if it were… shifting.

The pressure in his heart, the crushing burden of the storm—it was still there, but—something fought against it.

His fingers grabbed at the dust, pulse hammering.

Was he imagining it?

No.

The wind changed direction.

The storm veered clear of the drelf kingdom.

Finnian's breath came quicker now, his eyes watching the roiling clouds. The unnatural flashes of green that blinked, pulsed, then flickered back to silver, just for an instant. But he saw it.

His instincts screamed — ***move.*** The tempest was headed his way.

Chapter 26

Thalendir's breath came sharply, and his pulse pounded in his head. The name Ironwing still hung heavy, like a sword had been driven into his chest.

That was it; the name his mother had spoken that night so long ago. She had whispered it to the stars, her fingers tracing the very pendant that now hung around Gantar's neck.

Now he knew who she meant.

Lyria Ironwing.

The drelf. The one that carried the prophecy. The one who would alter the harmony of the realms.

Steel pranced beneath him, hooves striking the ground with restless energy. The stallion tossed his head, nostrils flaring as he caught the edge of his rider's unease. Every muscle in his sleek frame rippled with alertness as if preparing for a threat yet unseen.

Thalendir forced a breath into his lungs, dismissing the memory. "You knew," he said. "You knew who she was all this time."

Gantar did not respond. The sage's face was unreadable in the torchlight, but his eyes said everything.

Thalendir exhaled, a bitter laugh escaping him. "And yet, you let my brother leave with her? Commit treason for her? Risk his life for—"

Gantar's gaze did not waver. "For a prophecy beyond our comprehension."

The words struck like a thunderclap.

Thalendir yanked his horse's reins to a stop. "She is a drelf, Gantar. Do you even hear yourself?" He scoffed with a toss of his head. "A cursed half-breed marked by a prophecy that should have died with the rest of her kind."

Gantar tilted his head. "And yet here you are, riding into the same storm your brother is facing. Riding toward her."

Thalendir bristled. "I am riding for Eldrin."

Gantar's eyes gleamed. "Are you?"

The prince's jaw clenched. "Do not play word games with me, old elf."

Gantar exhaled, his fingers resting on the pendant against his chest. "The storm is not just a storm, Thalendir. You see what it is. You feel the darkness. We must stop it."

Thalendir did not want to acknowledge it. The unnatural lightning, the oppressive weight in the atmosphere—the storm was *alive*. And now…

And now, the eye of the tempest had turned.

Instead, it barreled toward something else.

Thalendir's stomach coiled.

Was it heading toward… Eldrin?

And if the storm was inexplicable, if it was tied to the shadows, to the shift in darkness, then—

He exhaled, jaw locking.

"Eldrin is in grave danger, isn't he?" He said voice strained. "This is a war against the shadowy forces."

Gantar nodded. "Let us hope we are not too late."

Thalendir's hands flexed. He had been trained to lead his people, to fight for his father's kingdom, and to protect Elven's blood.

But now, he faced another choice.

A choice that would lead him not to his father's war but to his brother's. To aid the very creatures he'd spent a lifetime hating.

Thalendir flexed his gloved hands. He had spent his life defending the honor of his people, believing the strength of the elves alone would be enough to withstand anything.

But this was no longer about honor, no longer about what he had been taught to believe.

This was survival.

Not just for him. Not just for Eldrin.

For his people. For his kingdom.

Gantar spoke quietly. "If we do not stop the darkness now, it will not end with the drelves. They will come for us next. For our lands. For our people. For your father's throne."

Thalendir realized in that moment the price of being heir to a king.

It was more than duty. More than the title.

It was a sacrifice.

It was a choice—one that Eldrin had already made. Risking his life for others.

Thalendir realized that he had made a decision a long time ago when he promised his mother that he would protect Eldrin. And he would not dishonor his mother.

Gantar contemplated him thoughtfully, then nodded slowly. He nudged his horse forward.

Thalendir exhaled, steeling himself one last time. Then—

"I'm with you."

His horse lunged forward, muscles coiling, hooves pounding against the earth. Gantar followed, his cloak billowing behind him.

The storm thundered ahead.

And they rode into it.

Nyxari, the Seer, turned, striding toward the entrance of her dwelling.

"Where are you going?" Kaelis demanded.

Nyxari didn't pause.

"To tell the council what they refuse to believe."

With that, she was gone, her long indigo braids clinking as she vanished into the winding tunnels.

Kaelis cursed under her breath and followed.

By the time she arrived at the great stone chamber, the Council was already arguing. Tension charged the air, as suffocating as the storm itself. Wings twitched in agitation, and tails flicked in frustration. Ever since Lyria vanished — the council had been divided. Half believed she had betrayed them, the other half fearing something far more sinister.

"She's gone!" one of the elderly warriors snapped, his tail lashing against the floor. "We should have declared her dead moons ago!"

"The Prophecy marks her," Nyxari's voice pierced through the noise.

The chamber fell silent.

The seer strode into the meeting—unannounced, uninvited, unstoppable.

"She did not leave of her own accord. Lyria was forced by the mark that now circles her neck."

Kaelis shoved through the gathered drelves, stepping into the firelight beside Nyxari, her eyes blazing as she slammed her hands onto the head table.

"I tried to tell you. All of you! That Lyria would not just leave us. That there was a reason behind her disappearance. But you would not listen."

A murmur of unease spread through the elders.

"And now, darkness has descended upon us."

Nyxari stepped forward, and her wings half-unfurled, her gaze like cut obsidian.

"The foretold prophecy, the one that you have ignored for ages, is now in progress. Lyria bears the tattoo," she said. "And while you argue over the past, the enemy gathers at our gates. If you will not listen—"

An unnatural blast of wind shook the chamber as a low, ominous horn carried through the tunnels from the outer watchtowers.

Deep. Resonant. A warning older than the kingdom itself.

The war horn had sounded, and Nyxari's following words came like a funeral toll.

"—then death will come to us all."

Kaelis' heart thumped against her ribs.

She spun around and sprinted for the tower.

War was here.

And they were out of time.

Chapter 27

Finnian's breath was shallow and labored, his chest heaving. The storm raged overhead, swallowing the sky with thick, rolling black clouds. The wind roared, but it paled compared to the sound emanating from the depths below.

They were coming.

He could hear them—a writhing mass of shapes moving in the mist, their twisted forms slithering between the remains of ancient reptiles. Glowing eyes shone in the gloom, dozens of them watching. Waiting.

He rose, each movement stiff, deliberate. Tears streaked his face, but his tears had dried. No more begging the wind to answer.

He grabbed his swords.

Twin hilts met his palms like old friends. Familiar. Steady. Anchors in a world spiraling into darkness as he tightened his grip.

Above him, the tempest raged—vortexed clouds tinged with sickly green, the air alive with static and hunger. The shadows howled, and through the gale came a shriek that did not belong to the wind or any beast. It was something ancient, something waiting to devour.

Finnian's breath steadied. His blades shone in the Vale's eerie glow.

"You want me?" he muttered through clenched teeth. "Come and get me."

The ground trembled. The mist parted.

And Finnian charged.

A deep growl echoed through the fog.

Then—a flurry of movement.

A panther leaped from the shadows, its black form twisting, claws reaching—

Finnian moved.

Faster than thought, faster than instinct. A blade met flesh, silver steel cleaving through the unnatural creature as he pivoted, twisting away just before another set of claws raked through the void where his throat had been.

He would not go down easily.

Finnian shifted into a defensive stance, twin swords gleaming under the sickly green lightning flashing above. He released his breath calmly and peacefully. This is what he had trained for his whole life. He was an elf. Fast. Furious. Faithful.

And if this was how he died, so be it.

Out of the fog, a beast three times his size hurtled forward. Finnian didn't flinch. He welcomed it.

He turned with the motion, blades slicing into the mist as another one charged. Finnian stepped aside at the last second, one sword slashing its chest, the other stabbing up through its jaw. Black ichor sprayed across his tunic as the creature shrieked and crumbled.

Another came—he met it with a roar of his own, spinning low, his blades flashing in the tempest light. Steel tore through sinew, bone cracked, and the feline fell, twitching before him.

Then, two more.

He pivoted between them, parrying with one blade, striking with the other.

They were coming too fast, their numbers unrelenting. He sidestepped, slashed, and rolled between them, moving like a ghost among shadows as he danced over the graves. But he felt the heaviness in his arms, the burn in his lungs. He wouldn't last forever.

A claw almost tore through his ribs. Finnian twisted away, deflecting the blow. Too close.

He exhaled, murmuring gently, "I hope Eldrin can see this from the depths because I would love to rub it in that I was the better fighter."

Another cat lunged.

Finnian struck—steel met bone, met darkness, met death. Again. Again. Again.

Black stained the earth below him. His vision blurred at the edges, his chest rising and falling rapidly, his arms trembling. But he did not stop.

Not until the last bloody one was dead.

Only the whisper of the wind curling through the bones of dead dragons remained.

Finnian staggered a step back, blades hanging loosely by his body. His breath tore from him in broken gasps, the fight draining from his limbs like water from a cracked vessel. Blood—too much of it—coated his tunic, his hands, his face. Some of it was his. Most weren't.

He turned, the storm rumbling above as if mourning its fallen kin.

And then—his gaze turned.

To the edge.

To the place where they had vanished.

His jaw clenched, grief rising like bile in his gullet. He wanted to scream again. To curse her name. The drelf. The mark. The prophecy. All of it.

But the words wouldn't come.

He stood there, fists trembling … but found only silence.

The storm had taken Eldrin. The shadows had swallowed Lyria. Despite it all, here he was—still breathing.

Why?

His gaze fell upon the place where her bandages had dropped. Torn. Abandoned. She had jumped after Eldrin.

She hadn't run. She hadn't saved herself.

She had followed him into the void.

And at that moment, Finnian realized…

He didn't hate her.

He never had.

Not really.

Perhaps it had always been fear—fear of what she meant, fear of what she might take from them, from Eldrin. From him.

But now, standing here, swords dripping and heart pounding, Finnian understood—she was never his enemy.

Something moved amidst the gale.

Finnian's fingers itched.

It wasn't over.

More were coming for him.

Chapter 28

The great hall of Eldermyst Keep stood eerily quiet, save for the distant rustle of banners swaying in the evening wind. King Eldermyst sat upon his throne, fingers steepled, his piercing gaze fixed upon the cold stone floor. The echoes of the last council meeting still played in his mind—whispers of rebellion and uncertainty and, worst of all, the risen doubt in his own heart.

He had always assumed Thalendir would stand by his side, come what may. His eldest. The prince. The heir. Thalendir hated the drelves almost as much as he did. The king had made sure of that.

Eldrin's leaving was a disappointment, too—but it was simpler to understand. Eldrin had always been more like his mother. He carried her big heart, her restless spirit, her quiet belief in far-fetched prophecies.

After his wife's death, grief had devoured the king, and in that grief, he had needed someone to blame. The drelves had been a convenient target. They were the living result of the broken covenant—their very existence was a public mark of betrayal.

Proof that the grand alliance between elves and dragons had failed.

A moment of passion shattered everything the elves and dragons had once built together.

The drelves caused her death.

The reason for the banishment.

At least, that's what he had told himself.

And he had made sure Thalendir believed it, too.

And now?

Now, with both his sons gone and the storm rising beyond his borders, he wondered if everything he had believed was a lie. Maybe he had repeated the lie so often that he had forgotten what had really happened.

That felt like a dagger to the ribs—sharp and merciless—settling into his bones with a weight he could not shake.

The truth was that the dragons were to blame. They were the ones who had broken promises… betrayed the elves… caused the world's fracture.

But it was more convenient to hate the drelves because they symbolized the forbidden union—one the elves could never erase.

And he felt truly alone.

He still longed for Thariel—her touch, the comfort she brought, the love she showed to everyone around her. She had been a true partner. A beautiful queen, a steady companion, and an alluring lover.

But she was gone.
And if he didn't act soon, both of his sons might be gone too.

The realization of what he faced came in waves, each more suffocating than the last.

His legacy was in jeopardy—if his sons perished, the line of succession would die with them.

The Council remained divided, too blinded by pride and tradition to notice the storm approaching.

And as king, the final decisions rested with him.

First, the fate of Eldrin—whether to brand him a traitor. Then Gantar—the only person who had known Thariel's mind, her heart, and her secrets. Their loyal friend for centuries.

But harboring a drelf was treachery—to the kingdom, to the elves, and the king himself.
And treachery, by their laws, came with a death sentence.

Still, it was the prophecy that haunted him the most. The foolish tale his wife had obsessed over—the one he had dismissed as ancient nonsense.

Now, it was stirring to life before his eyes. And he had to confront it.

Gantar had known a great deal more than he revealed—the king was sure of it.

For it was Gantar who had encouraged Thariel in her search for answers—who had helped her pore over ancient scrolls by candlelight, whispering about meanings beyond what was written.

And it was Gantar she had chosen for the Aetherstone—both the pendant and the stone itself.

Eldermyst stared out over the moonlit courtyard beyond his chambers. The torches below flickered but offered no warmth. Nothing could.

Gantar still had her pendant —the one Thariel had cherished for years. The same delicate silver chain that had once graced her neck now rested against Gantar's chest. Not a lover, no, never that—but not her husband.

The Aetherstone itself, too. She had entrusted it to Gantar, hidden it from her own king.

From him.

Not even in death had she returned it to his care.

Her dying words, soft as smoke yet sharper than any sword, cut deep into his memory.

"Gantar is to have the Aetherstone... and my necklace. Please, forgive me..."

He had tried to forget. Wanted to bury it beneath duty, beneath crown and council and war. But the wound remained. Quiet. Deep. Unseen.

She had trusted Gantar — with the destiny of a prophecy the realm had long tried to forget.

Not Eldermyst, the father of her children.

Not her king.

She had given to Gantar what was rightfully his. Her greatest treasure—besides their sons—was that stone and necklace. And she gave it… to him.

To the sage, who still wore her pendant like a promise. Who had kept the Aetherstone hidden away all these years… even from him?

Eldermyst's hand clenched against the stone windowsill.

The betrayal wasn't loud.
Or vicious.

It was worse than that. It was the kind that slowly burned away at his heart and soul.

She was gone.
And he was left with only a throne and the echo of a name he hadn't spoken aloud in years.

Thariel.

He whispered her name like a confession.
Not to call her back. She would not come.

But to remember how it felt to believe still she might.

The candle beside him flickered, then stilled.

Somewhere behind him, the breeze changed direction.

For the first time since her death, King Eldermyst was not by himself in the room.

He turned from the window, jaw tightening, the burden of crown and grief settling heavier on his shoulders. Eldrin and Thalendir had both made choices that aligned with the prophecy. Now, the king had choices to make.

The soft creak of leather stirred from the shadows beyond the pillars, and King Eldermyst's gaze flicked upward, sharpening like a dagger, though he already knew who stood there.

Orendir.

The High Warden was ever near a specter that could not be shaken — although unspoken words were sure to follow of things long buried, forbidden.

"You do not have to linger in the shadows, Orendir," Eldermyst said, his voice roughened by days without rest. "If you have something to say, speak it."

Orendir stepped forward into the firelight, the silver clasp of his cloak glinting at his shoulder — the same crest that had marked him as protector of Eldermyst's family for centuries.

"Forgive me, my king," Orendir breathed, his gaze fixed on the rough stone floor, though there was no mistaking the steadiness in his voice. "But I have stood by your side through many battles, through darker nights than this. And I have never seen you hesitate to act."

The king exhaled, a bitter smile curling at his lip.

"You presume much, Orendir."

"Perhaps," Orendir replied. "But I presume only because I have watched you shoulder this kingdom's burdens longer than any other living soul."

Quiet reigned between them, heavy with memory.

At last, Eldermyst rose from his throne, moving to stand before the hearth, where flames danced and cracked like faint memories of war.

"What would you have me do?" Eldermyst asked, at last, his back to Orendir. "Ride into a war that isn't ours to fight? Throw away what remains of my kingdom for a fool's prophecy?"

Orendir faded — but only for a moment.

"I would have you remember, my king," his voice quiet yet firm. "Remember what she believed in."

At that, Eldermyst turned, his eyes full of fire.

"Do not speak of her."

But Orendir did not back down.

"Thariel always believed the prophecy held a deeper meaning... that there was more to the drelves," he said, meeting the king's gaze at last. "She believed there was a future where we did not let our hate blind us."

Eldermyst stared at him, the firelight reflecting off eyes that had seen too much loss. "And she died for those beliefs."

"She died because her heart was broken," Orendir said. "Because you were too proud to see the future."

The king's shoulders drew tight, tension coiling through him like a drawn bowstring.

"And now you would have me fight for the creatures who destroyed her?"

"I would have you fight for your sons. And their future."

The words slid between ribs like a sharp blade—quiet, deliberate, unflinching.

Eldermyst staggered a half-step, the impact of the words cutting deeper than he'd expected.

Orendir stepped closer now, voice softening.

"Thalendir may be proud and blind to the truth, but he has gone to help his brother. Eldrin... has risked everything. Not for rebellion, but perhaps because he sees what you do not."

The king stayed silent, shoulders bowed, burdened by it all.

"If you do nothing, my king," Orendir finished, "you may lose them both. And the kingdom with them."

The fire crackled between them, projecting long shadows across the walls.

"You speak like a man who knows more than he says," Eldermyst said, eyes narrowing. "What else did Thariel tell you, Orendir? What truths do you keep from me still?"

Orendir's jaw tensed — and he looked older than his years as if the centuries pressed upon him all at once.

"Some truths are not mine to tell," Orendir murmured. "But I am certain of this: she believed Eldrin would be the solution to restoring our realms — a part to play that is much bigger than the two of us ever imagined."

Eldermyst turned away, pacing before the hearth, his hands clasped behind his back.

"You would have me lead my army into a battle that is not ours, based on the whispers of a dead queen and a prophecy we don't understand?"

Orendir's voice was steady but softer now — more personal.

"I would have you lead them because you are their king. Because it is the right thing to do. And… because it is what Thariel would want you to do."

Orendir's words resonated, heavy and sharp, keen like a dagger that would not be sheathed.

The king returned to the fire, watching the flames twist and writhe as if they, too, were bound by choices made long ago.

His hands, once steady as stone, now trembled.

Aid the drelves. March to war beside those who shattered the Covenant — the Covenant he had devoted his life to upholding? Trust in a prophecy that had stolen his wife and now threatened to steal his sons?

"A fool's prophecy," he had called it. But what if it wasn't? What if Thariel had been right all along?

Eldrin had staked everything on a drelf. And Thalendir — the ever-proud heir — had left to fight for blood and brotherhood.

Perhaps his sons had already seen what he had refused to see.

His eyes rose to the high arched windows of the hall, where the night pressed close, and beyond that, the storm building on the borders of his kingdom.

If he remained behind these walls, he would not just lose his sons. He would lose himself. Perhaps his kingdom and...

Thariel's dreams for them all would be shattered.

His breath shuddered within him, loud in the stillness of the great hall.

At last, he turned back to Orendir — and although the fire still blazed in his eyes, something deeper now tempered it.

"Prepare my armor," he commanded. "If we are going to war, then I will lead the charge."
The words were as piercing as a sword being drawn after decades of rest — not rusted but reforged.

Orendir bowed. But this time, it was not out of duty — it was an ancient force, something deeper.
Pride shimmered across his eyes.
This was the king he had followed into battle and the

unknown.

The king he thought he'd lost.

"As you will, my king."

And with that, the High Warden exited the hall, leaving Eldermyst alone with the fire — and the onus of the path from which he could not escape.

Chapter 29

Kaelis Skythorn climbed the stone steps, two at a time, her pulse hammering with each echo of the horn. Cries came from the bottom of the tunnels now—shouts of warriors preparing for battle, the clanging of armor yanked from racks, and the scrape of swords drawn from their sheaths.

She hoped they were ready. She had trained them and pushed them hard to prepare for this, and now... all that remained was the fight.

Kaelis burst into the open air of the tower, the wind tearing at her purple braids, her sharp gaze sweeping the horizon—and her stomach twisted.

Darkness churned near the mountains, a blackened storm not born of nature. Shadows moved within it—writhing shapes too large for men, too fast for normal beasts.

Nemods, she thought. *And more.*

A guard, pale and wide-eyed, faced her on reaching the parapet.

"Commander," he said—because that's what they called her now, though it still felt foreign on his tongue. "Orders?"

Kaelis swallowed hard, forcing herself to stand straight, tall, and unyielding — as Lyria would have done if she were here.

I must take the lead…until she comes back.

"Light the fires," Kaelis commanded, her voice steadier than she felt. "Summon every able drelf to the wall."

The guard hesitated for half a breath too long.

Kaelis stepped in front of his face, her eyes sharp as blades, and shouted.

"Now!"

He jolted as she'd struck him, then nodded.

"Yes, Commander."

Her eyes followed him as he ran to relay the order, and a second later, the first beacon fire ignited, casting bright light into the darkening sky—a rallying cry that every drelf warrior in the city would see.

Below, horns answered the first call, a chorus of warning and defiance mounting to meet the shadows.

Kaelis gripped the stone wall, her knuckles white.

Lyria, where are you?

The sky churned as the first shapes broke free of the clouds—sleek, shadow-wrapped figures sprinting toward the walls, their eyes fiery like coals.

Nemods. An entire legion of them.

We don't have enough warriors to hold them.

Still, Kaelis straightened, raising her chin.

We fight to the last, no matter what.

The wind swept past her, transporting the acrid stench of shadow.

She turned abruptly, descending back down into the keep, her voice ringing through the stone halls.

"Ready the archers! Shields to the front! And someone, find Nyxari—we'll need every ounce of magic she has."

Warriors scrambled past her, some unarmed, others clutching bows and swords with trembling hands.

They're afraid, she thought, jaw tightening. So am I. But courage isn't the absence of fear—it's choosing to stand, anyway.

And as the shadows closed in, Kaelis positioned herself at the ramparts, sword in hand, leading the defense of her people. Her sharp eyes scanned the skies, hoping Lyria was out there somewhere, headed her way. If not, then Kaelis would be enough.

She had to be.

Finnian stood alone, sword raised, the mist curling around his boots like icy fingers. Shapes moved through it—shifting, slithering, hungry. The next wave of panthers emerged from the fog, prowling beasts with eyes gleaming, their jaws agape in anticipation.

His arm shook—not with fear, but with rage. A raw, burning fury coiled deep inside like an extra heartbeat.

I wasn't there.

The thought was more damaging than any knife. The wind tore at his cloak, snapping it to ribbons. He gripped his swords until his knuckles burned.

I should've been by Eldrin's side. Should've stopped it. Should've—

He had failed.

Just like the Vale said, he would.

And now… they were gone.

His breath came faster, hotter. His blood thundered in his head.

"You want blood?" he snarled, stepping forward, blades catching the eerie luminescence of the sky. "Come get it."

The shadows hissed, slinking through the gloom, sensing his fury.

Good.

Let them come.

Let them *all* come.

Because if this were where he died—he'd make it a reckoning.

"This is for Eldrin," he spat. "And... for Lyria."

He bared his teeth, eyes narrowing when the first creature lunged—and he met it head-on, blades flashing like lightning.

Shadow panthers slithered from the crevices, their eyes like coals, low growls echoing off the skeletons.

Finnian drew a sharp breath, squaring his stance.

"Let's see what you've got," he hissed through clenched teeth.

The panthers crept closer, and muscles coiled, fangs bared.

Finnian took one last deep breath, blood and ash thick on his tongue. His knees threatened to give, but he stood anyway—because should he die, he would die on his feet.

Every nerve screamed, yet his grasp remained firm. His vision blurred, but his focus sharpened. He faced them—half-dead, half-mad, and unafraid.

"Well?" he growled, showing his teeth. "What are you waiting for?"

The wind shrieked in answer.

And then—

—they pounced.

The first panther hit like a shadow-given form. Finnian twisted, dodging its full weight. Its claws sliced across his ribs, tearing through leather and skin. Pain flared white-hot, yet he didn't scream—he struck back. Steel hissed and bit deep, cutting across the beast's shoulder in a spray of blood.

The second crashed into him from behind.

He hit the ground hard; the breath knocked from his lungs, but his grasp was still firm. His sword rose blindly and caught the panther's jaw, driving it back in a howl of fury.

Another swipe. Another slash. He moved on instinct now, driven by rage and grief and the burning refusal to fall.

The beasts pressed him from every side. But he refused to give up.

He spun, kicked, stabbed—one blade lost in a corpse, the other gripped so tight it cut into his palm. A panther leapt; he ducked beneath it and thrust his blade upward into its belly. It screamed as it fell, thrashing—even so, he didn't stop.

His tunic stuck to him, drenched in ichor. His shoulders sagged. The world spun.

But his fire burned.

"Come on then, you twisted cowards!"

Another shadow emerged from the haze.

Finnian roared and turned to meet it—sword flashing in one last arc of defiance.

A claw scraped down his back, sending fire through his nerves. He staggered, almost falling—but caught himself, turning with a snarl and slashing wildly at the creature that struck him.

Another crept closer, hissing through razer sharp fangs, its eyes glowing an eerie red, reflecting what little light remained. More followed—dozens fanning out near him in a wide half-circle, boxing him in.

The graveyard loomed about him — a sea of bone and shadow, twisted with fog and the stench of ash. The great skeletal remains of ancient dragons towered like silent sentinels—guardians that could not fight.

Unlike him, they could rest.

Finnian wiped sweat and grime from his brow and compelled himself to stand, swaying as pain lanced through his ribs. His legs wobbled, barely holding, but he would not fall. Not yet. Not until the last of them did.

Within the storm above, thunder cracked like splintering bone.

Finnian lifted his sword, torn, bloodied, but upright. Defiant.

"You hear that?" He rasped into the void. "I'm still here."

The wind didn't answer.

But something else did.

From afar, the storm brewed — but here, in this forgotten field of death, the wind carried a sharper bite, as if even the bones remembered the battle.

And from the other side of the graveyard, the darkness was moving again.

He could see them — slithering, skittering shapes pouring over the ridge. Nemods, their jagged talons scratching against stone. Above, leathery wyverns shrieked, circling like vultures awaiting their feast.

Finnian's heart thundered as he set his jaw. He forced his aching body upright, shifting his grasp to the hilt. His left arm was almost useless, but his right still held steel—and that would have to be enough.

A large cat caught him off guard and crashed into him, sending him tumbling. His sword clattered from his hand. Finnian gasped, reaching for his sword—but before he could move, shadows enveloped him.

He looked up.

Two more.

Their eyes gleamed crimson in the gloom, muscles rippling beneath inky fur. They stalked him on silent feet, jaws snapping, guttural sounds escaping their maws.

Finnian's stomach twisted.

He willed himself to rise, and his fingers clasped the hilt of cold steel.

If he were going out, it would be with blood on his sword and fury in his spine.

"Come on," He rasped, spitting blood. "If this is it, come take me."

The panthers circled him, moving in slow, deliberate steps—cats toying with a mouse.

For a moment, everything else fell away—no storm, no war horn, no kingdom to defend—just the sound of his ragged breathing.

Eldrin… Lyria… I'm sorry I wasn't enough. I'm sorry I wasn't there to save you.

His throat tightened, and genuine fear surged inside him.

The first panther lunged.

Finnian dodged, but not fast enough—claws slashed his arm, splattering crimson over the surrounding bones.

The second followed close behind. Finnian swung—his blade catching only air. He stumbled, falling to his knees.

This is it. This is where I die.

The panthers drew closer, poised to strike.

Finnian tasted dirt mixed with blood on his tongue.

At least I'll die fighting.

He struggled upright, blade trembling in his grasp, and faced them while the darkness pressed in.

"Come on," He growled, teeth bared. "Finish me."

And then— Claws. Steel.

A scream torn from the throat and sky.

And—nothing.

Just silence. Just bone.

Kaelis positioned herself on the wall. Below, the darkness churned—and from its depths, the nemods poured forth like a black tide.

She could hear the warriors scrambling behind her — the clash of swords, the creak of bowstrings as drelves rushed to their posts. Some fumbled with their weapons, their hands shaking as they prepared to fight.

Too long we've sat idle, Kaelis thought. *For too long, we've hidden in secrecy, thinking the storm would pass us by.*

But it hadn't passed them.

It had come straight for their throats.

A shout erupted from the lower towers as the opening volley of arrows soared upward, streaking like black lightning into the fog. The arrows rained down over the advancing nemods, cutting many down, but the creatures didn't slow.

Not enough. Nowhere near enough.

Kaelis's hand dropped to her sword, fingers curling tight.

Hurry, Lyria! She thought, her heart twisting. *We need you. I need you beside me.*

She shoved the thought down.

I will stand until you arrive.

Another shriek echoed as a wyvern broke from the clouds, banking hard toward the walls, its talons gleaming like hooked blades. Kaelis stood tall, ready for battle, her voice ringing out sharp and clear.

"Archers—loose!"

The crack of bowstrings snapping filled the air, and a second volley of arrows launched skyward, some finding their mark, striking the wyvern's leathery wings. It shrieked as it spiraled sideways, crashing into the lower battlements in a rain of shattered stone and blood.

But more followed behind it.

Kaelis swallowed the rising panic, turning as another guard ran up to her side—wide-eyed, breathless.

"Commander, they're scaling the east wall! We can't hold them back — there are too many!"

Kaelis turned a frantic pulse drumming within her.

"Get every soldier we have. We hold them here," she ordered.

The guard hesitated.

Kaelis grabbed him by the shoulder, her gaze fierce.

"We hold them here!"

He nodded, dashing back down the stairs.

Kaelis turned again to the battlefield—to the dark wave crawling up the stone walls.

Like cockroaches slipping through every crack. Climbing higher.

She drew her sword, the metal shining in the wavering light of beacon fires.

"Ready yourselves!" she shouted to the warriors behind her. "They are coming!"

And then—the first nemod reached the top of the wall.

Kaelis struck hard, blade flashing as it severed the creature's shoulder. It shrieked, talons swiping at her, but she stepped aside and plunged her sword through its throat.

Another climbed up behind it. Then another.

The wall exploded into pandemonium as drelves met the brutes head-on, blades clashing, shields splintering under claws and teeth.

So many…

Kaelis fought hard. She was a whirlwind of motion, shoving a nemod back with her shoulder, slicing its chest. Another lunged, throwing her to the stone floor—but she drove her dagger up beneath its chin, blood spraying her armor.

Behind her, she heard warriors crying out—some in defiance, others in pain.

Too many of them.

And then the shadows shifted again.

From the black storm, the panthers emerged—sleek and deadly, sliding from thin air. They hit the lines like black lightning, demolishing the drelves' defenses as though they were paper.

Kaelis froze momentarily as she watched them—monsters made of pure night, all muscle and gleaming fangs, their eyes blazing.

We can't hold them for long.

Still, she compelled herself to stand.

But we will die trying.

She lifted her sword high.

"Hold the wall!" she shouted, voice raw with defiance. "Hold!"

Yet even while she yelled, she knew—they would soon be overcome.

The dark panthers leapt onto the battlements, claws raking, jaws snapping. Warriors fell beneath them, screaming.

Kaelis turned to face the nearest panther, sword raised—and as she struck, all she saw was shadow and blood.

Chapter 30

The world surrounding Finnian burst into light.

Just as the shadows pounced, a sound ripped through the sky—not the cry of a panther, but something ancient and primal. The ground shook beneath him as if the earth itself had stirred from slumber. His sword slipped from his fingers as he knelt, raising an arm against the blinding glare.

The shadows shrieked, recoiling mid-leap, their bodies twisting in agony as the light illuminated the night. They scattered like insects as if the very atmosphere had transformed into fire.

Finnian sucked in a breath, stunned by the sudden shift from death's edge to overwhelming radiance.

Am I dead? The thought scraped across his mind like sandpaper.

He blinked against the brilliance, his vision swimming as he struggled to comprehend the shape rising from the abyss.

Something massive and magnificent unfurled—wings of silver fire, each beat resonating like thunder cracking the sky.

The tempest overhead seemed to hesitate. The very air grew still.

She rose.

A majestic white dragon—her scales like molten stars, her breath casting light in ripples across the ruins. Power rippled off her like heat from a forge, and in her roar, Finnian felt something unearthly. Not wrath. Not rage.

Revelation.

Her wings struck once, sending a pulse across the fog like the heartbeat of creation itself. In her wake, two figures ascended, cloaked in brilliance.

Finnian squinted through the glare, his heart hammering.

Eldrin appeared first, lifted by the wind, his cloak no longer the dark hunter's green but silver, rippling like spun starlight. The Aetherstone beat inside its pouch, and his dagger gleamed with a cold, relentless blue flame.

Then Lyria. Her wings, once crimson and torn, had changed—once the color of blood and fire, now the essence of moonlight and snow. Silver-white translucence stretched widely behind her, every movement shimmering as if the dragon's soul had woven itself into her very being.

They weren't just alive.

They were transformed.

Touched by light.

Finnian staggered to his feet, awe and disbelief warring within him. "Eldrin… Lyria…"

His voice cracked, barely more than a breath, as they faced him.

Alive. Radiant.

And it washed over him.

Hope.

Lyria turned, her gaze soft as she met his eyes. "You're not alone, Finnian," she said, though power still crackled in her voice.

Eldrin grinned, stepping to Finnian's side and holding out a hand to help him up. "Miss us?"

Finnian laughed as he took Eldrin's hand and rose shakily. "I thought you were ..."

Eldrin's eyes darkened, but he nodded. "So did we."

Above them, Seralyth circled, her great wings churning the inky blackness, driving back the mist and shadow. The white light of her body burned in contrast to the dark sky—a beacon in the night.

She hovered, her eyes glowing as she looked down at them. And then, in a voice that emanated as though from the depths of the earth itself, she spoke:

"The choice has been made. Unity forged in sacrifice, the light born from darkness. The realms rise—or fall—as one."

Her words echoed across the valley, rolling like thunder into the darkness. The earth stilled beneath her voice, and for a moment, all was still—before she turned, rising higher into the heavens, her wings slicing across the clouds until she disappeared into the vast expanse.

Finnian stood between his friends, breathless, as the wind stirred around them.

He glanced from one to the other and shook his head. "I don't know what happened down there... but I've never been so glad to see anyone in my life."

Eldrin slapped him on the arm, smiling. "You held the line. That's more than enough."

Lyria nodded, a spark in her eyes. "You did pretty well... For an elf."

From beyond the ridge, another shriek tore through the night—far away but growing closer.

Finnian straightened, retrieving his blades with renewed strength. "Thanks, but we're not done yet."

Together, the trio faced the storm—ready to fight.

Kaelis bit down hard on her lip as she twisted, her tail cracking as it sent a nemod hurtling off the wall. Her blade met another mid-lunge, cleaving through its heart with a wet crunch. Black blood sprayed the stone, hissing where it landed.

All around her, soldiers battled, a whirlwind of metal and fury—wings beating hard against the smoke-choked air, tails lashing, swords gleaming. But the enemy pressed on in waves—climbing, clawing, howling—crawling onto the walls like rot through stone.

A wyvern shrieked and dove above. Kaelis ducked as a spout of dark fire scorched the battlements behind her. Heat washed over her shoulders, the air laden with smoke and ash.

Her warriors were holding—but barely. It was in their eyes: the edge of exhaustion. The hint of doubt. The fear that came when questions arose, wondering if they were already beaten.

Kaelis's grip tightened around her sword, muscles screaming with every breath.

Lyria? Where are you?

And then, an explosion of silver fire erupted far off, streaking across the heavens like a comet sent by the gods themselves.

Kaelis staggered, throwing an arm across her eyes.

The blast ripped open the sky, radiant, defiant. Nemods shrieked, descending from the heights. Wyverns scattered like startled birds. Even the panthers, those death-born beasts, vanished into the fog.

Gasps rose along the battlements. Some drelves fell to their knees. Others just stared.

But Kaelis kept her gaze fixed.

She couldn't see the source.

Didn't need to.

Her heart thundered.

It's her.

She could feel it in her bones—in the blood they shared as kin, not by birth, but by bond.

"Lyria..." Kaelis whispered.

She straightened, wings twitching, her sword rising above her head. Nearby, warriors turned toward her voice.

"She's coming!" Kaelis shouted, her voice penetrating the stone. "Hold the line!"

The drelves rallied. Teeth bared. Eyes burning. Hope flaring like kindling amidst the gloom.

But Kaelis looked again at the wall, and she gasped.

The darkness still moved. Nemods clambered over fallen beasts. The wyverns regrouped, screaming for vengeance. And within the fog below, something bigger stirred—something old and waiting.

The light had struck.

But the night had not yielded.

Not yet.

As Seralyth melted away into the evening sky, Eldrin faced Lyria. "We must hurry. The enemy has reached your kingdom."

Lyria's gaze rested on the storm brewing beyond the ridge, her jaw set. The mark at her throat pulsed with silver light, and something inside her ignited—fierce, focused, and unrelenting.

"I won't let them fall," she whispered, more to herself than to others.

Finnian gave her a crooked grin. "You mean *we* won't let them fall?"

Lyria blinked, glancing at him—and after a moment, her mouth curved into a slight smile. "Looks like we're stuck with each other."

Her gaze spanned the graveyard, and then she spotted them—three dark shapes, partially obscured by the haze. "our horses..." she breathed.

Finnian followed her gaze, relief apparent on his face. He gave a sharp whistle to his trusty mount. "Embermane!"

The buckskin raised his head at once, ears pricking as he whinnied in reply.

"Think they're ready to face that storm?" Finnian asked.

"They are war horses," Eldrin said, a grin spreading across his face. "They don't ask. They charge."

Lyria inhaled, steadying herself. "Take Duskrunner for me."

Finnian blinked. "You sure?"

Her wings unfurled behind her—no longer torn but whole and radiant. Pale feathers edged in silver shimmered gently, the storm light catching on each arc of her wingspan like runes cast in moonlight.

Before she could answer, a piercing shriek rents the air.

A shadow dropped fast—a wyvern, leathery wings tucked tight, claws outstretched and aimed for her back.

"Lyria, look out!" Eldrin shouted.

She spun, wings folding, bracing for impact— But the wind surged, catching her as a current. It lifted her, snapping her wings wide as the wyvern's claws slashed at the void.

She rose, off-balance for a moment—then found her rhythm. Her wings fluttered once, twice, and she steadied, hovering with sharp, controlled grace above the others.

A breath flew from her lips. Then, a grin.

"Yes," she said, eyes fierce. "I'm sure."

Lyria laughed, glancing behind her. "I'll meet you at the walls."

Before they could protest, she reached the heavens—a flash of silver splitting the darkness like a shooting star in reverse.

"Show-off," Eldrin muttered, although his lips tugged upward, softening his features—as a new light reached his eyes.

Finnian glanced sideways at him. "Think you'll ever pull that off?"

Eldrin smirked. "I'll stick to riding."

As Lyria flew into the storm, Eldrin prepared to mount—but paused, frowning when his eyes noticed Finnian's injuries, where blood still seeped through his torn tunic.

"You're hurt," Eldrin said, brow furrowing.

Finnian smirked, although it was strained. "Yeah, well, you should see the other guys."

With a jerk of his head, Eldrin reached for something at his belt. "Here—what's left of Gantar's elixir? Drink it. You're no good to anyone if you collapse before we reach the walls."

Finnian hesitated—but at Eldrin's pointed look, he took the vial and downed it, wiping his mouth with his sleeve.

"Thanks," he muttered, a little of the strain easing from his countenance as the potion took hold.

Eldrin put a hand on his shoulder. "Don't make me carry you."

Finnian chuckled. "You couldn't if you tried."

Eldrin grinned, curling his arm. "Don't be so sure."

Finnian hesitated—but as he swung into the saddle, there was new strength in his body as the bleeding slowed and the wounds closed.

Together, the two elves mounted and headed to help the drelves. Far above them, Lyria soared—a glint of silver piercing the storm.

Gloomy skies churned, but now, a light burned against them—rising higher, pushing through the shadows. And though the darkness had not yet fallen, *the mark had risen.*

Chapter 31

The shift felt like a sudden blow to the chest.

Drakor hovered above the storm-tossed valley, and his wings extended wide against the churning clouds. His claws unsheathed, scraping the air as though he could tear it apart. The winds screamed around him, but he was quiet, watching, listening, as something within the magic twisted and turned against him.

A power he had thought extinguished—rekindled.

His lip curled in a snarl, a wisp of smoke escaping his nostrils as his eyes narrowed against the night.

She had risen.

He felt it in the way the darkness faltered—*his* darkness, the shadow magic that had seeped into every crack of the Drelf realm. Now, it recoiled like a snake burned. And only one thing could have done that.

The marked one.

Somehow, she had survived the fall. And emerged stronger.

Drakor's claws flexed again as he surveyed the darkened horizon. The storm raged around him, a roiling sea of cloud and shadow—until a silver flame sliced through it.

The drelf.

Her wings edged in silver light, sliced the nocturnal sky, rising higher as if she could challenge the storm itself.

Drakor's growl intensified.

No.

She would not reach the drelves. She would not carry that spark of hope through his storm.

He beat his wings once, rising into the black clouds, his eyes fixed on her silver form below. For all her brilliance, she had not yet seen him.

"Foolish drelf," he growled, voice like grinding stone. "You think because you've tasted power… you can defy me?"

A violent gust slammed past him, heavy with the scent of charred earth and lightning. Drakor spread his wings wide, riding the current higher, above her path—above her light.

"You may have survived the fall, little mark-bearer," he hissed, "but you will not survive *me*."

With a flap of his wings, Drakor shot forward—a flash of shadow across the storm, the gale screaming in his wake. Lightning licked across the clouds as his body cut through them like a knife, eyes glowing with hunger and hate.

He locked onto her like a war hawk, wings tucked, heart pounding with a fury surpassing the storm.

The sky split with thunder.

And into it he dove—fangs bared, death at his heels.

The walls shook beneath Kaelis' feet as another wave of wyverns screeched overhead, their leathery wings churning the storm winds.

Nearby, the drelves fought fiercely—tails cracking like whips, blades flashing, slicing into nemods that clawed over the battlements. Some took flight, diving and dodging as they clashed with wyverns.

Kaelis swept her weapon in a tight arc, killing a nemod that lunged for one of her warriors and spinning to block another strike aimed at her.

We won't last much longer. She thought as her blade met flesh and tore through bone.

A dark panther leapt onto the wall, fangs gleaming and claws raking. Kaelis ducked beneath its lunge and plunged her blade up beneath its ribs, twisting hard. The beast shrieked as it collapsed—but already two more were climbing after it.

From her right, a voice called out—calm, assertive, despite the chaos.

"Kaelis!"

She turned to see Nyxari stepping onto the wall, her dark cloak billowing around her.

"You shouldn't be here!" Kaelis shouted over the roar of wind and battle.

Nyxari's eyes gleamed, sharp as glass in the shadowy light. "And yet, here I am."

Kaelis barely parried a blow before spitting blood and barking a bitter laugh. "Unless you've come to tell me help is flying through that storm, I don't have time for riddles."

Nyxari's eyes rose to the sky, where the clouds churned violently.

"Help is coming."

Kaelis froze for half a heartbeat, blade still raised.

Nyxari's voice dropped low but firm. "But until she arrives, we hold."

Another wyvern screamed as it dove toward the wall—but before it could strike, Nyxari raised her taloned hands, an aura of violet and silver sparking between her palms.

A wave of crackling magic shot upward, slamming into the wyvern's chest and sending it spiraling out of control. The creature crashed beyond the walls, a tangle of wings and limbs.

Kaelis blinked, stunned. "Since when can you do *that*?"

Nyxari smirked, though sweat already glistened on her brow. "Since I had no other choice."

More nemods crested the wall. Kaclis and her warriors moved to intercept, but Nyxari stepped forward, weaving her hands through as if shaping the vapor itself.

A barrier of glimmering light surged between the drelves and the attackers—like a wall of translucent crystal, holding the enemy back momentarily.

Kaelis addressed her. "Can you hold it?"

Nyxari's jaw tightened. "Long enough."

Kaelis gripped her sword tightly, calling down to the warriors still on the lower levels.

"Retreat and regroup at the inner wall!"

The drelves below scrambled to obey, wings snapping as they leapt between platforms and towers.

Despite their retreat, Kaelis could see cracks in Nyxari's barrier forming, splintering like ice under pressure.

"How long, Nyxari?" she called.

Nyxari's gaze stayed on the enemy beyond, her magic pulsing in waves.

"Long enough for her to get here," Nyxari whispered.

Kaelis swallowed hard, her throat tight, but her hold on her blade did not waver.

Upon the battlefield, wyverns were already circling back for another strike—and the dark shapes of felines slinked between towers, looking for weaknesses.

Kaelis took her place beside Nyxari, sword raised, wings tattered but strong.

"If we die," Kaelis said, her voice fierce, "we die holding the line."

Nyxari's lips lifted. "We're not dead yet."

And as another roar echoed in the storm—far away, yet approaching—Kaelis felt a flicker of hope penetrate the night.

Maybe... just maybe...

Far from the tempest and battle, in the blackened peaks of the dragon spires, Vartharax stirred.

The surrounding shadows twisted and writhed, slithering along jagged stone walls. His massive form lay coiled atop the ruins of an ancient throne, talons raking deep furrows into the rock.

Something in the darkness shifted—and his eyes snapped open, burning dark coals in the gloom.

A tremor in the magic.

For the first time in a dragon's age, the shadows did not obey.

A guttural sound rumbled deep within when he arose, wings unfurling, scraping against the cavern ceiling. Vapor escaped his nostrils.

"She still lives," he hissed.

The mark pulsed somewhere beyond his reach, stronger than before, burning like a silver flame in the night.

A pulse of unity.

Vartharax snapped his jaws with a thunderous roar.

How had she survived?

She should have died in the fall.

And yet... the mark surged with renewed light.

The thing he had most feared was the union of the two realms.

"They seek to unite," he snarled, smoke and flame flickering between his teeth. "To tip the balance in their favor."

He rose to his full height, wings flaring wide as his tail lashed out, shattering a column of stone with a roar that shook the mountain.

No.

He would not allow it.

In the heights above the turbulent valley, Drakor sliced through the air, his wings driving the wind in thunderous beats.

The silver flame that was Lyria streaked across the night, her wings slicing the sky, trailing light like a meteor that would not succumb.

Drakor's eyes narrowed, his lips curling into a silent snarl.

"I must stop her," he growled, his voice lost in the storm's fury.

The mark pulsed in her—and each time she flapped her wings, the darkness recoiled from her light.

She was undoing all that Vartharax had wrought—all that Drakor himself had crushed beneath claw and shadow.

And if she reached the drelves, *would she join them in this fight?*

Never.

She would not make it that far.

He angled his wings, diving hard against the wind, shrieking past him.

Lightning flashed, and he could see her clearly—her silver-lined wings reflecting the light, her face fierce and determined.

"She thinks she can stand against me?" Drakor snarled, smoke pouring from his maw.

Closer now. He could smell the warmth of her blood and feel the pulse of her brand.

His claws extended, already tasting the power he would claim when he tore it from her dying body.

Kill her—and the mark will pass to me.

The thought snaked through his consciousness like a serpent. *Vartharax may think it belongs to him. But he is old. Weak. Blinded by the past.*

I will seize the power.

A growl escaped deep from within his throat as he tucked his wings and shot downward, closing the gap.

Below them, the drelf nation was ablaze, the walls crumbling beneath waves of darkness. But Drakor's eyes never left his prey.

Closer.

Closer.

Almost mine.

Lyria's wings faltered in the breeze, buffeted by a sudden gust—and Drakor's eyes gleamed.

"Fly, little drelf," he hissed, teeth shining in the flashes of lightning. "Fly while you still can."

She pushed higher, wings battling the storm as if she could outrun fate itself.

Drakor's growl intensified.

"No one escapes me," he whispered.

With one last ferocious wingbeat, Drakor surged forward, straight into her path.

"Time to end this."

Chapter 32

Lyria's wings struggled against the howling wind, every inch aching as rain lashed her face.

Below, the Drelf realm lit up with fire, its walls buckling under the assault. But it was the roar behind her—deep and jagged like thunder dragged across broken stone—that chilled her more than the weather.

Her wings faltered as she risked a quick look behind her.

A dragon.

But unlike any she had ever imagined.

Ashen-gray scales, mottled and cracked, clung to a body too lean—a crooked shape that seemed stitched together from darkness itself. Sickly yellow eyes seared across the tempest and wind, zeroing in on her with a gaze that felt like knives sliding beneath her scales.

Her heart twisted.

This couldn't be Vartharax. But something worse?

Who—?

Her pulse thundered, her body aching from the strain of holding her flight steady. Her wings strained, battling the wind, and doubt gnawed at her—*Could she outfly him?*

A bolt of lightning split across the sky, and in its flash, she caught another glimpse of him—cutting across the sky with lethal grace.

Closer.

She banked hard, diving to avoid a jet of fire that roared past her, searing through the air. Heat licked at her wings, and she faltered, gritting her teeth.

I can't outrun him.

Her pulse roared in her head, her mark burning against her collarbone—even so, she couldn't shake the dark shape closing in.

Another roar pierced through the maelstrom, and her wings buckled under a sudden gust as Drakor surged after her.

Eldrin... Finnian... Her thoughts flickered to them, racing toward the Drelf walls—too far to help her now.

Her hand reached inside the pouch at her side, fingers seeking the stone flower Fizzlewing had given her. The cool surface pulsed—a faint warmth that increased the longer she touched it.

Fizzlewing...

Could he even hear her now?

She swerved hard as Drakor's claws slashed behind her, the power from his wings sending her tumbling sideways. Her breath left her in a sharp gasp as she struggled to right herself, wings straining, muscles trembling.

Her fingers locked around the token.

Please, she thought. *If you ever meant it—to come when I called—I need you now.*

The flower flared with a gleam of light—a sudden thrum of magic pulsing from its core.

Behind her, Drakor unleashed a savage snarl, barreling toward her like a raging storm.

The stones' glow flickered in her palm, and for one breathless moment, the surrounding wind stilled. Her heart slammed against her ribs.

Her eyes widened.

Nothing.

"Fizzlewing—!" she cried, her voice ragged.

BOOM.

With an earsplitting clap, color and light exploded out of nowhere—right between her and Drakor—sending the sinister dragon veering off course with a furious roar.

"Well, well, well… if it isn't my favorite mark-bearer dangling in the wind!"

Lyria's head shot up, swallowing her breath.

There—floating sideways in the sky as though he'd been there all along—was Fizzlewing.

She blinked. "You came!"

"Of course, I came," he said with a wink as if they weren't flying straight into death itself. "You know how I love drama."

His translucent wings, laced in gold, trembled with a crackling sound. His smile faltered as a renewed roar erupted from Drakor, who circled back toward them.

"Oh, no…," Fizzlewing muttered. "Not now… "He stifled a gasp while his tail sputtered and jerked, threatening to send him plummeting.

Drakor roared and dove toward them. Lyria leveled her gaze, wings flaring.

"Do something!" she shouted.

Fizzlewing straightened midair. "Right, then…" he said more seriously, his usual mischief burning into resolve. His wings burst open wider, crackling with light as his tail spat again — but this time, it held steady.

"*Move* when I say," he muttered out of the side of his mouth, eyes narrowing on the oncoming dragon.

Lyria ground her teeth, wings beating hard to hold position. "Ready."

Fizzlewing raised his tail, the tip sparking wildly, gold and violet threads swirling around them. He spun once in midair, faster and faster, as if winding himself up—and with a sharp cry, slammed it down like striking a bell.

A shower of golden dust and light erupted outward, whirling around them in a sudden torrent. The wind caught it, twisting it into a shimmering cyclone that stretched between them and Drakor.

The dark dragon roared, his flight jerking when the storm hit him. He banked sharply to his left, talons slashing at the swirling magic as it stung and blinded him.

"What is this?!" Drakor bellowed, his voice muffled inside the spiraling gold.

"Just a little something I like to call pixie grit!" Fizzlewing shouted, though sweat now beaded his brow. "Nasty, isn't it?"

Lyria stared in shock as the blinding vortex pulsed around them, flickering like molten sunlight and stardust.

Fizzlewing looked towards her, eyes suddenly serious. "Go!"

"But—"

"I can't hold him forever," he said. "You've got friends who need you. Now go—before scaly here makes a meal of you!"

Lyria's wings flared, determination settling in her soul. She nodded once.

"Thank you."

With a strong flap of her wings, she launched upward—toward the drelf kingdom where the storm still raged, and her people fought for their lives.

Behind her, Drakor's bellow shook the clouds as he tore against the golden storm. But it was holding—for now.

Fizzlewing's voice drifted after her, a familiar chuckle buried in his words.

"Next time, don't wait until the eleventh hour to call me, eh?"

Lyria grinned as she flew straight into the midst of the battle, the golden light still trailing in her wake. She flew with all her might, the wind screaming past her ears, rain lashing her face. Every beat sent fire through her muscles, yet she didn't slow. She couldn't. Not now.

Below, fire engulfed the drelf lands.

From above, she saw it all—proud towers battered and crumbling, walls crawling with shadow. Black shapes swarmed the battlements, steel and violet magic flashing as her people struggled to hold them back.

Her heart clenched. Kaelis. Nyxari. Her people. Fighting. Bleeding. Dying.

A wyvern shrieked in the clouds ahead, breaking from its flight pattern to dive straight for her. Its eyes locked onto her jaws wide as it emitted a piercing cry. Jagged wings sliced the wind as it barreled toward her, talons outstretched.

Lyria's teeth locked together, and she tucked her wings close as she rolled sideways, the beast's claws raking the space where she had been a breath before. Panting, Lyria forced her wings to steady. They burned, each stroke more intense than the previous one, but she refused to slow.

Below, Kaelis stood, blade raised high as a panther lunged toward her. Beside her, Nyxari fought, hands glowing with magic, as waves of nemods clawed over the stone. Lyria angled her wings and, with a shrill cry, dove, piercing the storm like a silver arrow.

The wind whipped around her, rain slicing her skin, but she focused on Kaelis, locked in combat, blade raised for what might be her last strike.

The shadow panther leapt, claws outstretched—its fangs flashing in the firelight.

Lyria's wings unfolded a heartbeat before she hit, and with a burst of speed, she collided with the panther in midair, sending it tumbling over the wall in a mass of claws and smoke.

Kaelis stumbled back, shock flashing across her features—then fierce, sharp-edged relief.

"About time," she growled as Lyria floated to land beside her. More shadow panthers prowled below, their red eyes gleaming. For a brief instant, the two friends' eyes locked—battle-weary, fierce, and unspoken words passing between them.

Kaelis reached out, gripping Lyria's shoulder, and Lyria gripped hers in return—a warrior's embrace, brief but solid. Lyria's chest heaved, her wings folded tight against her body as she steadied herself, eyes burning as she took in the battlefield.

A crooked grin crossed Kaelis's face. "Glad you're back."

Fizzlewing flickered across the sky, wings buzzing as his remaining magic scattered in glowing trails. Sweat dripped down his brow, adhering to the soot smudging his face.

Below him, the kingdom blazed with gloom, smoke, and screams. The tempest raged like a wounded beast—and still no trace of that brooding elf-boy or his cheerful sidekick.

"Where are they?" he mumbled, teeth gritted as another violent lurch in the weather nearly bucked him sideways.

Drakor emerged from behind a cloud of golden grit, coughing smoke and fury. His wings thrashed against the lingering shimmer, scattering the last traces of Fizzlewing's dust. His snarl morphed into a growl as he surveyed the sky, looking for his target.

Too late.

She had disappeared.

His claws clenched. The odor of scorched air and dragon fire still lingered.

Then—something shifted.

A low vibration rolled within the clouds, deeper than thunder. Older than any wyvern's cry. It slithered through the cosmos like a living thing.

Drakor's head snapped around, his gaze sharpening.

A deafening roar pierced the heavens.

Furious. Unmistakable.

Fizzlewing froze mid-air, wings trembling. "Oh... that's definitely not good."

The tempest overhead split like shredded cloth.

Something massive dropped through.

A dragon—enormous, crimson as molten stone, its wings serrated like blades, its eyes gleaming red hot. It descended like vengeance, fire curling from its throat.

Drakor recoiled midair, wings flaring wide.

His snarl turned into something sharper—surprise.

"Korrath," he spat.

A howling wind blew as the red ball of fire barreled toward his target, and in an instant, the storm held its breath. Another roar shattered the heavens, shaking the very stones beneath the Drelf kingdom.

Drakor twisted midair, eyes squinting, as he prepared to confront the new threat. He might be smaller and twisted, but he was wicked-fast.

The sky erupted in flames and darkness, twisting into war.

"They're going to rend the heavens," Fizzlewing whispered.

Far below, Lyria ducked beneath a collapsing tower wall, her wings still aching from flight. Kaelis met her just beneath the battlements, sword slick with ichor.

A sudden *flash* lit the sky—red and green crashing in a spiral of flame and fury.

Kaelis turned. "What in the universe?"

Lyria's gaze snapped upward, her wings rising. "Only one creature makes that kind of noise…"

"Dragons," said Kaelis, staring at her friend. "Let's just hope they annihilate each other."

The sky writhed with light and smoke. Another roar rolled like thunder, shaking the stone beneath their feet.

Drakor growled, voice a rasp of venom and rage. "This isn't your fight," he hissed. "Go back to whatever hole you crawled from."

Korrath's eyes blazed like molten embers, his massive wings beating once—twice—before folding them tight to his body and diving straight at Drakor in silence.

Drakor rolled sideways at the last instant, tail lashing. "Fool," he spat, smoke hissing from his jaws. "You think you can steal what is mine?"

"What you have no right to claim," Korrath thundered, his voice deep as tectonic plates grinding together. His talons scraped across Drakor's flank, drawing sparks and blood.

They collided midair—talons locking, wings buffeting, jaws snapping—spiraling downward in a storm-fueled knot of scales and fury.

"You are weak, Drakor," Korrath growled, driving him back with sheer weight. "Just like the one you grovel for."

Drakor's snarl intensified. Rage flared. He spat black fire, forcing Korrath to veer wide, but the red dragon was fast—too fast. He came in low, jaws snapping, claws flashing. One blow cut across Drakor's jaw. Another scored his shoulder.

Drakor roared in rage, as scale met scale.

Fizzlewing, still hovering nearby, yelped and zipped backwards, his wings sputtering as the shockwave of the clash hit him. "Oh no, oh no, oh no…!" he muttered, watching wide-eyed as the dragons grappled.

But Drakor wasn't giving up. As Korrath surged past, he twisted, sank his jagged teeth into Korrath's wing joint—and *wrenched.*

A sickening rip tore through the storm.

Korrath roared in agony, fire and blood pouring from his wing as he spiraled sideways, a chunk of his wing membrane fluttering about. He *screamed* a cry that cracked the clouds. And then he turned—fast—rage igniting every fiber of his being.

Drakor spat the shredded piece heavenward, triumphant. "Still chasing scraps, Korrath?" Drakor hissed, fumes escaping from his snout. "You'll never claim the mark. It is mine."

Korrath lunged, jaws wide, flames pouring forth in a stream of molten light. He barreled forward, fury renewed, claws slashing with punishing speed. "You don't have the strength to take it."

Drakor was driven back, unable to keep up with the raw power behind each blow. Talons tore across his flank. Teeth snapped close to his neck. The predator was now the prey.

Korrath charged into him, tail coiling, and hurled Drakor into the side of a broken spire. Stone exploded. Lightning flashed through the heavens as he roared in pain, blood flowing from his snout. His wings beat desperately as he pulled clear of the crumbling tower, circling high to escape the onslaught. His eyes burned with hatred as he wheeled to face his rival.

The two dragons circled each other—wind shrieking, thunder booming around them.

Korrath twisted in midair, arching his vanes and angling for the next strike. "You've grown weak—hiding in shadows, licking Vartharax's claws like some broken whelp."

"And yet I still live," Drakor hissed, circling.

Above them, thunder cracked like the earth splitting open.

And then Drakor saw it.

Movement against the wall.

A shimmer of silver.

The mark.

Her wings gleamed, her mark pulsing with that same cursed light—the light that had haunted him from the moment she received the mark. The power Vartharax wanted.

Drakor's eyes squinted. He felt the fury raging within him, but something else moved beneath it—icy, calculated.

He couldn't win this fight by force.

But he could still *win*.

He slowed his wings. Let the wind carry him.

Below, drelves and nemods alike looked up as the sky erupted with light—fire and black smoke rolling together in a maelstrom.

"You want the mark?" Drakor rasped, voice hushed and coiled.

Korrath bared his fangs, eyes blazing like forge embers. "I will take it—and burn everything in my path to do so."

They collided again, a brutal clash of fire with ice—teeth snapping, talons gouging. But as they broke apart, Drakor didn't pursue it.

His wings stilled. His gaze turned glacial.

He watched Korrath—watched his gaze flick toward the prize, the silver glow calling to him like a song. His smile returned, slow and serpentine, as he hovered in the storm, blood staining his scales, his body heaving with the effort to breathe, begging for relief.

Let the red beast waste his strength chasing the mark.

Let him think he's won.

When Vartharax turns on him—when the power of the prophecy crushes him—I'll be there.

Korrath's wings struck once, driving him higher above the battlefield. He sneered down at Drakor, his voice rumbling like stone cracking beneath the heat. "Go crawl back to your master, worm. Leave the real war to those with fire in their blood."

Drakor's eyes sparked.

Korrath snorted and turned—toward the glow, the mark.

With wings tucked in, he dove, a streak of flame piercing the dark.

"That mark belongs to me," he roared, his voice booming. "You were chosen, drelf, but I'll claim it for myself."

And high above, Drakor released a plume of smoke, fading into the distance like a promise unkept.

His whisper rode the wind.

"We'll see who survives."

Chapter 33

From the ridge beyond, two riders burst into view, their cloaks snapping like torn banners in the wind's fury. Lightning lit the sky above them, illuminating the battered walls below—and the chaos raging atop them.

Finnian leaned low over Embermane's neck as the horse galloped hard, hooves striking against the stone. Beside him, Eldrin gripped his reins tightly, keeping his eyes focused on the battlefield ahead.

The wind ripped past them, bearing the clang of metal and cries of the wounded. A streak of red fire streaked through the mist, cutting through like a falling star.

Finnian's head snapped up, eyes wide. He wrenched Embermane's reins sharply, nearly bringing the horse to a standstill, and pointed with a trembling hand.

"Eldrin!" he yelled over the thunder. "Look—there!"

Above them, the clouds pulsed crimson—like veins of blood—as a massive dragon, deep red and burning like molten ash, cut across the blackness, wings spread vast.

Eldrin's heart slammed into his ribs the moment his eyes spotted the diving fireball—and Lyria, battling atop the ramparts, oblivious of the danger barreling toward her.

Her silver wings flared in her fight against shadow panthers, blade flashing under the stormy sky.

"She doesn't see him!" Finnian cried. "We'll never make it in time!"

Eldrin's pulse pounded in his skull.

The Aetherstone flared hot, pulsing against his side with a rhythmic thrum. His mother's dagger blazed to life, wreathed in blue fire that licked up the blade, crackling like a tempest bound in steel. He gasped, glancing down as searing heat shot through it—magic surged, wild and untamed.

As if the Aetherstone knew. As if it had been waiting for just this time.

Across the battlefield, Lyria's mark blazed in answer—silver light flaring like a beacon.

A connection. Something ancient. Something deeper than both of them.

Finnian turned, eyes wide, as he noticed the burning dagger. "What in the—?"

But Eldrin wasn't listening. He was deaf to the turmoil that raged around him… as a song rose in his heart—the words long-forgotten… suddenly there.

"Through storm and shadow,
Through fire and night,
We rise as one,
Bound in the light..."

The stone glowed brighter with each word, and the blue fire of the dagger arced to meet it, lightning crackling between stone and steel, as though two parts of the same power had awakened.

Across the wall, Lyria's head lifted, her eyes locking on Eldrin—and she heard the words clearly, as if he had spoken them aloud.

She had heard the song before—in the Vale, when he hummed it in his sleep.

And she remembered Fizzlewing's warning. "Don't wake him… someday he may need to remember the words."

Today was that day.

Her hand touched her mark as it blazed brighter—silver and blue now twining between them, streaking like threads of living light.

"Together we rise,
Together we stand,
Light in the darkness,
Hope for the land..."

The words pulsed through Eldrin's mind—half memory, half instinct—and though his mouth barely moved, the storm carried them, as if the sky itself listened.

Above, the weather raged, winds shrieking like wounded beasts as Korrath dove—molten fury, a streak of incandescence hurtling straight at her.

But as Eldrin's song resonated within the storm and the bridge of light connecting both races pulsed brighter, something cracked open a flare of raw magic, alive and wild, resembling a hurricane breaking loose from above.

Lyria's gaze met Eldrin's, their connection pulsing as a vibrant thread of light—her mark flaring brighter, answering to the call from his dagger and the Aetherstone. Power surged between them, fierce and unstoppable.

But above—a shadow loomed.

Her eyes flicked up, and her breath hitched.

A dragon.

Diving straight for her, molten fire blazing in his gullet, jaws wide—a spear of flame meant to finish her. The mark burned hot on her flesh, the silver light ascending to join the storm.

Lyria grasped her sword. Her wings flared, weathering the wind.

She knew what she had to do.

But Korrath was upon her now—so close she could feel the intensity of his fire rising. His roar shattered the sky as his eyes found hers, triumphant.

He saw victory.

He tasted it.

This was the end.

His jaws opened wide, flame swelling deep in his throat—a final, consuming blaze.

And then—

"Now!" Eldrin's voice broke across the storm, fierce and unyielding.

As if on cue, Lyria hoisted her sword high, the silver spirals flaring brightly, while Eldrin lifted his dagger, blue fire licking up its blade, the Aetherstone pulsing in time.

The light between them pulsed once—twice—and then erupted outward in a dazzling surge of silvery-blue light. A beam of pure energy.

Korrath reared back, shrieking as the beam struck his chest, flames and shadow blasting away. His ember-lit scales cracked and splintered under the force, the light tearing across him.

"No!" Korrath roared, wings beating, but the light swallowed him whole, hurling him backwards—a falling comet, wings folding while he plunged into the maelstrom.

The shockwave of magic tore across the walls, throwing shadow panthers and nemods like scattered leaves. Even the clouds above peeled away, pushed back by the unleashed power.

As the light dimmed, the silence fell—before the storm winds crept back, howling through the broken towers.

Lyria stood at the parapet, panting, sword lowered, her eyes wide as she fixed her gaze on the sky where Korrath had been.

On the battlefield, Eldrin gripped the handle of his blade, breathing hard, the Aetherstone glowing faintly now, as though drained by what they had done.

Nothing moved, as if frozen.

Then Kaelis stepped up beside Lyria, her eyes opened in stunned awe.

"What was that?"

Lyria blinked, still catching her breath. "I don't… know," she whispered.

Finnian rode to Eldrin's side, gaping at the sky. "Remind me… never to get on your bad side."

Eldrin chuckled, shaking his head. "That wasn't just me."

They both looked toward Lyria, standing fierce and unyielding atop the wall, her silver wings stretched out against the fading storm.

It was all of them. United.

Chapter 34

The shattered gates of the kingdom loomed ahead, half-broken but still holding, as shadows clawed against them.

Smoke billowed from the walls. Drelves fought atop the battlements, firing arrows down at the nemods swarming below, while others launched into the skies on tattered wings, clashing with wyverns in midair. Blades flashed, and the shrieks of shadowy cats rose from below as they tried to scale the walls.

Finnian reined Embermane to a sharp halt, breathing hard, eyes searching the chaos. "No way we're breaking through that mess," he muttered, jaw tight.

Eldrin's eyes narrowed as he surveyed the scene—shadow panthers circling, nemods surging, and wyverns screeching above. More drelves leapt from tower to tower, their movements sharp and weary, arrows loosed in quick succession as they fought to hold back the enemy.

Above, the wind roared, but in the darkness, the essence of the bond he and Lyria had forged still shimmered—fragile but unbroken.

Eldrin dismounted his horse in one smooth motion, reaching for his bow. "Then we start here," he said, slapping his horse on the butt to send him off.

Finnian grinned, pulling his bow from his back as he stepped out of the saddle and onto the battlefield. "Archery contest, then?" he asked, a sharp grin breaking through the fear.

"Loser owes the winner a bottle of Gantar's best," Eldrin shot back, although his eyes burned with focus.

"You're on."

Both elves nocked arrows in unison—and as a horde of nemods charged toward them, the first arrows flew.

Thwip. Thwip.

Two brutes fell before they had crossed ten paces, arrows buried deep in their chests.

Finnian breathed, "Two."

Eldrin's second arrow flew as he moved, graceful and precise—dropping a shadow panther mid-leap. "Three."

A shriek split the air—a wyvern diving for them.

"Down!" Eldrin barked, both of them dropping low as the beast's talons raked the spot they'd been.

As the wyvern wheeled back around, Finnian rose, bowstring drawn, and loosed a shot that struck the creature in the wing, sending it spinning wildly into a tower. Drelves on the ramparts finished it, arrows raining down like a deluge of silver.

Finnian grinned, glancing sideways. "Four."

"Not bad," Eldrin admitted, lips twitching despite the chaos. "But watch this."

He spun, drawing and releasing in one motion—his arrow striking a nemod just as it lunged for a wounded drelf near the wall, sending the creature sprawling lifelessly to the mud. The drelf, a young warrior with torn wings, shot Eldrin a grateful nod before returning to the fight.

"Five," Eldrin said.

Finnian huffed a laugh. "Now you're just showin' off."

But the raging battle left no time to banter further—the ground surged with more nemods, charging from both sides, and two wyverns circled overhead, closing in fast.

As the creatures attacked, a female drelf with emerald wings descended from above, burying her sword into the back of a nemod that was charging at them. She launched back into the air with a sweep of her tail, nodding to Eldrin and Finnian.

"Glad they're on our side," Finnian muttered, respect audible in his tone.

"Yes," Eldrin said. "But they can't hold on much longer. Neither can we."

More panthers circled. Finnian reached for another arrow, breathing hard. "Where's an old sage when you need him?"

Almost as if summoned by his words, Gantar appeared. Aetherstone necklace shining brilliantly. As a wyvern dove, Gantar thrust his sword upward—a blast of shimmering force exploding from its tip, slamming the wyvern backwards with a shriek. The light permeated the air, crackling and alive.

Eldrin grinned, the dagger burning in his hand. The Aetherstone beat in rhythm. "What took you so long?"

Gantar's eyes twinkled as he twirled his sword. "I'm a little slower than I used to be."

"Glad you're here," Eldrin said, mopping sweat from his forehead.

Another surge of nemods poured toward them—too many. Eldrin raised his bow, but his arm was now trembling, his quiver nearly empty.

"There's too many," Finnian growled, stepping closer. "We're not gonna—"

And then the snarl as another beast lunged.

"We could use more help, Gantar!" Eldrin shouted through gritted teeth.

Gantar chuckled low, eyes sharp despite the storm raging around them. "Then it's a good thing I brought your brother."

Eldrin froze. The words barely sank in before a snarl ripped through the silence—a massive nemod lunging straight for him, claws outstretched. Finnian swore, scrambling to draw his bow—but before either could shoot, an arrow whistled through the air and pierced the beast's throat, dropping it in a pile at Eldrin's feet.

Spinning, chest heaving, Eldrin's mouth dropped open. For a moment, he was sure he was seeing things.

But no—there he was.

Thalendir.

Standing a few feet away, bow half-lowered, another arrow already nocked to the string. The rain drenched his golden hair, and his eyes gleamed sharp and steady.

Eldrin started, breathless.

Thalendir smirked, raising one brow. "Good thing I showed up to save you, little brother."

A breathless laugh escaped Finnian. "You always know how to make an entrance."

Thalendir gave a dry, humorless smile. "And you always know how to get into messes."

Eldrin's head swayed, half in shock, half in exasperated relief. "Since when are you in the business of saving me?"

Thalendir's gaze flicked to him, sharp and unreadable—but something softer stirred beneath. "Since always."

Twin panthers circled them, a red luminescence gleaming in their eyes. Thalendir stepped in beside Eldrin, drawing his blade in a clean, fluid motion.

"Now—shall we show them what two brothers can do?"

Eldrin gave a tight nod, blades ready. "Let's make Father proud."

Thalendir's smirk twitched into something real. "For once."

Finnian grinned, shifting into place beside them. "Don't forget me."

And then Gantar moved up behind them, his makeshift staff glowing, a wry grin playing on his mouth.

"A fine trio," Gantar remarked. "But I'm not letting you boys have all the glory."

And together, they formed a line of fire, steel, and light—and plunged into the fight.

Lyria's blade flashed, destroying a nemod that had clawed its way over the wall.

Beside her, Kaelis swung wide, slashing through a panther mid-lunge. Its body crumpled backwards into the shadows, as another surged forward to take its place.

Yet, they were holding.

Along the wall, the drelves fought with fierce precision—blades flashing, arrows flying in rhythmic volleys. Tails snapped like whips, sending more brutes to their deaths. From the towers above, longbows sang—silver-tipped bolts streaking into the clouds, burying deep in wyvern flesh.

And just beyond the wall, the silver-blue glow of Lyria and Eldrin's bond still shimmered above, casting a light that made the darkness flinch and falter.

"They're pulling back," Kaelis breathed, glancing at Lyria with a grim but hopeful smile. Her hair clung to her face, soaked in rain and sweat, but her eyes burned bright.

Lyria's wings flared, rain streaming from their edges as she brought down another nemod. Her sword gleamed, still thrumming with magic from the surge that had cast Korrath from the heavens.

Nearby, Nyxari stood her ground—arms lifted, hands glowing with woven light. A dome of shimmering magic rippled around her, shielding a cluster of injured drelves from a fresh volley of wyvern fire.

"I won't allow them to take any more," Nyxari said, her voice tight, her face pale. Sweat shimmered across her brow, but her magic didn't falter.

Lyria faced the battlefield and saw Eldrin with Gantar beside him, casting pulses of radiance that slammed into enemy lines. Finnian was darting into the fray, twin swords dancing like flames.

The tide had shifted.

The darkness—once unrelenting—was now staggering. Step by step, it was breaking.

Kaelis stepped to Lyria's side, flashing a bloodied grin. "You really are full of surprises, Ironwing."

Lyria exhaled, her breath fogging in the frigid air. Her mark still glowed against her throat. "Let's make sure we live to tell of them."

Far above, shrouded within the swirling clouds of the storms, a pair of yellow eyes watched in silence.

Drakor's ashen wings beat slowly and unwaveringly, his gaze glowing like twin agates. Below, the battlefield burned—but the light was winning. His nemods lay broken, wyverns scattered, shadow panthers driven back beneath the fury of sword and spell.

And still... his troops fought.

A low grumble emanated from deep within him, vapor escaping from his nostrils like coiled serpents.

"The drelves think this is over," he snarled, voice drowned by wind and rain.

He circled once, wings whispering against the tempest while he watched Lyria's silver wings flare in the distance—as

Eldrin's blade flashed, and Gantar's magic shimmered in defiance.

A cruel smile curved his lips.

Let them celebrate. Let them believe the light had prevailed.

With an abrupt twist, Drakor angled his feathers and soared higher, into the vortex. He threw back his head and hissed words older than bone, older than breath—guttural and cold, tearing through the sky like a curse.
"One last gift…"

The storm shuddered.

And from the void beyond the trees, the shadows answered.

A crack of thunder rolled over the distant landscape as the ground split open past the outer ridge. Out of the fog, they came—not dozens, not scores, but hundreds.

Shadow panthers.

More than any realm had seen.

Eyes burning. Claws slicing through mud and stone. They surged forward like a tidal wave of death—silent, disciplined, relentless.

Toward the drelves. Toward the elves. Toward the mark.

Drakor hung above the maelstrom, his eyes gleaming.

"Let them taste unity," he whispered. "Let them bleed for it."

A gale blew, tearing through anything in its path as Eldrin pressed a hand to his side, catching his breath. His dagger pulsed, its blue flame dimmed but steady, while Finnian stood nearby, an arrow nocked and ready, eyes scanning the battlefield.

Thalendir wiped blood from a cut on his cheek, casting a sharp glance towards Eldrin with a nod.
"You alright?"

Eldrin managed a tight smile. "Still standing."

"A miracle, considering how you usually fight," Thalendir muttered, though his eyes were soft—Protective. Watchful.

Gantar remained several steps back, the Aetherstone pendant around his neck glowing like a fragment of moonlight. "We've pushed them back for now," he said, voice rough but steady. "But this isn't over."

Eldrin looked up to the walls where silver wings flashed—Lyria. Still fighting. Still alive.

A smile spread across his lips—until a sound froze them all in place.

A deep, rolling growl.

Not from one throat—but from many. Dozens. Hundreds. Maybe more.

Thalendir's hand shot to his sword hilt as Finnian looked towards the treeline beyond the battlefield.

"What is that?" Finnian whispered.

The earth trembled below them, as if something vast passed beneath the earth. Then came the glint of red eyes—burning like embers in a dying fire.

Gantar breathed. "More shadows."

Eldrin turned. His heart raced as shadows amongst the trees rippled and broke — and the first of a new horde of panthers emerged.

Not five. Not ten. Hundreds.

Their sleek, black forms moved like smoke, their eyes glowing crimson, their fangs gleaming.

"By the stars…" Finnian whispered.

Thalendir's jaw tightened as he said, "They're going to overrun the walls."

Eldrin swallowed hard, but his grip clenched around his dagger. "Then we hold the line."

Thalendir shot him a sharp look—then nodded, something fierce and proud in his eyes. "We hold the line."

Finnian exhaled, loosening his shoulders. "Guess this is where we die, looking good."

Thalendir smirked. "Speak for yourself."

As they braced for the onslaught, a distant cry echoed over the storm—a great sound that made even the panthers pause, their eyes flashing with malice.

Eldrin's head snapped up, looking for the source.

And then—

Silence.

Even the storm appeared to pause.

Then it came—clear and powerful, splitting the night: the blast of a horn...

Gantar's head lifted, eyes narrowing. "That's definitely not a drelf horn."

Another blast echoed, followed by the thunder of hooves, and from the far ridge, figures burst from the downpour and mist streaming down the hill in perfect formation.

Elves.

Thousands of them.

Clad in gleaming armor, with banners in silver and green snapping in the breeze, swords drawn and bows raised. And at their head—

King Eldermyst.

Mounted on a white steed, his silver crown glinting in the rain, the Elven king had answered the call.

Eldrin's breath caught as he watched, disbelief and hope warring within him.

Finnian blinked, jaw slack. "I don't believe it..."

Thalendir straightened, pride and something like relief behind his gaze. "He came."

"I told you," Gantar murmured, a slight smile beneath his beard. "The king does not abandon his sons."

As the Elven army swept down the slope, arrows arcing in graceful flight toward the panthers, Eldrin found his voice.

"Well," he whispered, a faint grin teasing at his lips. "Looks like our help has arrived."

Thalendir glanced sideways, smirking. "Don't get used to it."

Together, the four of them turned to face the horde with renewed strength, as the elves poured in behind them, and the tide of battle turned once more.

Chapter 35

The elves surged forward as an enchantment washed over the battlefield—a wave of radiance that forced the darkness back.

Lyria sensed it first—her mark flaring with renewed brilliance, flowing across her body, and a sigh escaped her.

Below, Eldrin's dagger burned brighter, the Aetherstone pulsing with radiant heat. The power coursed through him—no longer untamed, but sure and steady. Unified.

And together, elves and drelves fought as one—blades flashing and arrows singing in the gale.

King Eldermyst rode at the vanguard, a storm of steel and resolve. His white steed charged through the chaos, hooves striking sparks from the stone, and his silver blade flashed in wide arcs as nemods fell before him. Rain sheeted from his armor, turning him into a figure carved from moonlight.

But something shifted.

From the chaos of battle, the shadows parted—and something larger stepped through.

A massive brute. Twice the size of the others. Its flesh pulsed with dark veins, eyes burning embers. It moved with eerie elegance, its claws slicing the dirt as it stalked toward the king.

Thalendir swiveled—

His heart stuttered. "Father!"

But Eldermyst didn't hear. Or perhaps he did—and stood his ground, anyway.

The king wheeled his horse to meet the threat, lifting his sword, blood trailing from the blade's edge.

Time seemed to fracture—a breath caught between thunderclaps.

Then the beast lunged.

Claws tore through silver armor. The impact crashed like a boulder. The force of the impact threw Eldermyst from his saddle; he crashed hard onto the earth, his sword flying from his hand.

His majesty was down.

Thalendir broke toward his father, killing a nemod that jumped in his path—but more surged in, snarling and snapping, blocking his way.

On the ground, the king scrambled to his feet, reaching for his weapon as he jumped up. The silver blade dripped black as he grasped the handle. He reacted swiftly, in time to intercept the giant nemod's charge—its jagged blade coming down like a hammer.

Steel met steel with a brutal crash, the impact jarring through the king's frame. He stumbled back a step, teeth clenched, muscles trembling. With a quick twist, he knocked the creature's weapon aside and slashed across its arm. Black blood splattered onto the earth.

The beast howled but didn't retreat—it circled, its eyes glowing with hatred.

Eldermyst stood tall, rain streaming down his face, sword raised once more. "Come on, then," he growled, a fire behind his gaze.

The nemod lunged again—faster this time. The king turned the first strike, but the beast's claw sliced through his chest, shredding armor and flesh. He went down on one knee, breath ragged.

He struggled to rise.

His sword came up—shaking, but ready—at the very moment the nemod lifted its claws for the killing blow.

Eldermyst braced—

—and a silver streak tore across the maelstrom.

With a fierce cry, the spear slammed through the nemod's back, piercing its heart. The creature shuddered, emitted a strangled snarl, and fell with a loud thud.

King Eldermyst staggered back, stunned. His gaze lifted.

Orendir stood above the corpse, yanking his spear free, breath rasping in the frosty air.

Their eyes locked—two warriors, two friends. No words. Just the heaviness of everything they'd lived and lost.

"Orendir…" the king breathed, voice thick with more than pain.

Everything stilled—the storm, the screams, the battle. Rain pounded the earth, hissing against fresh blood.

Then—

A flash of movement. From the side.

Another nemod, charging through the smoke.

"Orendir!" the king shouted.

The beast struck hard, its claws ripping into Orendir's side and dragging him down in a deluge of mud and blood. The commander grunted, staggering—but he did not fall. He turned, teeth clenched, and swung his spear in a wide arc, catching the nemod in the ribs and forcing it back.

"Stay back!" Orendir barked at the king, voice raw, rain streaking down his bloodied face. "I'm not finished."

But more nemods closed in—three, four, circling like wolves that had caught the smell of weakness.

"No!" Thalendir roared, felling a beast as he charged into the fray, blood splattering across his blade. "Hold the line!" he shouted, voice slicing through the mayhem.

Eldrin was right behind him, his dagger blazing blue, and his eyes filled with horror as he witnessed Orendir fall, a hand pressed to the open wound on his flank, while more savages closed in.

A nemod lunged for the king.

Thalendir leapt over the bodies in his path, meeting the brutes head-on—his sword slashing across the rogue beast, slitting its throat in a clean, savage arc. The form collapsed before him.

Eldrin reached the king's other side, slaying a second nemod that charged for them. Battle obliterated its scream.

"Get him up!" Thalendir shouted, locking blades with another foe. "We have to move!"

King Eldermyst caught Orendir as he sagged, stepping before him with his sword raised to stop another strike.

"Stay with me," Eldermyst said to his charge, voice hoarse—beneath it, something deeper stirred. Fear.

Orendir's grasp clamped on the king's shoulder, strong despite the tremble in his hand. His words came ragged, each one pulled from a place of pain.

"There's something..."

"Don't talk," the king snapped, almost pleading. "We'll get you out of this—"

But Orendir shook his head.

His vision was pure. Sharp. Unafraid.

"Thariel… didn't betray you."

The king froze. The storm stilled.

"What?" Eldermyst breathed, leaning closer.

Orendir, his voice now faint. "She gave the Aetherstone to Gantar… for Eldrin."

The king's jaw clenched. Rain traced down his cheeks, indistinguishable from anything else.

"She knew," Orendir said. "He… was the key. To the prophecy."

Lightning flashed. None of them moved.

Orendir's voice faded, thread-thin. "But she never stopped believing in you."

Eldermyst gazed at him, unmoving, then bowed his head when the final breath left his old friend's lungs.

The hand on his shoulder slipped away.

And Orendir fell still.

The king knelt beside him—silent, motionless—as the tempest lashed about him like judgment made wind.

For a long moment, he didn't speak. Didn't breathe.

Then he reached out—gently —and closed Orendir's eyes.

His hand lingered there, trembling slightly, before falling back to his side.

"I was blind," he whispered to the storm. "But no longer."

Then, slowly, Eldermyst rose—not as a grieving king, but as the warrior his people remembered.

His sword hung beside him, rain mixed with tears tracing lines down his cheeks.

He spotted Eldrin.

And then—the Aetherstone.

It pulsed at Eldrin's belt, silver-blue and steady. The same stone Thariel had once carried. The one she'd entrusted to Gantar. The one she'd meant for their son.

His throat tightened. His voice was roughened not by battle, but by memory.

"She believed," the king said. "All this time… she trusted what I could not see."

His eyes found Eldrin's—and held.

"You carry her light," Eldermyst said. "And I see it now… I see *you.*"

He looked at Gantar, and something like an apology flickered in his expression. "Thank you… old friend."

Gantar gave the slightest nod—not with pride, but with quiet sorrow.

Eldermyst shut his eyes for one heartbeat.

Then they opened them again, and they were on fire.

He faced the battlefield. His sword lifted.

"We end this," he said, voice steady as stone. "For her. For him. For all of them."

The king brandished his blade with renewed fury, decimating a nemod with a cry that split the storm. Beside him, Thalendir fought like a beast, his sword a blur as he carved through the enemy ranks.

And Eldrin stood with them, the Aetherstone glowing, his dagger wreathed in blue flame. Grief and rage surged through him, and with each swing, the dagger burned hotter, its light forcing the shadows back.

Lyria felt it from where she stood—a surge of magic pulling at her mark, as if Eldrin's power called to her own. The light on her neck flared, her wings extending wide as their forces converged once more—ribbons of silver and azure weaving into a single brilliant force.

Nemods and shadow panthers faltered as the combined power roared through them, burning away the blackness that clung to their forms. The United Realms' fury pushed back the remaining enemy forces.

Silence fell—the quiet that comes only after ruin.

Vapor billowed from the bodies… nemods, panthers, and wyverns lay scattered like broken dolls, and amid them, too many elves and drelves who would never rise again.

Against the fortress walls, Lyria stood with Kaelis and Nyxari, all three worn and bloodied, wings torn and heavy with rain. Their swords hung at their sides, forgotten, as they looked out over what remained.

Kaelis exhaled, wiping her blade clean. "We did it."

Nyxari swallowed hard, voice soft. "Barely."

Lyria remained silent—her gaze sweeping the field below, landing at last on a familiar figure. Eldrin.

His gaze met hers—and in that instant, the chaos and blood faded away, leaving only them. A quiet understanding passed between them—unspoken, but undeniable.

From the ruins, Finnian emerged, mud-splattered, his bow in hand, eyes wide as he searched the battlefield. He jogged the last few paces, breathless, to Eldrin's side.

"Well," Finnian gasped, bracing himself with his hands against his legs, glancing around at the carnage. "We won… right?"

Eldrin chuckled, "I think so."

"I'll drink to that," Finnian murmured.

From behind them, a gentle utterance disrupted the quiet.

"I hope you aren't planning on celebrating without me."

Eldrin turned, a weary smile playing upon his lips as Gantar approached, leaning on a wooden staff. His robes, soaked and torn, his beard matted with rain and soot, but his eyes took in every detail—the carnage, the casualties, the living who still stood.

Finnian released a breathless chuckle. "You look like you crawled through the battle."

"I did," Gantar said with a tired smirk. "But I'm standing. And that counts for something."

As Gantar came to stand beside them, Eldrin's gaze lifted—drawn to the battered wall where silver wings caught the first pale glimmers of sunlight breaking through the clouds.

Lyria stood there, her sword lowered, watching him. Her eyes, bright and weary, locked on his.

Silently, she stepped to the cusp of the wall—and leapt.

Her wings spread wide, catching the wind as she glided down from the battlements, the storm's remnants parting around her as if recognizing her victory. She landed with a soft thud a few paces from Eldrin, her wings folding in close, rain cascading off their edges.

For a short time, neither spoke.

Then Lyria exhaled slowly, her voice soft and rough from battle. "You're alive."

A breathless smile escaped Eldrin's lips, with something warm—and vulnerable—surfacing from his exhaustion. "So are you."

A laugh escaped her, full of relief and disbelief. Without thinking, her fingers reached out to him—and Eldrin, moving just as naturally, reached back.

Their hands brushed, fingers curling together with talons, lingering, as though neither could quite bear to let go.

It wasn't quite an embrace, but it was more than just a fleeting touch—a silent promise hanging in the air… Deeply felt yet unspoken.

Finnian cocked an eyebrow, glancing at Gantar with a smirk. "Well, I'd say about time."

Lyria flushed, releasing Eldrin's fingers.

Before anyone could speak, the soft sound of hooves on wet earth made them turn.

Out of the cloud of rain and smoke, King Eldermyst strolled toward them, one hand holding the bridle of his splendid horse. The beast moved with careful steps beside him, its silver mane darkened by rain, but its head held high—a quiet strength amid the ruin.

Although his armor was battered and bloodstained, and his cloak torn, he stood tall. Grief shadowed his eyes, carved deeply into his features like time etched into stone. He surveyed the battlefield—the fallen elves and drelves, the broken bodies of beasts, the mud and blood soaking the earth.

But when he saw his sons standing side-by-side, and Gantar among them, something in him steadied. A trace of the elf he once was—and could still be—surfaced. His mount gave a low snort, nudging the king's shoulder. Eldermyst lifted a hand, resting it against the beast's neck.

"You're all alive," he said, voice subdued and hoarse.

Thalendir straightened, nodding once. "We are."

Eldrin met his father's gaze with the heaviness of a thousand words—regrets, truths, of what had been lost and what had been found—yet for the moment, the silence was enough.

Then the king's eyes shifted to Gantar, and briefly, something softer passed between them—a silent exchange between old friends who had weathered more than war together. The grief didn't leave the king's face, but the weight of it seemed shared now, not carried alone.

Then Eldermyst's eyes fell upon Lyria.

For a long time, they regarded one another. The king's face was unreadable, although his eyes shifted—to where her hand had been in Eldrin's. No open hostility. But no simple acceptance.

"You fought bravely," he finally said, his voice cool, but not cruel. "Your drelves have paid dearly for this day."

Lyria dipped her head. "So have your elves."

A stillness fell between them—uneasy, but honest.

"Thank you," she said, her violet eyes shining with unshed tears.

As the group stood together, a pale ray of sunlight pierced the clouds, slicing through the war zone like a fragile blessing. The first light of dawn.

Lyria looked up, her wings shifting as she breathed in deep. The rain slowed to a faint drizzle. Eldrin followed her gaze…

And there—a flash of violet and gold burst through the fading mist, swirling like a flicker of lightning and smoke.

Finnian blinked. "What in the realms—?"

With a shimmer of iridescent wings, Fizzlewing spun into view, hanging upside down before flipping upright with a flap of gossamer wings.

"Well, well, well…" he said, grinning as if they hadn't just battled to the death. "Having a party without me?"

Gantar chuckled low, moving his head from side to side. "Fizzlewing."

Lyria lifted one eyebrow. "Yes. And you're late."

Fizzlewing gave a midair bow. "Fashionably."

Eldrin stared, incredulous. "It's over, Fizzlewing. We won."

The pixie's smile wavered—as something sharp and knowing gleamed in his depths. He glanced towards Gantar, who caught his gaze. The sage's smile faded, a knowing look in his eyes.

Fizzlewing twirled a lazy loop overhead, his tone turning grave. "This is far from over."

Eldrin frowned. "What?"

Fizzlewing drifted closer, eyes gleaming. His tone became hushed. "My friends… this is just the start."

Eldrin tensed. But before he could speak…

Fizzlewing's eyes twinkled again, mischief layered with truth. "We have to find the bearer of the second mark. Before the darkness does."

Finnian exhaled sharply, muttering under it. "Bloody elves. There's another mark?"

Lightning cracked above, cleaving through the stillness like a warning. The heavens trembled.

Far above—veiled at the center of the storm—wings carved through the darkness, and eyes of fire blazed.

Still watching.

Still waiting.

And somewhere far away, deep in the Elven wilds, a second mark stirred to life—oblivious of the tempest it would bring.

Continue the adventure in the Elves, Drelves & Dragon series:

Book Two: ***Whisper of Elves***

ELVES, DRELVES & DRAGONS
BOOK 2
WHISPER OF ELVES
C. STAR

If you enjoyed this book, please take a moment to write a review.

It will help others find my books (so I can keep writing in this series).

Thanks for your review!

C. Star

Character & Creature Guide

Main Characters

- **Lyria Ironwing** *(LEER-ee-uh)* — Drelf mark-bearer, part dragon, part elf.
- **Eldrin** *(ELL-drin)* — Elven warrior, son of King Eldermyst.
- **Finnian** *(FIN-ee-an)* — Eldrin's loyal friend.
- **Gantar** *(GAN-tar)* — Elven sage and healer.
- **Thalendir** *(THAL-en-deer)* — Eldrin's older brother.
- **King Eldermyst** *(ELL-der-mist)* — King of the Elves, father to Eldrin and Thalendir.
- **Kaelis Skythorn (KAY-liss SKY-thorn)** — Lyria's fiercely loyal best friend from the Drelf Kingdom.
- **Orendir** *(OR-en-deer)* — High Warden to King Eldermyst.
- **Nyxari the Veilkeeper** *(NICK-sar-ee)* — Drelf seer.
- **Seralyth** *(SERR-uh-lith)* — Ancient white dragon.
- **Thariel** *(THAR-ee-el)* — Eldrin's mother.
- **Fizzlewing** *(FIZZ-uhl-wing)* — Mischievous pixie guide from the Shrouded Vale.

Elven Council

- **Lady Alariel** *(AH-lar-ee-el)* — Mistress of Lore.
- **Lord Thalion** *(THAL-ee-on)* — Commander of the Elven Guard.
- **Elder Faelorn** *(FAY-lorn)* — Master of Nature.
- **Lady Seraphina** *(SERR-uh-fee-nuh)* — Ambassador of Alliances.
- **Elder Sylthir** *(SILL-theer)* — The Shadow Watcher.

Horses

- **Silverwind** *(SILL-ver-wind)* — Eldrin's mare.
- **Duskrunner** *(DUSS-kruhn-er)* — Gantar's gelding, ridden by Lyria.
- **Embermane** *(EM-ber-mayn)* — Finnian's buckskin gelding.
- **Steel** *(STEEL)* — Thalendir's black stallion.

Creatures & Terms

- **Nemods** *(NEEH-mods)* — Shadow-forged creatures.
- **Wyverns** *(WHY-vernz)* — Winged beasts.

- **Shadowmanes** *(SHAD-oh-mayns)* — Nemod mounts with black hides, clawed hooves, and glowing eyes.
- **Aetherstone** *(AY-ther-stone)* — Ancient stone of power.

Dragons

- **Zyressa** *(ZAI-ress-uh)* — Fierce green dragon.
- **Korrath** *(KOR-ath)* — Crimson dragon, rival of Drakor.
- **Drakor** *(DRAY-kor)* — Servant of Vartharax.
- **Vartharax** *(VAR-thuh-raks)* — The Dark Dragon Lord.

More Elves

- **Master Aldareth** *(AL-dah-reth)* — Elven weapons trainer.
- **Caelith** *(KAY-lith)* — Fellow warrior who trains and patrols with Eldrin.
- **Aelar** *(AY-lar)* — Forest scout under Aldareth.
- **Dareth & Erynder** *(DARE-eth / AIR-in-der)* — Scouts patrolling the Elven borders.

www.ingramcontent.com/pod-product-compliance
Lightning Source LLC
LaVergne TN
LVHW020522100826
845148LV00010B/1311

* 9 7 9 8 9 8 5 0 6 8 1 8 4 *